IDENTITY CRISIS

BOOKS IN THE B.K. INVESTIGATIONS SERIES

BOOK TWO IN THE B.K. INVESTIGATIONS SERIES

IDENTITY CRISIS

Little Angela Patten is kidnapped by a madman—a man
who's convinced she's his dead daughter.

JEAN HACKENSMITH

INKWATER
PRESS

PORTLAND•OREGON
INKWATERPRESS.COM

*Scan this QR Code
to learn more about
this title.*

Publisher: Inkwater Press | www.inkwaterpress.com

    Hackensmith, Jean.
      Identity crisis / by Jean Hackensmith.
      pages cm -- (B.K. Investigations series ; book 2)
      LCCN 2014902443
      ISBN 978-1-62901-075-5 (pbk.)
      ISBN 978-1-62901-076-2 (Kindle)
      ISBN 978-1-62901-077-9 (ePub)

      1. Private investigators--Fiction. 2. Police dogs--
Fiction. 3. Detective and mystery stories. 4. Suspense
fiction. I. Title. II. Series: Hackensmith, Jean.
B.K. Investigations series ; bk. 2.

    PS3608.A2478I34 2014   813'.6
                QBI14-600045

Paperback ISBN-13 978-1-62901-075-5 | ISBN-10 1-62901-075-8
Kindle ISBN-13 978-1-62901-076-2 | ISBN-10 1-62901-076-6
ePub ISBN-13 978-1-62901-077-9 | ISBN-10 1-62901-077-4

1 3 5 7 9 10 8 6 4 2

To My Husband, Ron:

You were my biggest fan, and I know you're happy to see me back on track and this book finally completed. I hope you can read it in heaven. I love you, and I miss you.

ACKNOWLEDGMENTS

First of all, I would like to thank my family for giving me the motivation and the courage to put my grief aside and start writing again. It took a while, but I'm back on track now and it's all due to them. Once again, I would also like to thank Chris Byrne from Stonehill Kennel, www.k9one.com, for his willingness to work with a virtually unknown author and bring my new canine character, Sinbad, to life. Last but not least, I would like to thank my publisher, Inkwater Press, for their wonderful staff who are always willing to go the extra mile for their authors.

PROLOGUE

June 12, 2009

Two-year-old Courtney Lanaski pointed to the tattoo of a mermaid on her father's left arm. "Is she your little mermaid, Daddy?"

Six-foot-four Collin grabbed his daughter and began to tickle her mercilessly. "No, *you* are my little mermaid!"

Courtney giggled uncontrollably until her mother stepped in. "That's enough, Collin. You're going to make her pee her pants."

"That's right," he said as he ceased the play and sat down in a chair at the dining room table. He plopped his daughter on his knee. "And we can't have that, since she hasn't peed her pants in over a week!"

"I'm a big girl now, Daddy, right?"

"You sure are, honey, and Mommy and Daddy are so proud of you."

Courtney nestled her head against the shirt of her father's

Air Force DCU, desert combat uniform, more commonly known as "fatigues." "I don't want you to go to a war, Daddy."

"I know, honey. Daddy doesn't want to go either, but I have to."

"Will you come home for my birthday?"

Tears clouded Collin's eyes. His daughter would turn three in only four months, and he had yet to be there for one of her birthday parties. He wasn't there when she was born, either. "No, honey. I can't. But I'll send you a present."

"Can you send me a *Little Mermaid* dolly?"

He glanced at his wife, Lynn, and she nodded, assuring him that she would buy the doll and put his name on it. "I sure will, honey."

"Okay." She fingered the dog tags that lay against his chest. "Why do you wear a necklace all the time, Daddy?"

Collin laughed. "It's not a necklace, honey. They're my dog tags."

Courtney giggled. "But you're not a *dog*!"

"Are you sure?" He nuzzled her neck. "Grrrrr! Don't I sound like a dog?"

The little girl sat up suddenly. "Can I get a dog, Daddy? I want a puppy, though, because they're cute."

"I'll tell you what. If you're a good little girl while Daddy is gone, we'll get a puppy when I come home. Okay?"

"Promise?" she asked excitedly.

"I promise." He glanced at his wife again, and she just rolled her blue eyes and shook her blonde head. "And I'll tell you what else I'll do."

"What?"

He pulled an extra dog tag, complete with chain, from his pocket and put it around Courtney's neck. "I got an extra one of these yesterday, so *this* one you get to keep. That way, every time you look at it, you'll think about your Daddy and know that I'm thinking about you, too."

"Okay."

"How did you get an *extra* one, Collin?" his wife asked. "They issue only two tags, and you need to have both of them to get on the plane."

"So I told them I lost one of mine, okay?" He looked at Courtney again. "And this dog tag will help keep you safe, cuz it's *magic*." He whispered the last word close to her ear.

"Really?" she asked, her big blue eyes wide with wonder.

"You bet. So you have to keep it on all the time, okay?"

"Okay. Is that why you have to wear yours when you go to a war, because they keep you safe?"

"Yup. All the soldiers have to wear them, one around their neck and one laced into their boots, so they can come home to their little girls."

"I won't ever take it off, Daddy, until you come home. I promise."

Collin dropped a kiss on top of her head. "That's a good girl. Now, give me a big hug, because I have to go."

Courtney wrapped her arms around her father's neck and squeezed. He stood then, and handed the little girl to Lynn. "You be a good girl for Mommy now, okay?"

"I will."

He pressed another kiss to his daughter's cheek, and dropped a peck on his wife's lips. "Bye. I love you both."

"I love you, too, Daddy," Courtney returned.

He looked at Lynn expectantly. "I love you," she murmured.

A slight frown puckered his brow, but he let his wife's apparent hesitancy to say the words pass. He started for the door then, but paused when Courtney wriggled free from her mother's embrace and slid to the floor again. She ran to grab his leg in a desperate hold.

"Don't go, Daddy! Please!"

"Lynn, I have to leave!" he exclaimed softly.

She moved to pick up her daughter again. "What do you say we go bake some cookies!"

"Can Daddy wait until they're done, so he can take some to the war?"

Lynn hesitated just a moment before answering. "Sure he can." She turned to carry her daughter into the kitchen, but mouthed the word "Go!" to her husband over her shoulder.

Collin watched them until they had disappeared through the swinging door, then wiped a tear from his eye and left the house.

CHAPTER ONE

"So, you found Miranda Bennington's body, huh?" Captain Brian Koski nodded his dark head slowly. The sluggish movement combined with a profound sadness in his normally vibrant gray eyes to relay his grief to his friend. "You heard about that, huh."

Zach Riker took a sip of Miller Lite and returned the bottle to the patio table in front of him. He pushed a stray lock of sandy hair back from his suntanned brow before responding. "It's been all over the news, Brian. We'd had to have been deaf, dumb and blind not to. "

"Yeah, well, we may have found the body, but we're no closer to catching her killer. And, between you and me, I don't know if we ever will."

"Her parents must be devastated," Caryn Riker commented softly.

Brian's gaze shifted to his friend's lovely wife. As usual, the woman's copper locks were pulled back from her face and wound into a tight French twist. "That's putting it mildly.

Miranda was only twelve years old, and Lord knows what she went through before she died. The coroner hasn't determined if she was sexually assaulted yet, but judging from the state her body was in, I'd bet on it. What's especially hard on the mother is that she *told* Miranda to wait in the schoolyard if she was late picking her up. Her teacher and the principal are kicking their asses, too. They both saw Miranda sitting on a swing in the playground area the day she disappeared, and neither of them took it upon themselves to stay with her until her mom got there."

"I would never do that," Caryn replied emphatically. "In fact, I stay with kids all the time if their parents are late."

Brian took a swig of his own Miller Lite before continuing. "Yeah, and you teach second grade at Lebhart. Your students are what? Seven years old? Miranda was in sixth grade. Her mother figured she was old enough to look after herself until she got there. And you can't tell me that there haven't been times when Evan has had to wait for you or Zach to pick him up."

"Evan rides a bus, Brian," Caryn corrected gently. "And Zach and I always make sure that one of us is home by the time he gets here."

The subject of their conversation exited the log home via the back door and stepped onto the deck. "I'm done with my homework, Dad. Can I play video games for a while?"

Zach looked at his ten-year-old son. "Sure, but only for an hour." Evan disappeared inside the house again as his father's attention was momentarily drawn to the large black German Shepherd that lay on the deck near his feet. A low growl rumbled in the animal's chest. "Quiet, Mika."

Brian smiled. "The bear again?"

"More than likely," Zach returned. "That's the only reason she ever growls. At least it doesn't come near the house when she's outside."

"No, it waits until the middle of the night when she's

in the house and we're all asleep," Caryn added. "Then it wreaks havoc on the deck and in my flower garden."

The cop laughed. "Such is life in the country." Brian looked at the dog again, then at Zach. "So, are you going to take her out to Connecticut and have Chris Byrne from Stonehill Kennel train her?"

"I haven't decided yet. We don't really need a full-fledged protection dog anymore. It would cost between five and eight grand to get her trained, and I'm not sure it's worth it. She can handle *bears* without training, and that's about all she has to worry about out here."

"Unlike her predecessor," Brian commented.

Zach glanced at his wife. Even after nearly three years, Caryn's cheeks still paled at the thought of the horror Dan Hamilton had put them through. "Yeah, unlike her predecessor."

"So, how's Kelsey doing?" Brian quickly changed the subject, referring to Zach's daughter from a previous marriage as he took yet another swig of the Miller Lite. "She enjoying college?"

"She's only been at the main U in Laramie for two weeks, but yeah. She likes it. It helps that Brandon is there to show her the ropes." The fire chief glanced at his wife again, this time with a wan grin. "In fact, Kelsey and Brandon are *dating*."

Brian laughed. "*Your* daughter and *Caryn's* son are dating? That must be a little awkward. For you guys, anyway."

"A little," Caryn admitted. "In fact, Brandon was hesitant even to tell us. But, like I told him, they're not blood related, so there's nothing wrong with it." She lifted her slender shoulders in a shrug. "Actually I'm surprised it didn't happen before now. Brandon and Kelsey formed a close bond after that night with Dan. All the kids did."

"Yeah, well when a family faces death together, it's bound to create some close ties. Even *extended* families."

"And on that note," Caryn said as she pushed herself up, "I'm going to go start supper." She looked at their friend. "You staying, Brian?"

"Do I ever pass up one of your meals?"

She laughed. "Okay. I'll set four places."

Caryn started toward the back door and froze when an echoing report was immediately followed by a resounding *thwack*. Shards of wood exploded from the house only inches from her head. Brian tackled her to the floor of the deck an instant later. Zach, in turn, grabbed the lunging Mika's collar, preventing the dog from charging from the porch. He tipped the wooden patio table on its side, using the thick oak as a shield for himself and the canine. Brian and Caryn crawled to join him as another five bullets marred the deck around them.

"What in the hell—!"

"I don't know," Brian answered his friend's quiet exclamation, "but obviously somebody still wants the two of you dead."

"What are we going to do?" Caryn cried softly.

"Dad?"

Zach's alarmed gaze swung toward the now open door to the house, more than ten feet away. "Get back inside, Evan! Now!"

The boy obeyed without argument.

"Can we make it to the door?" Caryn asked in a voice that shook with fear.

"You're gonna have to try," Brian returned. "From the sound of the shots, I'd say the guy's got a 30-30. That means he's out of bullets...for now." He looked at Zach. "Let Mika go."

"What?" the fire chief asked in amazement.

"Let her go, Zach. She'll cover the ground between us and the shooter a hell of a lot faster than you or I can. She'll keep the guy busy while the two of you get inside."

"Damn it, Brian, I'm not going to lose another dog!"

"I said he's out of bullets. Let her go, Zach, before the guy can reload!"

However reluctantly, Zach relinquished his hold on Mika's collar. The dog was off the deck and on her way across the driveway a split-second later. Her ferocious barks carried back to those on the porch.

"Get inside!" Brian ordered. He pulled the police-issue Glock from his shoulder holster and sprinted after Mika.

"Carl Hamilton. Why am I not surprised?"

"Get this fucking dog off me!"

Brian couldn't help but chuckle as his gaze moved to where the snarling Mika had a die-hard grip on the shooter's right wrist. Unlike her predecessor, this dog had not been trained to release on command. Blood oozed from the wound in Carl Hamilton's arm. Beside him on the ground lay a Winchester 30-30.

"Mika, come here," Brian ordered firmly.

The dog continued its assault, totally ignoring the command.

"Mika, come here!" Brian moved to grab the dog's collar, but paused upon hearing Zach's voice from behind.

"I'll get her."

The cop stepped back, allowing Mika's master to force her to relinquish her prize. Zach hauled the German Shepherd away from Carl Hamilton and commanded her to sit. The dog did as told, but a low growl continued to rumble in her chest. The fire chief looked at their assailant again as the other man struggled to his feet. His voice took on a scathing tone. "You just couldn't let it rest, could you? It's been almost three years since Dan died—"

"No, it's been almost three years since my son was *murdered*," Carl snarled as he brought his injured wrist to his chest and cradled it with his other hand.

Zach and Brian exchanged quick, apprehensive glances before the former looked at Dan Hamilton's father again. "What are you talking about?"

"I'm *talking about* the fact that *he*—" he glared at Brian "—shot Dan in cold blood!"

"That's ridiculous," Zach countered. "He was going to shoot Caryn, and Brian had no choice—"

"And that's bullshit! That may be the story you all concocted, but I found out different." His fiery gaze swung to Brian again. "You murdered him, just as sure as I'm standing here, and I'm going to make you pay." He looked at Zach again. "All of you."

"You're not going to do anything," the cop returned easily, "because you're going to prison for attempted murder." The police captain moved in and an instant later the suspect was handcuffed and muscled toward the driveway.

"Caryn called 911," Zach told his friend as he followed along behind, the decided limp in his gait a testament to Dan Hamilton's cruelty three years earlier. A still agitated Mika trotted along after them. "A cruiser should be here any minute."

"Good," Brian returned. "This guy—"

"If I'm going to jail, then you're going to be sitting in the cell right next to me!" Carl spouted, cutting Brian short. "You can be damned sure that I'll let the whole fucking town know what you did to my son!" He turned his glare on Zach. "And you and your whore of a wife can join him! There are laws against conspiracy, too, and covering up the facts!"

"I didn't cover up anything," Zach ground out.

"That's a lie, and you know it! Dan was *unarmed*. In fact, he was *handcuffed* when your friend here shot him at point blank range!" His hate-filled gaze moved to where Caryn now stood on the deck listening to them. "And she saw it, too."

The blare of sirens in the distance filled the air for the next few minutes until, finally, three patrol cars and an ambulance careened up the driveway. The still spouting Carl Hamilton was now under guard where he sat in the open doorway of the ambulance. Two paramedics tended the wound on his wrist. The 30-30, his weapon of choice to kill his former daughter-in-law and her new husband, had been tagged and taken into evidence along with six spent shell casings.

"I'll be at the station in a few minutes," Brian told one of the officers. "I want the pleasure of booking that bastard myself."

The patrol cop grinned. "You gonna do the report, too?"

"Gladly," he muttered.

The three squad cars and ambulance headed back toward town a few minutes later, with Carl Hamilton in tow. Brian and Zach returned to the deck. Mika obediently followed.

Caryn went into the latter's arms. "Are you two okay?"

"I'm fine, honey." Zach stepped back and looked at his friend. "But I'm a little worried about Brian."

The cop's brow wrinkled in confusion. "Me? Why?"

"He *knows*, Brian. I don't know how he found out, but somehow Carl Hamilton knows what really happened the night Dan died."

"And do you really think anyone will believe him? It'll be fine, Zach."

"I hope so," the other man returned doubtfully. "The new Chief of Police isn't your biggest fan, Brian. At the very least, you could lose your job over this and, at the most, you could be sitting in prison for the rest of your life."

"And, I repeat, it'll be fine." Brian dismissed the subject and his eyes strayed to the now docile Mika. "So, you think maybe she needs some training after all? She almost took Carl's arm off."

Zach chuckled, though it was far from heartfelt. "Yeah, I may have to give Chris a call after all."

CHAPTER TWO

B rian fidgeted nervously in a chair outside the office of the Chief of Police the following day. The meeting had been scheduled only two hours earlier, and the police captain had not been told why. Chief Stanley had said only that he needed to discuss something "very disturbing" with one of his least favorite employees.

Brian and Martin Stanley had a history that went way back. They had once been partners, in fact. Brian was a rookie straight out of the academy. Stanley was a field training officer assigned to show the "newbie" the ropes. The man reveled in every minute of it. He enjoyed wielding power over the inexperienced cop. He enjoyed correcting him at every turn, whether it was warranted or not. In short, he enjoyed watching Brian squirm.

All that ended the day Brian witnessed his partner take a bribe from a local drug dealer. After much soul-searching, he reported the incident to the then Chief of Police. On that day, Brian became a whistle blower within the department. Stanley was cleared of the charges, despite Brian's testimony at a departmental hearing. The other officers in their precinct eventually forgot the rookie's betrayal of a fellow cop; Brian had proven himself time and again and had saved the life of more than one of them. Stanley never forgot—and two months earlier, he had been promoted to Chief of Police.

Brian had his suspicions as to what the conversation with Chief Stanley would entail. He hoped he was wrong, but feared he was not. Carl Hamilton had wasted no time in doing exactly what he said he would. The entire city of Cheyenne, Wyoming, now buzzed with the accusations—accusations that one of the city's most honored police officers had killed an unarmed prisoner in cold blood.

The door to the Chief's office opened and the overweight, gray-haired man addressed the officer waiting in the outer room. "Come on in, Brian."

Brian did as asked. He waited until the door had been closed again before confronting his boss. "What's this all about, Chief?"

"I think you know what it's about, Brian." He indicated one of two chairs before the desk. "Have a seat."

Brian remained standing. "If you're referring to the bullshit Carl Hamilton is spouting—"

"It's not bullshit, Brian. I think you know that as well as I do." The Chief took his place behind the desk, then leaned back and studied the plain-clothed man before him. "You want to tell me what really happened that night? In your own words?"

"It was all in my report, Chief…a report written almost *three years* ago."

The older man brought his hands up, rested his elbows on the arms of the chair, and laced his fingers. "Refresh my memory."

Brian's suit-jacket–covered shoulders lifted in a sigh before he moved to take the proffered seat before the desk. "It was Christmas Eve, 2010. Dispatch got a 911 call from Caryn Riker's daughter, Melissa. She was still Caryn *Deaver* back then."

"That's right. She took back her maiden name after she divorced Dan Hamilton," the Chief stated rather than asked.

Brian nodded. "Anyway, Melissa said that her family was being held hostage by Hamilton. She and her two small children, along with Zach Riker's daughter, Kelsey, had managed to get into the panic room Zach installed in their downstairs bathroom. They were safe, but the others—Melissa's husband and brother and Kelsey's brother—were still in the living room with Zach and Caryn—and Hamilton. He had a gun and had shot Zach in the leg. In fact, he shot him in *both* legs before it was over. He also killed a guy who was playing Santa Claus *and* he killed the two cops I left stationed at the house in my absence."

"You were on your way to California to visit family when all this was going down, right?"

"Actually, I was driving back from Salt Lake City. My flight had a layover there. I had a gut feeling that something wasn't right, so I rented a car and started back to Cheyenne. I arrived at the Riker house just before the SWAT team infiltrated the place."

"And, according to your *report*, when the SWAT team stormed the house, Hamilton had the gun pointed at Caryn Deaver, correct?"

"Yes," Brian repeated the well-practiced lie. "All the curtains in the house were drawn, so we had no way of assessing the scene. The SWAT team leader and I conferred and decided we had no choice but to storm the house. When we did, Hamilton was in the process of swinging his gun toward Caryn—"

"And you had to use deadly force in order to save her."

"Correct."

"You're lying, Brian."

He bristled. "With all due respect, sir—"

Surprisingly, the Chief laughed. "Cut the crap, Brian. You have no respect for me, and the feeling is mutual. We're both cops, though, and as your *boss*, I have a job to do." Stanley pulled a pack of Marlboros from his shirt pocket and lit one before continuing. Brian was well aware of the fact that smoking was not allowed in any city-owned buildings, but refrained from commenting on the issue as Martin continued. "Apparently one of the SWAT team members had a little too much to drink a few nights back and started to ramble about the events of that night. Unfortunately for you, Dan Hamilton still has a few friends on the force, and one of those *friends* was also in the bar. He heard everything. How you stormed the house, how Hamilton was down at the time—he'd been shot in the shoulder by Caryn Deaver—how you taunted him, how the officers on scene handcuffed him and started to haul him out, how *he* threatened Caryn, told her it would never be over; that he would make it his mission to escape from prison and kill her or, if he couldn't, he'd have one of his prison buddies kill her for him. Either way, she would die. But you made sure he couldn't do that, didn't you, Brian? You made sure your *friends* would be safe. You pulled your gun and shot Hamilton in the chest—*while* he was handcuffed. Of course, the handcuffs were removed and Caryn's gun placed in his hand before you allowed the paramedics inside to treat Zach Riker, so your story held up."

Brian had paled visibly during the Chief's long oration.

"Needless to say, it was that *friend* of Dan Hamilton's, the guy who was in the bar that night, who went to Dan's father and told him everything. Hence the incident at the Rikers' the other day. Carl Hamilton was out for revenge when he started taking pot shots at the three of you. Granted, that doesn't make what he did right, and he *will* do a long stint in prison, but it was understandable."

"None of that is true, sir," Brian ground out. "That night went down exactly as it says in my report."

"That's what the SWAT team officer said, too—after he sobered up. He denied it all; said that Hamilton's friend made the whole thing up. The other cops on the scene that night are sticking to their stories, too."

"Because it's true!"

"I highly doubt that, Brian, but right now, that's beside

the point. The media is having a field day with this and, consequently, the Mayor is on *my* ass to get to the bottom of it. Fortunately for you, those SWAT team members *are* sticking to their stories. So are Zach and Caryn Riker and their children. I have no proof, Brian, but you know better than anyone that a cop has to follow his gut, and *my* gut is telling me that this whole thing stinks like a pile of shit." He lifted his broad shoulders in a shrug. "But, again, I can't prove it. If I could, I'd see you put on trial for what you did that night, and I'd relish watching you rot in prison."

Brian bristled, but didn't respond.

"You're a good cop, Brian. A damned good cop, but even *good* cops make mistakes." He emphasized the last statement, making it obvious to Brian that Martin Stanley referred to himself. "You were protecting your friends, and I can't blame you for that. What I *do* blame you for is the turmoil you've caused; the damage you've done to this department. No one trusts a rogue cop, Brian, no matter how admirable your actions might have been, and it's up to me to come up with a solution." Chief Stanley met the junior officer's unwavering stare with an equally steely one. "The way I see it, there is only *one* solution. I'll accept your resignation, Brian, effective immediately."

Brian's gray eyes widened in disbelief. "What?"

"It's the only way out, Brian...for you, and for me. Even your resignation won't be enough to satisfy some people, but I'll deal with that." The Chief's jaw hardened to match his eyes. "You have two choices, Brian. Either resign right now, or suffer through my own private investigation into what happened that night at the Riker house. And, believe me, I'm a good cop, too. I *will* get to the truth and, when I do, you'll spend the rest of your life in prison for murder."

Brian bounded to his feet. "So I'm supposed to just buckle under and give up my career? This job is my life, Martin!"

The smirk that creased Chief Stanley's face left Brian with the overwhelming desire to punch the man. "You can always do what most other rogue cops do. You can become a private detective. You don't need a license in Wyoming, but your practice *would* be regulated by the local jurisdiction." The smirk turned into a full-fledged grin. "That would be me."

"I don't want to be a private detective. I want to be a *cop*! I *am* a cop, and a damned good one!"

"Not anymore. Your career with this department is over, Brian. And this little indiscretion will follow you anywhere else you might try to get a job. I'll guarantee you that. No, whether you decide to resign or to stay under very heavy scrutiny, your prestigious career as a law enforcement officer is over. And, trust me, if you do choose to stay, you'll spend your days tracking down stray dogs until I can put you away."

Brian no longer bothered to hide his dislike or his lack of respect for the man before him. "You're enjoying this, aren't you? It may have taken twenty fucking years, but you're getting your revenge."

Stanley leaned back in the chair again. "I have no idea what you're talking about, Brian. I'm just doing my job, which includes ridding this city of bad cops."

"I thought you just said I was a *good* cop."

"That was prior to December 24, 2010. You crossed the line that night, Brian, and that decision cost you your career."

"I am so sorry, Brian," Caryn murmured early that evening where she, Zach, and the former police captain sat in the Rikers' great room. A roaring fire burned in the massive fieldstone fireplace that separated the living and dining areas of the house. The fire helped to take the decided chill out of the air, but not out of Brian's bones.

"And I repeat, it is not your fault." He looked at the just-as-guilt-ridden Zach. "Either of you. What I did that night was my choice. It was the only way the two of you were going to be rid of Dan for good. He would have killed you, Caryn. Zach, too. Maybe not that day or the next, or a week or month or a *year* later, but he would have succeeded eventually. I couldn't let that happen. He was an animal, a cruel, sadistic, *insane* animal who needed to die."

"And we're not arguing that fact," Zach countered. "In fact, I'll be forever grateful for what you did that night, but it cost you your job, Brian! Your pension is gone, all your benefits...everything you worked for for over *twenty years!*"

"I'll make do. Luckily I was able to tuck away quite a bit of money over the years." A crooked smile creased his lips. "I guess, in that way anyway, it pays to be single."

"And you'll find a job in another city," Caryn tried to reassure him. "I have no doubt. They can use good cops all over the country, Brian."

"Not *this* cop," he replied ruefully. At the questioning lift of Caryn's eyebrow, Brian explained. "Stanley made it pretty obvious that he'll see I never get another job in law enforcement." He shrugged. "Any prospective employer would have to call him for a reference. He may not be able to prove that I *stepped over the line*, as he put it, but he can make damned sure that any other departments know I was accused of it."

"So what are you going to do?" Caryn asked softly.

"Strange as it sounds, I may have to consider Stanley's suggestion."

"His *suggestion?*" Zach echoed.

Brian smiled. "He said I could become a private investigator—like most *rogue* cops do. They have to be licensed in a lot of states, but not in Wyoming, so I could virtually start right away. I would be regulated, though...by local law enforcement."

"Great," Zach muttered. "So Stanley would still have control over you."

"To a certain extent. The main problem would lie in the fact that the average P.I. gets most of his jobs from police referrals. That's where people go when they have a problem, and if it's something the police can't or *won't* handle because of lack of evidence, they refer the person to a P.I. You can be sure Stanley won't allow that. And you can also be sure that *I'm* not going to spend the rest of my life tracking down cheating husbands. I want to continue to do what I do best, and that means solving crimes and apprehending criminals."

"So when do you plan to start doing this? Working as a private investigator, I mean?" Caryn asked.

Brian took a deep breath. "Tomorrow. The first thing I'll have to do is find an office space and hire a secretary." He winked. "A hot one, of course—"

"Don't you think you should take a little time to regroup?" Zach was quick to advise, ignoring Brian's attempt at humor, which he knew was a defense mechanism. "This whole thing hasn't really sunk in yet, Brian, and when it does, it's going to hit you like a ton of bricks."

Brian bounded to his feet. "And I told you, *I am fine*! I can handle this! I'm not about to let Martin Stanley and his *ultimatum* set the course for the rest of my life! He's doing this out of revenge, plain and simple. He expects me to fail, Zach. He *wants* me to fail. Hell, he probably hopes I'll hit rock bottom and confess all my sins so he can lock me up!" The former police captain's jaw firmed with determination. "I'm not gonna let that happen, Zach. I'm going to prove him wrong. I'm going to survive this. Hell, I'm gonna do more than survive. I'm going to *thrive*! Do you have any idea how nice it will be to not have to conform to *department* rules and regulations anymore? I'll be my own boss, Zach. No more Stanleys. No more D.A. Cochranes or Mayor Kreigers to contend with. Just me, fighting crime on my own terms."

"And I hope it works out for you, Bri. Really I do, but—"

"No. No *buts*. I don't need your concern, Zach. I don't need your sympathy. What I need is your *support*. I need you and Caryn, my *best friends*, to believe that I can do this."

Caryn stood and crossed to stand before him. "We do, Brian. You were a good cop, a *great* cop, and you'll be an even

better private investigator. Heck, I'd hire you in a heartbeat."
Her expression became speculative. "If I needed a private
investigator, which I don't, but if I did, I'd hire *you*. And I *will*
recommend you if I come across anybody who needs one…"

Brian pulled her against his chest and enveloped her in a
hug. "Thanks, honey. I appreciate it."

"Mom, I'm hungry. Are we going to eat soon?" Evan
asked as he entered the great room from the kitchen.

Caryn stepped back and looked at her son. "I'm going
to start supper right now." Her gaze moved to Brian again.
"You're staying, right?"

"I'd better," he returned drolly. "If this plan doesn't work,
it might be the last decent meal I'll ever get."

CHAPTER THREE

B rian sat behind the desk in his orderly office, contemplating the heavy snowfall that continued to pile up outside the two dormer windows. Three months had passed since he had been forced to resign from the job he loved and go into business for himself. An impressive website, as well as ads in all the area newspapers, touted his experience. The newly released phone book and the Yellow Pages online included him in the "Private Investigator" listings. Even the sign displayed prominently on the outside of the building declared his presence to a bustling community. And what had it netted him? One client: a woman who needed someone to track down her wayward ex-husband so the state could go after him for back child support. She was a teacher at Lebhart Elementary and had been referred by Caryn Riker.

Money was running low. Bills were running high. By his calculations, he could stay in business two more months, three, maybe four if he laid off his "hot" secretary, Sherry Corbin. Despite his reputation as a playboy, Brian had not been able to find the energy to hit on the twenty-seven-year-old voluptuous, single, and very capable blonde. He was just too tired.

The subject of his thoughts entered the office from the

reception area. Brian looked up as she laid several envelopes on his desk. "The mail," she told him. "The utility bill is in there. It's $219.00."

"Thanks, Sherry. I'll take care of it."

The blonde started to leave, then reconsidered and turned back. "Would it be okay if I leave early? It's getting pretty nasty out there."

Brian nodded. "Sure. Drive safely."

Sherry started to exit the office again and, again, turned back. "Are you okay?"

Brian's shoulders lifted in a sigh. "No, I'm not, Sherry, and you won't be either if business doesn't pick up soon. I... might have to let you go."

She moved to perch on the edge of one of the chairs before Brian's desk. Even the sight of her ample cleavage did little to lighten his mood. "Hey, don't give up the ship yet. You *could* still try the bounty-hunting angle. You'd just have to get a bail bondsman to hire you—"

"I told you, Sherry, I'm a P.I. Not a bounty hunter. I don't want to traipse all over the country tracking down fugitives. I want to work right here in Cheyenne."

She sighed. "Okay, well, if worse comes to worst, we can sell that big, fancy photocopier and get one of those little all-in-one printers. That might get us by for another month or two."

Brian couldn't help but smile. "You really *do* want to keep your job, don't you?"

"In this economy, are you kidding? Don't forget, I have a baby to take care of. You know, formula, diapers... And, besides, you're a great boss. I love working here."

"I bet you'd prefer to be a little busier, though, wouldn't you?"

"Granted, I can fill the coffee pot and clean my desk only so many times in a day, and I do get a little tired of playing solitaire on the computer, but I'll manage."

Brian could do nothing but laugh at the futility of it all.

"Get the hell out of here. I have a lot more brooding to do, and I prefer to do it in private."

Sherry cast him a sympathetic smile as she stood. "It'll work out, Brian. I'm sure of it. Word will get around about what a good private investigator you are and people will be beating down your door."

"Right. I'd be happy just to have someone walk *through* the door...a paying client, that is." He returned her smile. "See you tomorrow...unless the storm gets too bad, then don't bother. You can just come back after Christmas. I don't want you sitting in a ditch somewhere."

"Will do. I'll see you tomorrow and, if not, have a Merry Christmas!" Sherry returned to the outer office then and, a moment later, fought the howling wind as she opened the door and exited into the storm.

Brian leaned back in the chair and resumed his unseeing perusal of the would-be blizzard outside. *I have to do something so that woman can keep her job. Christ, she's got a kid...*

"Damn you, Stanley!"

Brian couldn't help but feel that the new Chief of Police was somehow responsible for his lack of clients. In his former position as captain of Cheyenne's 6th District Brian had referred people to local private detectives at least once a month, and he was just one cop. He knew others had, too. In fact, the P.I.'s in Cheyenne did a very lucrative business *because* of police department referrals. Or at least the five main ones did. The fact that he had gotten *no* referrals led Brian to believe only one thing with certainty. Martin Stanley had issued a citywide order that *no one* was to refer prospective clients to B.K. Investigations.

And the Police Chief had gone one step further. Apparently he had approached every bail bondsman in Cheyenne, also. Typically, these companies would jump at the chance to have a former cop, and a police *captain* no less, in their employ as a bounty hunter. Despite what he told Sherry earlier, Brian *had* talked to virtually every bail bondsman in the city. Granted, that was *not* what he wanted to do—travel the country tracking down bail jumpers—but at this point he would do about anything to keep the office open. Stanley had made it impossible for him to follow that route, too. Apparently the man was determined to humiliate him at best and put him out of business at worst.

The door to the reception area opened and closed again a few minutes later. Brian smiled as he stood and made his way to the doorway between the two offices. "What? Did you decide to take the photocopier with you for insur—" He paused in mid-word when confronted with the woman who was in the process of stamping snow from her boots just inside the front entry. The hood of her jacket shadowed her face, but her petite stature relayed that she was definitely *not* his secretary.

"Are you Brian Koski?" she asked breathlessly.

"Y-yes, I am," he stammered in surprise. "How can I help you?"

The newcomer removed the glove from her right hand and held it out before her. "My name's Melody Patten. I live just down the street...and I might be interested in hiring you."

Brian ignored the sudden rapid beating of his heart and stepped aside. He indicated for the woman to precede him into the other room. "Well, in that case, let's go into my office and you can tell me what the problem is."

"Thank you."

Brian waited until Melody had paused before his desk. "Can I take your coat?"

"I suppose that would probably be a good idea." He could feel, if not see, her smile, nervous though it was. "Considering that I'm dripping all over your rug."

She removed the coat, and Brian hung it on a rack in the corner of the office. He did not miss the rewarding view of Melody's slender, shapely body and short, stylishly cut brunette hair. He was a man first, after all, and a private investigator second. He indicated for her to sit, and then did the same himself behind the desk.

"So, what can I do for you, Miss—"

"It's Mrs. Mrs. Jeff Patten. But, please, call me Melody."

"Okay, Melody. And, again, what can I do for you?"

"You handled the Dan Hamilton stalker case a few years back, didn't you?" she returned with a question of her own. "When you were still on the police force?"

Brian bristled. *Where is this going?* "Yes, I did."

"So, you're familiar with how stalkers work and how to deal with them?"

"I'm very familiar, yes." He sat back in the chair. "So, do you think someone is stalking you?"

"Actually, I think it would be closer to the truth to say that he's stalking my daughter, Angela."

Brian's brow knitted in a concerned frown. "Really? That's disturbing." He stood again and rounded the desk to perch on the edge in front of Melody. "And who would *he* be?"

"His name is Collin Lanaski. He's my daughter's teacher. Or rather, he *was* her teacher. We managed to have her moved to a new classroom a few weeks ago."

"Okay, let's back up here a minute. How old is Angela?"

"Seven," Melody answered.

"Seven?" he repeated incredulously.

"Yes. She's just a little girl, Mr. Koski. She can't defend herself!"

"Okay. Calm down. What school does she attend?"

"Lebhart Elementary."

The same school Caryn teaches at, Brian's mind volunteered. "2nd grade?"

"Yes."

"Who's her teacher now?"

"Mrs. Riker."

The private detective smiled. "I know Mrs. Riker. Your daughter is in good hands." Brian crossed his arms over his chest. "So, this Collin Lanaski, what makes you think he's stalking your daughter?"

"It began last fall, shortly after school started. Apparently, he took the class into the gym one day to play dodge ball and took off his shirt. He still had a T-shirt on—it wasn't like he was being inappropriate. Anyway, Angela saw the dog tags he wore around his neck—he's ex Air Force. He said she told him that she owned a dog tag like that a long time ago. She said that her father gave it to her." Melody shrugged. "I think he misunderstood her, though he claims he didn't. My husband was never in the service and Angela has never owned any dog tags. She did play with *my* father's dog tags a few times when she was little, though, so that might be what she was referring to. Anyway, that simple assertion was enough to convince Collin Lanaski that Angela was *his* long-lost daughter; apparently he had given his little girl a dog tag years ago when he left for Iraq."

"And he told you all of this?"

Melody nodded. "A couple of months ago when he first came to the house."

"To *your* house?"

"He comes there all the time, Mr. Koski. At first he would actually come up to the door and, when we'd answer it, he would rant and rave about how Angela was his daughter. How he had *proof*. After he showed up a few times, my husband told him that he wasn't welcome and that we would call the police if he ever bothered us again. Now he just stands on the public sidewalk out front and watches the house. Or, if Angela is playing in the yard, he'll stand on the other side of the fence and watch *her*. We've come out of the movies, or a restaurant, or a shopping mall and found him waiting in the parking lot. Wherever we go, Mr. Koski, he is always there!"

Melody's last words were accompanied by a rush of tears. Brian handed her a box of tissues that had been sitting on the desk and waited for her to dry her eyes before asking his next question.

"*Did* you contact the police?"

She nodded. "I did—and Jeff was not happy."

"But I thought he told Lanaski that he *would* go to the police if he didn't stop harassing your family."

"It was just a threat. Jeff says there is nothing the police can do, because he hasn't actually *done* anything, and he was right. In fact, they've had dealings with Mr. Lanaski, too. He's gone to the police with the same story—that Angela is his daughter and *we* took her."

"Is there any possibility that he might be right? Is Angela adopted?"

"No!" Melody exclaimed. "She is *my* daughter. I gave birth to her seven years ago!"

"Okay, okay. Calm down. I had to ask." Brian pushed himself up and wandered the small room. "So, do you know if Lanaski actually has a daughter?"

"I asked that same question of the police. Collin Lanaski *did* have a daughter; she died in a car accident out on Hynds Boulevard four years ago when he was serving in Iraq. His wife died, too."

Brian turned back to the prospective client with a raised eyebrow. "Really? If that's the case, it sounds like this guy might have suffered a psychotic break—and that could make him very dangerous."

"That's what we're afraid of, Mr. Koski. He's convinced that Angela is his daughter, and there's no telling what he might do."

Brian nodded slowly as he moved to sit behind the desk again. He pulled a pad of yellow legal paper from one of the drawers and laid it on the desk top. "Okay. Collin Lanaski," he mumbled as he wrote down the name. He looked at Melody again to confirm the spelling. "L-a-n-a-s-k-i?"

"Yes."

"Do you happen to know his address?"

"No."

"That's okay. I can find it out from the school."

"So, are you saying that you'll take the case?" Melody asked hopefully.

"Let me go talk to the guy, see what he has to say, and then we'll go from there. If you can give me your address, I'll stop by after I've talked to Lanaski. I'll need your phone number, too."

Melody relayed the information. "My husband won't be pleased to see you," she cautioned.

One eyebrow dipped in confusion. "Why is that?"

"He doesn't know that I'm here. He thinks we can handle this ourselves." She shook her head. "I'm scared, Mr. Koski. Collin Lanaski is out of control. He really believes that Angela is his daughter. What if he just takes her?"

"That's what I'm here for, Melody...to make sure that he doesn't."

"Brian! What are you doing here?" Caryn Riker exclaimed from where she sat behind her desk in the empty classroom at Lebhart Elementary grading papers. Brian stood in the open doorway.

"Actually, I'm here on a case. I just finished talking to the principal."

"A *case*?" Caryn echoed.

"Yeah, and this client wasn't referred by you." He smiled.

She stood and moved to give him a hug. "Well, congratulations. I told you things would pick up."

"Yeah, well I haven't actually been hired by these people yet. I'm doing a little leg work for them first. And, even if they do hire me, *one* case is not going to cut it—so feel free to send more people my way."

Caryn smiled. "Will do. So, what is this case anyway, and why did it bring you to Lebhart?"

"It concerns one of the teachers. He may be stalking a student—one of *your* students."

Caryn stepped back, her brow furrowed in confusion. "My kids are only seven and eight years old, Brian. It's pretty unlikely that one of them would be stalked."

"Maybe," he returned noncommittally. "So, how well do you know Collin Lanaski?"

"Fairly well, I guess. I mean, I talk to him nearly every day—" Her eyes widened in sudden dawning. "Is he the teacher you were referring to? The one who might be stalking a student?"

"Possibly."

She moved to sit behind the desk again. "You're way off base here, Brian. Collin Lanaski is a very nice guy, and a good teacher. He would never hurt one of his students."

"Did he ever mention that he had a daughter?"

"Yes. She died in a car accident a couple of years before he started working at Lebhart. His wife died, too. He was stationed in Iraq at the time; he was in the Air Force. His wife and daughter were still living here, though, on the base."

"Warren?" Brian asked, referring to the Air Force base just west of Cheyenne.

Caryn nodded.

"So, since you think he's such a nice, normal guy, would it surprise you that he's insisting Angela Patten—your student—is his daughter?"

"You're kidding! Is that why they moved her from his class to mine a few weeks ago?"

"I would say that's a fairly good assumption. Angela's parents went to the principal and told her about Lanaski's accusations. Actually, I'm surprised she didn't fire him."

"There would be no grounds, unless he actually did something to Angela."

"So, hanging around outside their house, following them to the movies and the mall, that doesn't count?" Brian asked astutely.

"He's been *following* them?" Caryn rubbed sudden goose bumps from her arms.

Brian lifted an eyebrow. "Sound familiar?"

"Yes, a little *too* familiar. If he starts sending boxes of chocolates and flowers, then they have something to worry about."

"Boxes of chocolates, along with a cryptic message, right?" Brian's smile was sympathetic.

"Right." Caryn shuddered again, this time from head to toe.

"Anyway, I managed to get his address from Principal Sampson. I'm going to go have a talk with him now. Get his side of the story, as ludicrous as it might be." He reached out to squeeze Caryn's hand. "Be careful around this guy, honey. It sounds like he might have a screw loose."

"What about his kids, Brian? The kids in his class, I mean. Do you actually think he might be dangerous?"

"I don't know the answer to that one. I'll be able to judge better after I talk to him. If I *do* think he's a threat, though, you can be sure I'll be talking to Monica Sampson again tomorrow. As principal of this school, it's her responsibility to make sure *all* the children are safe, and if she has a psycho working here as a teacher, it's a given that there is going to be trouble ahead."

Brian had Sherry research the car accident that killed Collin Lanaski's wife and child before he headed over to the 2nd grade teacher's house the following day. He wanted to have all the information, *accurate* information, before he confronted what, from the sound of it, might be a very disturbed man.

"Mr. Lanaski?"

"Yes."

Brian held out his hand toward the tall, thirty-some-thing, blond man who stood in the open doorway before him. "My name is Brian Koski. I'm a private investigator. I was retained by Melody Patten to try and sort out this mis-understanding regarding their daughter, Angela."

"There's no *misunderstanding.* Angela is my daughter... and, by the way, her real name is Courtney. You want to know anything else, talk to my attorney." He started to slam the door in Brian's face, but the former police captain's quick actions halted the movement.

"You have an attorney?"

"Thomas Mathison. I retained him yesterday. He's going to work on proving Courtney's real identity."

"So, he wasn't bothered by the fact that your daughter is *dead?* That she died in a car accident, along with your wife, on December 16, 2009? *That* information is documented, Mr. Lanaski."

"Look, I don't understand how it happened any better than you do, but Angela Patten *is* my daughter. She didn't die in that accident. Somehow the Pattens managed to get their hands on her—and I intend to get her back."

27

CHAPTER FOUR

Christmas Eve dawned under a blanket of heavy snow. The storm had ceased late the previous afternoon, giving road crews just enough time to clear the main thoroughfares before thousands of motorists ventured out to visit family and friends. Brian had no close relatives; both of his parents had passed away the previous year. Thankfully he did have friends. He would spend the holidays with Zach and Caryn Riker and *their* family—children and grandchildren who would ensure a joyous Christmas for all.

"I still can't believe that Collin Lanaski might be psychotic," Caryn commented from where she sat beside Zach on the black leather sofa in front of the roaring fireplace. "I talked to him for a few minutes again the other day before we left for the Christmas break. He seems so *normal.*"

"You didn't say anything about the whole Angela Patten thing, did you?" Brian asked from the chair at a right angle to them.

"No, and neither did he...other than to ask how she was doing in my class."

"So, he *did* ask about her," Zach pointed out astutely.

"Just in passing," his wife defended her previous words.

"He's hired an attorney," Brian put in.

Caryn's emerald eyes shot to the other man. "Then Collin really *must* believe Angela is his daughter, and the attorney must believe it, too, or he wouldn't have taken the case."

"I haven't talked to the guy yet, so I don't know what he's thinking. I am going to meet with him, though, right after the holidays."

"He isn't going to be able to tell you much, with the whole attorney/client privilege thing," Zach cautioned.

"I know, but I can at least try."

"So, have the Pattens actually hired you then?" Caryn asked.

"Not yet. I want to talk to the attorney before I decide whether to take the case or not. If there's any possibility that Angela Patten might actually be Collin Lanaski's daughter, then I'd have to rethink *my* position."

"Lanaski's daughter is dead, Brian," Zach reminded. "There is no way Angela can be his child."

Brian shook his dark head. "God, this whole thing is so messed up." He heaved himself up from the sofa and moved to warm his hands before the fire. Seven huge stockings hung from the mantle amid a plethora of garland. The stairway to his left was decorated with yet more of the tinsel-adorned rope, as well as a myriad of brightly colored lights. "So, when are Steve and Melissa and the kids supposed to get here? And Brandon and Kelsey?"

"They all should be here any minute," Caryn answered. "In fact, I expected them before now."

"They probably had to drive slower because of the roads, honey," Zach assured her. "I'm sure they'll all be here soon."

"What about Matt?" Brian asked, referring to Zach's son as he turned back to them. "Is he coming?"

"Not until tomorrow. It's Katie's turn to have the kids on Christmas Eve. In fact—" he glanced at his wife "—that may be where Brandon and Kelsey are. They might have gone straight to Katie's parents. That's where they always open gifts." A rueful smile touched his lips. "And they all want to meet Brandon."

"Could you call and find out for sure?"

"Sure." Zach stood and went to use the kitchen phone as Evan exited his bedroom at the foot of the stairs.

"Hi, Uncle Brian!"

"Hey there, squirt. Merry Christmas."

The boy looked at his mother. "So how long *now* before Santa comes?"

Caryn just smiled. "We went through this earlier, honey. Santa doesn't come until the middle of the night when you're sleeping."

The boy released a heartfelt sigh as he moved to plop down on the floor in front of the massive, brightly decorated Christmas tree. He rested his chin in his hands as he stared at all the gaily wrapped presents. "I'm getting really tired of waiting." He looked over his shoulder at Brian. "My *other* Mom and Dad said they didn't have money to spend on stupid presents for me and Megan, and they said Santa wasn't real. That people just made him up. But my *new* Mom and Dad—" he craned his neck further to look at Caryn "—said that isn't true."

"So how about Mr. and Mrs. Kirby? Didn't they buy you any presents?" Brian asked, referring to the boy's foster parents, with whom he lived for over a year until Zach and Caryn adopted him.

Evan shook his head. "They didn't have Christmas at their house. They did give me a present on Hanukkah, though. It was a truck."

"Ah, so they were Jewish."

"I guess so." His eyes returned to the tree. "But I get *lots* of presents this Christmas. I did last year, too. There's *ten* of 'em under the tree with my name on 'em, but I can't open 'em until after supper."

Brian moved to ruffle the child's blond hair. "It won't be

long now, squirt. Your mom said we'll be eating as soon as Melissa and Steve and the kids get here."

"Kelsey and Brandon *are* at Katie's Mom and Dad's," Zach announced as he reentered the room. "They got there a couple hours ago. They're staying at Katie's tonight and will be over in the morning."

Caryn released a relieved sigh. "Good. I can quit worrying about *them* anyway."

"Did my Mom and Dad tell you that we're getting another dog, Uncle Brian?" Evan piped up again.

It was Brian's turn to glance over his shoulder at the boy's parents. "*Another* dog?"

"I forgot to tell you about that," Zach returned. "I got a call the other day from Chris Byrne. He sold a dog to the NYPD a while back, but they realized it gets skittish on subway platforms. It's scared of thunder, too. They had to return it. Chris can't resell it, so he's just looking for a good home."

Brian stood and crossed to his friend. "So, he's *giving* it to you guys? A trained police dog?"

"Yup, which means I probably won't have to get Mika trained after all, since *that* dog is trained. As long as an intruder doesn't arrive during a thunderstorm, we should be good." Zach laughed suddenly. "Actually, it was kind of funny...Chris said they could fire a gun right next to the dog's head and he wouldn't flinch, but take him out in a thunderstorm and he freaks."

"His name is Sinbad," Evan put in.

"So this one's a *male* dog?"

Zach nodded.

"Is he a German Shepherd?" Brian asked.

"Actually, he's a Belgian Malinois," Zach informed him. "Another breed of Shepherd that's smaller and more intense. They also have a boxier build than a German Shepherd. Chris said they're the most popular police dogs in the world right now. Sinbad is trained in cadaver scenting and search and rescue, too, so I might be able to use him at work once in a while."

"Do you have to go through the training again, the whole transfer of authority thing?"

"Oh, yeah. Chris will be bringing him next week and he'll put us through the entire gamut. He emailed me a picture of him. Want to see it?"

"Sure."

Brian and Zach started through the kitchen, headed toward the game room where the computer was housed, but paused when the back door opened and Melissa and Steve and the kids blew into the house.

"Grandpa!" seven-year-old Jacob exclaimed as he started toward Zach at a run.

"Uh-uh-uh," his mother caught him by the hood on his jacket and reeled him in. "Boots off first. You don't want to make a mess of Grandma's floor."

The little boy quickly did as told, and then tore across the room to be scooped into Zach's arms.

"Hey there, buckshot!" he greeted as his gaze strayed to where Caryn and Evan had just rounded the fireplace and entered the kitchen, also.

"It's Christmas!" Jacob declared. "Is Santa gonna come here tonight?"

"Doesn't he always?" the older man returned.

"Yup. But Mommy said the bad man *isn't* gonna come again, right?"

The adults exchanged quick glances. It was the heartfelt wish of all that Jacob would forget the terror on Christmas Eve three years earlier. Apparently, he hadn't, despite extensive counseling. Ashley was only two at the time and her immature brain had not held onto the memory.

"No, buckshot," Zach told him firmly. "The bad man can never come here again."

"Good. He was scary."

"Yes, Jacob, he was."

"So, did you have a good trip?" Caryn asked Melissa, quickly changing the subject as she responded to five-year-old Ashley's outstretched arms and picked up her granddaughter. "A harrowing one would be more like it," Melissa responded. "The roads were terrible."

"Well, hopefully they'll have them cleared before you head back to Loveland."

"I hope so."

"Can we eat now, Mom, so we can open presents?" Evan asked, barely able to contain his own excitement.

"Oh, I don't know." A mischievous twinkle lit Caryn's green eyes as she set Ashley on the floor again and stooped before her son. "I think maybe we should wait until tomorrow to open presents."

"Mom!"

Caryn laughed as she tousled the boy's hair. "Just kidding. And, yes, we can eat. It's all ready."

"Yes!" Evan pumped his right arm in sync with the exclamation, then raced to take his place at the massive dining room table as Caryn and Melissa began setting out the meal.

CHAPTER FIVE

B rian waited impatiently in the waiting room outside Thomas Mathison's office two days after Christmas. He had been informed by the man's pretty blonde secretary that the attorney was on the phone and would be with him shortly. His failed attempt to flirt with the law clerk had lasted exactly one minute; she wanted nothing to do with him, and the diamond ring on her left hand explained why. Brian was, therefore, left to sit in a hard leather chair, his right foot tapping out an aggravated beat on the carpeted floor.

The door to the inner office opened a few minutes later and the rotund, aging Thomas Mathison stepped into the entryway. "Come on in, Mr. Koski."

Brian bounded to his feet and followed the larger man into the next room.

"Have a seat," the attorney invited as he did the same himself behind the large, scuffed desk.

Brian did as asked.

"So, you're here about Collin Lanaski?"

"Yes," the other man affirmed. "I know you probably can't tell me much because of attorney/client privilege, but—"

"Mr. Lanaski is not my client, Mr. Koski, so I can tell you anything you want to know—but be warned. I don't know much."

Brian's forehead wrinkled in confusion. "He's not your client? But he told me that he had retained you."

"I met with Mr. Lanaski, yes, and I was admittedly ambiguous when it came to taking his case. I did *not* accept any money from him, however, and will do my best to avoid his phone calls in the future."

Brian's raised eyebrow prompted the attorney to go on.

"The man is clearly delusional, Mr. Koski, and quite scary. There is no basis in fact that Angela Patten is his daughter. Courtney Lanaski is dead. I know that better than anyone."

"Why do you say that?"

"Because I *was* his wife's divorce attorney—prior to her death and the death of her daughter."

"Her *divorce* attorney?"

The older man nodded. "Mrs. Lanaski retained me three months before she died in the accident. She wanted to wait, though, until her husband had returned from Iraq to serve the papers. She was a kind-hearted woman. She didn't want to spring the divorce on him when he was so far from home and serving his country."

"So you knew Mrs. Lanaski then?"

"As well as any attorney actually gets to know his clients, yes."

"And you know for a fact that Courtney Lanaski died in that accident," Brian stated rather than asked. He already knew the answer after reading the news article Sherry found, but wanted to hear the man's response.

"It was all over the news, Mr. Koski. It's also a matter of public record. You should know that better than anyone, being a former police officer."

"Traffic accidents, fatal or not, were not a part of my job, Mr. Mathison. I didn't respond to the scene, so I have no knowledge of what happened. That's why I'm asking you."

"Yes, well it was a terrible tragedy. There's no doubt of that." The lawyer sat back in his chair. "Mr. Lanaski *also* made the news when he was sent home for the funeral. He claimed, even then, that his daughter was still alive."

"Why would he say something like that? I mean, he must have had to identify the bodies."

"The car exploded on impact, Mr. Koski. Both bodies were burned beyond recognition. The coroner wasn't even able to perform an autopsy, because the damage was so severe. They were able to identify the mother through dental records, but there were no dental records for the child; she had not yet been to a dentist at her young age. The license plate on the car also served to identify the victims. It was registered to Mr. and Mrs. Lanaski."

"And he just chose to ignore all that and claim his daughter was still alive?"

"Mr. Lanaski is not a stable man, Mr. Koski. He lost touch with reality after the death of his family. He based his conclusions on the fact that the child in the car was not wearing a *dog tag*. Apparently he had an extra one and gave it to her before he left for Iraq. He claims she never took it off."

"I'm aware of the whole dog tag scenario. I *didn't* know, though, that he was using that argument even way back then."

"He was also spouting something about a discrepancy concerning the car seat that was found in the vehicle. I didn't get the whole gist of it. He was very distraught and wasn't making a lot of sense when he was here."

"A car seat?"

The older man shrugged. "That's what he said. Something about it being the *wrong* car seat. Again, the man is delusional. He rambled on about the dog tag and car seat for close to an hour, trying to convince me that there was merit in his claims. Frankly, I saw none. What I *did* see is a man whose level of anguish has caused him to lose touch with reality. He doesn't need an attorney. He needs a shrink. I wasn't about to tell him that, though. Hell, I didn't even have the courage to tell him that I wouldn't represent him. The man is clearly dangerous, Mr. Koski, and he firmly believes that

Angela Patten is his daughter. He told me that day in this very office that no one will ever convince him otherwise and, if necessary, he will kill to get her back."

"I'm willing to take your case, Mrs. Patten," Brian told the shapely brunette later that same afternoon where he sat across from the woman in the living room of their modest home on Oneil Avenue in Cheyenne. "Collin Lanaski is clearly delusional," he used Thomas Mathison's words, "and your little girl is going to need protection. So are you and your husband."

"Thank you, Mr. Koski. I can't tell you how much this means to me. I am so scared that he's going to do something to Angela…or that he might try to take her."

"And you should be concerned, but it will be my job to make sure that doesn't happen. Now, I hate to bring this up, but before we get into what I can do to help you, we'll have to discuss my fee."

"Of course. Whatever the cost, it will be worth it to see that Angela is safe."

"I'll try to keep my expenses down as much as possible, but I'll basically be on call for you twenty-four hours a day, seven days a week. You'll have both my home and cell numbers. My apartment is only ten minutes away and my office, as you know, is just down the block. No matter where I am, I can be here on virtually a moment's notice if the need should arise."

"That's good to know."

"Now the bad news." Brian smiled. "My retainer is $5000—"

"Who are you?"

Melody bounded off the sofa at the sound of her husband's voice and crossed the room in three long strides. Brian, too, came to his feet.

"Jeff! I didn't expect you home so early."

"Obviously," the stout, dark-haired man returned snippily. He looked at Brian again and repeated his earlier question. "Who are you?"

Brian moved to stand before the shorter man, one hand outstretched. "Brian Koski, Mr. Patten. I'm a private investigator."

The other man's brown eyes narrowed with suspicion as he shook the proffered hand. "Private investigator?"

"I contacted him, Jeff," Melody jumped in. "I was hoping he could help us with Collin Lanaski. Brian said he'll take the case—"

"We don't need any help. I can handle Lanaski."

"From what your wife has told me, Mr. Patten," Brian interceded, "the situation with Mr. Lanaski is escalating rapidly. It went from him simply being your child's teacher to him insisting that she is his *daughter* within the matter of only a couple of months. He's watching your home, he's following you...all so that he can keep track of Angela's whereabouts. He's also made threats against your lives—"

Both of the Pattens' eyes widened with this latest revelation. Jeff spoke first.

"What do you mean, he's made threats?"

"I spoke with a Thomas Mathison this morning. He's a local attorney. Collin Lanaski attempted to hire him to look into the whole parentage thing regarding Angela. Mr. Mathison was actually *afraid* to tell Lanaski that he wouldn't take the case. He also believes that Lanaski is delusional— and dangerous. Consequently, Mr. Lanaski thinks this guy *is* representing him. In fact, he's the one who gave me Mathison's name."

"But the lawyer *didn't* take the case, right?" Jeff pressed.

"No. Thomas Mathison was actually retained as *Mrs.* Lanaski's divorce attorney just before she died. He knew her...and he's all too aware that she and her daughter are dead. He attempted to tell Mr. Lanaski as much, but the guy wouldn't listen. Apparently, he started this whole *my daughter's alive* thing right after the accident. Then it was just conjecture on his part. Now, though, he's progressed to where there's an actual child that he's fantasizing about—"

"Angela," Melody breathed.

"I'm afraid so," Brian affirmed, "and Lanaski told this attorney that he would kill if necessary to get her back."

"Oh, my God!" It was Melody again who made the quiet exclamation. Her husband slipped a comforting arm around her shoulders as Brian looked at him again.

"You need me, Mr. Patten. Collin Lanaski is getting desperate, which also makes him dangerous. You need someone who can delve into his past and find out what makes him tick. You need someone who has the time to tail him and watch his every move. You need someone who, if necessary, can put the fear of God into him. In short, you need someone who can assure your family's safety and, as a former cop, I'm that guy."

"And you really think he's that dangerous?"

"He's psychotic, Mr. Patten, and he truly believes that Angela is his daughter. Yes, he's that dangerous."

The other man nodded slowly, and then got down to the crux of the matter. "So how much is this going to cost us?"

"My retainer would be five thousand dollars. That would secure my services for three months. It wouldn't include expenses, of course, but they should be minimal in this case—"

"Five thousand dollars!" Jeff apparently heard nothing except the initial fee. "I'm an explosives expert, Mr. Koski. I *work* for K.C. Demolitions. I don't own the damned company. We don't have that kind of money!"

"Yes, we do, Jeff," Melody interjected softly.

"No," her husband returned firmly. "We're not touching your inheritance. That's supposed to be for Angela's college education."

"And what good will it do to save for her education if Collin Lanaski takes her from us or worse!"

The front door opened, and a towheaded girl walked into the house, book bag in hand. She was unusually tall for her age—considering that she was only seven years old. Melody cast a nervous glance in Brian's direction before she moved to hug the child.

"Hi, honey. Did you have a good day at school?"

"Uh-huh." Angela looked at Brian with a question in her big, blue eyes.

He smiled. "Hi, Angela. My name is Brian. I'm...a friend of your mom and dad's."

"Hi," she returned shyly.

"Okay!" Melody exclaimed a little too brightly. "Let's go in the kitchen and get you a snack." She helped the child to remove her jacket and backpack, then took her hand and led her down the hall.

Jeff looked at Brian again. "Five thousand, huh?"

"I wish it could be less, Mr. Patten, but, believe me, it'll be worth it."

"And you really think that Lanaski might harm my wife or daughter?"

"I don't think he would harm Angela, not if he truly believes she's *his* daughter, but there's no telling what he would do to you and your wife if he should decide to actually try and take her. From what I've found out so far, it sounds like he suffered a psychotic break when he learned that his wife and daughter died in that accident. Over the years, he's become delusional. Obviously there's something about Angela in particular that triggered that delusion. He's been teaching at Lebhart for two years and this is the first time there's been a problem with one of the children under his care."

"All he ever said to me was that Angela told him she used to own a dog tag like the ones he wears. Apparently, he gave *his* daughter one at some point. He was convinced that she would have had it on when she died, but apparently the little girl in the car didn't. When I asked Angela about it, she said she was referring to the dog tag she saw in my wife's jewelry box. It belonged to Melody's father. Melody let her play with it now and then, but that was years ago."

"And did Angela tell Lanaski that the dog tag she played with belonged to her grandfather?"

"Yes, she did."

"And Lanaski just misunderstood?"

Jeff lifted his broad shoulders in a shrug. "Apparently so."

"One other thing," Brian continued. "Does Angela walk home from school by herself?"

"Actually she walks with a couple of friends who live just around the corner."

"I would strongly suggest that you not have her do that anymore, Mr. Patten. It makes her an easy target should Lanaski decide to try and take her."

"So you think we should take her to school and pick her up?"

"Is that possible?"

He nodded. "Melody doesn't work, so yes. She can walk her to school in the mornings and go get her afterward—if you really think it's necessary."

"I do."

"Okay... Well, I guess I'll have to go to the bank and get the money to pay your retainer. I still don't think it's necessary, but apparently Melody feels differently. And, if it'll help put her mind at ease, then it's worth it to me, too. It's her money, after all. She can do what she wants with it."

"I would also stop at the police station and apply for a restraining order against Lanaski. If a judge grants it, and I don't see why one wouldn't, then Lanaski will be in contempt if he comes within five hundred feet of Angela."

Jeff nodded slowly. "Okay."

"And I will start delving into Lanaski's history tomorrow. I'll also go have another talk with him. I'd like to talk to Angela first, though, if that's all right."

"Now?"

"It makes sense, since I'm here. I just want to hear her version of what happened that day with the dog tag."

"I...guess that would be okay. Can Melody and I be in the room when you talk to her?"

"Sure."

Jeff stepped out into the hallway and called for his wife and daughter. They appeared a moment later.

"Mr. Koski would like to talk to Angela."

The little girl immediately looked up at her mother, her eyes wide with obvious hesitancy.

"It's okay, honey. Mr. Koski is a nice man."

"And Mommy and Daddy will be right here the whole time," Jeff added.

"Okay," she replied softly.

Melody led her daughter to the sofa and moved to stand behind her. Jeff joined his wife, while Brian took a seat at a right angle to Angela.

He smiled. "Hi again."

"Hi," she returned.

"Angela, I wanted to ask you a few questions about your teacher, Mr. Lanaski."

"He's not my teacher anymore."

"That's right. Mrs. Riker is your teacher now, isn't she?"

The little girl nodded.

"I know Mrs. Riker, too. She's a pretty nice lady, isn't she?"

"She's real nice."

"Was Mr. Lanaski nice, too?"

"Uh-huh."

"Angela, can you tell me about the day you saw Mr. Lanaski's dog tags? I think it was in gym class."

"We were playing dodge ball. He took off his shirt, and they were hanging around his neck."

"What did you think when you saw the dog tags?"

"I thought they looked like the one—" she glanced at her father over her shoulder "—my grandpa had. It was in my mommy's jewelry box. She used to let me play with it when I was little."

"Did you tell Mr. Lanaski that?"

"Uh-huh."

"And what did he say?"

"He said that he gave a dog tag to his little girl when he had to go to a war, and that he told her to never take it off, even when she took a bath or went to bed. Sometimes her mommy would get mad because she said the chain on the dog tag could hurt her when she was sleeping. The little girl didn't like to take it off, though, because it made her remember her daddy, and he told her it would keep her safe when he was gone."

Brian smiled. "Boy, Mr. Lanaski told you a lot about that dog tag, didn't he?"

Angela's eyes found her lap. "Uh-huh," she mumbled.

"Did Mr. Lanaski tell you anything else about his little girl?"

"He said that if she was a good little girl, he would get her a puppy when he came home. She always wanted a puppy, but he said she had to get bigger so she could take care of it right."

"Well, that's true. Have you ever had a puppy?"

Her gaze dropped to her lap again. "Uh-uh. My daddy doesn't like them because they pee in the house."

Brian glanced at Jeff and saw the strained smile on his face. He looked at Angela again then, and reached out to ruffle the hair on top of her head. "That's all I needed to know, Angela. Thank you for talking to me."

"You're welcome. Can I go finish my cookies now?"

Brian smiled again. "Sure you can."

Angela slid off the couch and ran for the doorway to the hall. She turned to wave at Brian. "Bye!"

"Bye, Angela."

Melody followed her daughter out as Jeff rounded the couch. "So, did you get what you needed?"

He nodded. "She's a great little girl, Jeff."

"Yes, she is."

"Well, I think I'm going to head out. I need to go see the principal at Lebhart again."

"The principal? Why?"

"Like I told you, this guy is dangerous. He shouldn't be teaching anywhere, let alone at a grade school."

"Mr. Lanaski? I'm Brian Koski. We spoke last week?"

"I have nothing to say to you."

Once again, the tall, blond man attempted to slam the door in Brian's face and, also once again, he prevented the action.

"I'd beg to differ on that point. You've been harassing my clients, Collin, and in particular, their little girl. It has to stop before you land in jail."

"Angela, or rather Courtney, is *my* daughter," Lanaski ground out. "I may not be able to prove it right now, but I will. And, when I do, it'll be *them* sitting in jail. Not me."

"So, why don't you tell me about it, Collin? Why don't you invite me in and explain why you're so certain that Angela Patten is your daughter?"

The taller man, taller in fact by three inches, studied the private investigator for a long, arduous moment. His deep blue eyes almost seemed to look right through Brian, and the former cop had to quell the shudder that threatened to wrack his body. There was definitely something eerie about this guy, and Brian cautioned himself silently to stay on alert...if Lanaski agreed to let him inside, which apparently he had.

"Okay, I'll talk to you...but only if you agree to hear me out before you come to any conclusions."

"Agreed," Brian answered readily.

Lanaski opened the door wide, then stepped aside and allowed Brian to enter. The experienced cop sidled into the room, never letting his eyes leave the other man. When the door had been closed and Lanaski had seated himself at a table in the small dining area, Brian relaxed...at least somewhat. He moved to scan the myriad of pictures that hung on the wall in the equally tiny living room. Most contained the vision of a lovely, platinum blonde–haired woman. In some of the photos, Collin stood beside her. In all of them, with the exception of the wedding photo in the center of the collage, one or the other held a child—an adorable little towheaded baby girl ranging in age from birth to three years old. Other pictures featured only the child in various stages of growth. She definitely had the same hair color and facial features as Angela Patten, but the seasoned detective was well aware of the fact that, at that age, a child could resemble anyone you wished them to.

"Are these pictures of your wife and daughter?"

"Yes."

"They were beautiful."

"Yes, they were…and Courtney still is."

Brian turned…and got right to the point. "So, tell me about the dog tags."

"I'm former Air Force. First Lieutenant. I always wore my dog tags, even when I was home on leave. From the time Courtney was three months old, she would play with them whenever I held her. She was fascinated by them. Before I left for Iraq, I told my C.O. that I had lost one of them, so they issued me a *third* one, which I gave to Courtney. I wanted her to have something to remember me by."

"How long was that before the accident? When you went to Iraq, I mean."

"About six months."

"And your wife and daughter stayed here, on the base?"

"They couldn't very well go with me."

Brian ignored the snide remark. "And Courtney was what? Three years old when you left?"

"Actually, she was only two. She turned three while I was gone." His eyes teared suddenly. "You know, I was never here for even one of her birthdays. I wasn't even here when she was born." He looked at Brian. "And I haven't been able to be there for her birthday for the last four years, either."

Brian also chose not to comment on the other man's reference to *Angela's* last four birthdays and continued the questioning. "So, finish telling me about the dog tag you gave her. Why are you so convinced that your daughter would have been wearing it the day of the accident?"

"Because she wore it on a chain around her neck, and I told her to never take it off. I told her it was magic and would keep her safe, and she took me literally!" Collin stood to wander the room and, surprisingly a slight, reminiscent smile curved his lips. "Whenever I talked to Lynn—"

"Lynn was your wife?"

He nodded. "She would tell me how she couldn't pry the damned thing off Courtney. Even when she'd give her a bath, she had to leave it on or Courtney would throw a fit. She'd tell her, 'my daddy's, my daddy's.' She even wore it to bed, which actually worried Lynn, because she was afraid the chain might get tangled or caught and choke her." He turned to Brian. "She would have had that dog tag on the day of the accident, Mr. Koski, but when I viewed what was left of their bodies after I got home, it wasn't around her neck and the coroner swore he didn't take it off her. There was also the whole thing with the car seat."

"The car seat?"

"We bought a new one just before I left for Iraq; the old one was worn and just kind of nasty since she'd been eating, and sometimes peeing, in it for two years. I remember the new one vividly, because I had such a hell of a time getting it secured in the car. It was a *Dora the Explorer* car seat, a limited edition, more of a booster seat style. It didn't really have sides on it. The one that was in the car, though, was the wrap-around kind, like for a younger child. It was also on the wrong side of the car. Lynn always insisted on having the car seat on the passenger side in the back seat, so she could look over her shoulder and see Courtney. The seat in the burned-out car was *behind the driver* and, again, the police and the coroner insist that nobody moved it."

"I'll admit that's a little strange, but it doesn't prove—"

"Yes, it does! You would had to have known my wife to see that it *does* prove it. Lynn was a meticulous type person, especially when it came to Courtney. That car seat was always in the back seat on the passenger side, and it was found behind the driver's seat after the accident!"

"And there are any number of reasons why she might have moved it. The seat belt on the passenger side might have broken, or the seat itself became unsafe. The position of the car seat does not in and of itself prove anything. And, even if it did, you had only the one child and that *one* child was found in the car after the accident."

"Then what about the scar?"

Brian's eyes narrowed. "What scar?"

"The scar on Angela Patten's right shin. She fell out on the playground one day and skinned her knee. When I rolled up her pants leg to clean and disinfect the cut, I noticed that she had a scar on her shin. Courtney also had a scar—in the exact same place! She fell off a swing when she was just over a year old and cut her leg. Lynn had to take her in for stitches...and it left a scar!"

Brian's chest rose in a sigh. "Kids get bumps and bruises and cuts all the time, Mr. Lanaski. *All* kids. It's not that much of a stretch to believe that Angela could have injured herself in the same place that Courtney did."

"It *is* a stretch! When you combine it with everything else, all the other discrepancies, it's a stretch!"

"Your daughter is dead, Mr. Lanaski," Brian countered gently. "As painful as that is to accept, she died in that accident, along with your wife, and there was a body to prove it."

"My daughter is not dead! I know it! I would *feel* it if she was. I felt that pain when I viewed Lynn's body, but I *never* felt it when I saw Courtney because that child was not her! She's alive, and somehow the Pattens got ahold of her. They've been raising her as their own daughter, and she is mine!"

For the first time since arriving at the Lanaski home,

Brian caught a glimpse of the man that Collin Lanaski had become. His fists were clenched, his eyes wild, his jaw tense. Even the veins in his forehead threatened to burst with his level of agitation—agitation born of an incredible, all-consuming grief.

"Mr. Lanaski—"

"Get out."

"Mr. Lanaski, please, you have to be reasonable—"

"I said, *get out!* Get the hell out of my house! Go back to your *clients* and tell them that *I know!* I *know* they took my daughter and I will damn well kill them if I have to to get her back!"

"You'd better watch the threats, Mr. Lanaski."

"It's not a threat. It's a promise," he ground out.

"Are you aware that your wife had filed for divorce?"

Lanaski did a double-take, and the rage left his eyes in an instant. "What?"

"Thomas Mathison, the lawyer who is *not* going to take your case by the way, was actually retained *by your wife* a few months before the accident. She was going to divorce you, Collin. She just didn't want to tell you while you were in Iraq fighting for your country. She was going to wait until you got home."

"That's impossible." Lanaski's voice came out in barely a whisper. "We had a good marriage."

"Apparently she didn't think so."

"Get out," he growled.

"Is it possible that your wife saw this side of you, Collin? The side I'm seeing right now? The psychotic, delusional, *crazy* part of you?"

"I said, *get out!*"

"You need help, Mr. Lanaski. You're in full-fledged denial. You need help to accept your daughter's death, and you also need help with your anger issues. If you don't get that help, the anger is going to fester and the delusions are going to grow, and you're going to be a danger to everyone around you, including the children in your class at Lebhart that you've sworn to nurture and protect—"

Lanaski's eyes widened with a sudden dawning. "You got me suspended, didn't you?"

"What?"

"When I went into work this morning, I was called into the principal's office. She *suspended* me until the whole Angela Patten situation, as she put it, had been settled. That was *you*, wasn't it? You told her that I'm psychotic and *delusional!*"

"I did talk to Mrs. Sampson, yes. Whatever action she took was her decision. Not mine."

"You bastard!"

"You need professional help, Mr. Lanaski. Please, see someone before this escalates out of control."

Collin advanced toward Brian slowly, methodically. The former police captain held his ground, even as the final, scathing words poured from Lanaski's mouth. "Angela Patten is *my* daughter. I will *never* believe otherwise. The Pattens are the ones with a problem...a *big* problem...and that problem is me! They took my daughter—when and how I don't know yet, but trust me, I'll find out. And when I do, they'll damn well give her back to me or they'll find themselves lying dead in a ditch somewhere! And you, *detective*, if you try to stop me from proving my claim, will be lying right beside them."

CHAPTER SIX

Brian arrived at the office just after nine o'clock the fol-lowing Monday. He stepped into the reception area via the back door and paused. A small, gray-haired man sat in one of the chairs in the waiting room, his scuffed boot impa-tiently tapping the floor.

Sherry immediately came to her feet. "Brian, this is Mr. Watson. Henry Watson. He's been waiting to see you."

Henry got to his feet also, and stepped forward to shake Brian's proffered hand.

"Nice to meet you, Mr. Watson. What can I do for you?"

"I need you to find out who the old bat I'm married to is cheatin' on me with."

Brian glanced quickly at Sherry, who was doing her best to battle a smile. He hid his own amusement as he looked at the prospective client again. "I'm sorry, Mr. Watson, but I don't handle infidelity cases—"

"Brian!" Sherry jumped in. She moved to wrap her arm around his, tugged him a short distance away from Henry, and hissed in his ear. "We could really use the money. *One case is not going to feed my daughter for very long.*"

Brian sighed—and didn't deny himself the pleasure of ogling his secretary's ample bosom. He tore his eyes from the tempting sight and moved to stand before Henry again. "Okay, Mr. Watson. Like I said, we don't *normally* handle infidelity cases—" he glanced at Sherry again "—but I guess we can make an exception in your case. Why don't you come into my office and we'll have a talk."

The old man laughed. "Need the money pretty bad there, huh, son?" He preceded Brian into the other room then, shaking his head and chuckling all the way.

Brian's gaze slanted to Sherry again. "You owe me!" he growled before he followed Henry into the office and closed the door behind them.

"That secretary you got is quite a looker," Henry commented as Brian moved to seat himself behind the desk.

He smiled. "Yes, she is." He indicated the chairs before the desk. "Have a seat, Mr. Watson."

"So, you doin' 'er?"

Brian froze in a half-bent position, midway to the seat of his own chair. He looked at the other man beneath furrowed eyebrows, and then continued his descent. "Uh, no. I'm not."

"Well, ye should be. What's the matter with you?" Henry looked at him closely. "You ain't one of them *funny* boys, are you?"

It took every ounce of self-control Brian had to keep the smile that threatened to play on his lips from materializing. "No, sir. I'm very normal...in that way anyway. Now, what makes you think your wife is cheating on you?"

"She just ain't actin' normal, and she's gone a lot more'n she used to be."

"What do you mean when you say she's not 'acting normal'?"

"She's happy! The woman's usually a crotchety old bat, and lately she's been prancin' around the house like she's sixty!"

This time, Brian did smile. "How old is she?"

"Eighty-two—three years younger'n me. And she's started wearin' *pants*! That woman wouldn'ta been caught dead in a pair of pants a year ago, and now she's wearin' 'em all the time." The old man shook his head. "She's found somebody, I tell ye, and it ain't me, that's fer sure. I couldn't keep it up with a splint these days."

Brian brought a hand up to rub his eyes...and hide yet another smile. "What's your wife's name?" he finally managed.

"Rosie. We were married sixty-six years this past September."

"That's pretty impressive."

"And that's why I don't understand it, Mr. Koski—"

"Please, call me Brian."

"Well, in that case, you can call me Henry. I'm sure Rosie's parts ain't workin' any better'n mine are these days, so why would she go lookin' for some young whippersnapper?"

"Do you have any suspicions about who you think she might be seeing?"

"Yeah, it's that dern Oscar Tibbit. Always walkin' around showin' off his bulge to the ladies." Henry snorted. "Be willin' to bet he stuffed a pair of socks down 'is pants."

Brian was close to tears. "And how old is Oscar?"

"Oh, he's just a young'un. Only seventy-six. He actually slapped my Rosie on the behind at the Senior Center the other day. If my arthritis wasn't so bad, I'da punched 'im." His eyes lit up. "Hey, if you take my case, is that somethin' you could do? Your punch still packs a wallop, I'll bet."

"I don't think so, Henry. It would land me in jail."

"Damn. Well, I reckon I wouldn't want that. So, what *can* ye do?"

"I...could follow your wife, I suppose." Brian shook his head at the craziness of the situation. As desperate as they were, he couldn't take this man's money. His fee would probably be their entire Social Security check—and then some. "Look, Henry, I think the best course of action here would be for you to talk to your wife. If you've been married sixty-six years, then I think it's pretty obvious that the two of you have good communication skills—"

"Shit. We ain't said more'n ten words to each other in ten years."

Brian lifted an eyebrow. "Really?"

"When ye been married as long as me and Rosie, son, it's all been said. I spend mosta my day sleepin' in my chair, and she spends mosta hers sleepin' in hers. Except durin' *Jeopardy* and *Wheel of Fortune*. We manage to stay awake for those."

"Well—" Brian cleared his throat…another attempt to quell his laughter "—maybe that's part of the problem. Maybe you need to talk more. Maybe Rosie misses that—the conversations you used to have, the closeness you once shared—"

"And if she *misses* all that, then why's she so dadgum happy! I told ye, she's flittin' around the house like a schoolgirl!"

"Have you *asked* her why she's so happy all of a sudden?"

"Oh, no. I couldn't do that. Then she'd think I was accusin' her of something."

"You *are* accusing her of something, Henry."

"Only to you, not to her."

Brian leaned forward and rested his forearms on the desk. "Would it be okay if *I* talked to Rosie?"

Henry looked suddenly wary. "What would you say to her? Would you tell her that I know she's foolin' around with Oscar?"

"You *don't* know she's fooling around with Oscar, Henry, and you *won't* know unless I talk to her. I promise you I'll be very discreet."

"I suppose that would be okay," the old man grudgingly agreed. "But she's a real lady. You treat her like one now, you hear?"

"I wouldn't treat a woman any other way."

"Good man." Henry shifted in the chair, reached into his back pocket, and extracted a weathered wallet. "So, how much do I owe ye for this, son?"

Brian knew the old man's pride would not allow him to accept any service for free. "I think $20.00 will cover it."

"You sure that's enough?"

"I charge $20.00 an hour, Henry. I'm sure our conversation today, and my talk with Rosie, won't take longer than that."

"A fair price, son. A fair price."

Brian accepted the twenty dollar bill and stood to round the desk. Henry stood also, with a little more effort. "Leave your address with Sherry on your way out. I'll try and get over to talk with Rosie tomorrow."

"Oh, not tomorrow. They got Bingo at the Senior Center, and it's Liver and Onions day for lunch." He winked. "We never miss that, either."

Brian's stomach churned at the mere idea. "I can see why. So, Wednesday then?"

"Wednesday should work, son. Make sure it's before 3:00, though."

"*Jeopardy,*" Brian remembered.

"Yup. Never miss it."

"Will 1:00 work?"

"Sounds good." Another wink. "And I'll be sure to make myself scarce." Henry held out a gnarled hand. "Good doin' business with you, son."

"You, too, Henry. Stop in again on Thursday, and I'll let you know what I found out."

"Will do."

Brian headed out to Zach and Caryn's after work the following day. Chris Byrne from Stonehill Kennel had been due to arrive with the new dog that morning and curiosity led him to check out the newest member of the Riker family.

Brian saw no sign of Zach and Caryn, or the dog, when he pulled into the driveway, so he parked his black Dodge Ram in front of the log garage and made his way across the snow-dusted blacktop to the deck. He entered the kitchen without knocking. Caryn stood at the island counter preparing an early dinner.

She smiled. "Hi, there."

"Hi, yourself. So, did Chris Byrne get here with the new dog?"

Brian's question was answered when both Mika and a slightly smaller Shepherd entered the kitchen. The all-black Mika simply stood at Brian's feet, tail wagging, and waiting for the usual ruffling of her ears in greeting. The other dog, which he could only assume to be Sinbad, bounded toward him with a series of sharp, authoritative barks.

Brian instinctively took a step back.

"Sinbad, *fuss.*" The command came from Chris Byrne as he rounded the fireplace. Zach was right behind him. The dog immediately moved into the heel position at Chris's left side. A younger man accompanied them.

The dog was magnificent. The most prominent features were his black facial mask and ears. A short mahogany coat and black saddle covered the animal's back, lightening as it reached the underside and inner leg. He was easily twenty-six inches at the withers and weighed in somewhere around seventy-five pounds.

"I'd advise that you don't do that again, sir, once the transfer of authority has taken place," Chris advised.

"Do what?" Brian asked, confusion evident in his tone.

"Enter the house without knocking first, and then being admitted. Sinbad has already started to think of this house as his territory—the place he needs to guard. He might take offense at what he considers an uninvited guest."

"This is Brian Koski, Chris," Zach made the introductions. "A good friend of the family. Brian—Chris and C.J. Byrne. C.J. is Chris's son and Sinbad's agitator."

The three men shook hands, and then Brian smiled at the latter. "So, you're the one who pretends to be the bad guy, huh?"

"That's me," C.J. replied.

Sinbad's ears lay back against his head with his agitator so near.

"We were just going to have a light supper, Brian," Caryn

told him. "It should be ready in a few minutes. You can join us, if you like."

"That would be great." He followed Zach and the other men back into the great room. They all took seats before Zach looked at his friend.

"Anything new with the whole Collin Lanaski fiasco?"

"Haven't heard a word from him, and neither have the Pattens."

"Well, that's a good sign. Maybe your little talk with him the other day scared him off."

"We can hope so, but I doubt it. The guy's pretty determined."

The fire chief looked at Chris and C.J. and explained the whole Lanaski scenario.

"Sounds like the guy's got a screw loose," Chris commented a few minutes later.

"You got it, which *really* makes him dangerous." Brian looked at Zach. "So how's the training going so far?"

"Not good. Sinbad isn't taking to me too well. Caryn either. He'll let us pet him, but that's about it, and even that is at his whim. He won't come when called, except by Chris. Won't follow my commands, either. Like Chris said, the only thing he *has* taken to is the house itself."

"Really? You didn't have that problem with Mika, did you?"

"No, she responded to us right away." He glanced at the trainer. "Chris is a little worried that we might not be the right fit for Sinbad after all."

Sinbad approached the four men at the mention of his name. He paused before Chris, though, not Zach. The trainer made a concerted effort to ignore the dog and, strangely, it moved on to Brian. The former cop stiffened instinctively.

"Don't be nervous," Chris assured him. "He's just like any other pet at this point. He won't attack unless provoked."

Brian relaxed and, consequently, Sinbad sniffed his leg, and then his hand. To the amazement of all, the dog plopped down on its haunches at Brian's feet.

"Try petting him," Chris instructed.

It took Brian a moment to gather the courage to lay his hand on the animal's head. He had to laugh at himself. He had faced countless armed criminals over the years without flinching and yet this dog had him terrified. Finally, he reached out and stroked Sinbad's ears, then his scruff. He withdrew the hand and looked at Zach again. Sinbad moved back to the inattentive Chris.

"You won't believe who I got as a new client yesterday."

"Who?" the fire chief asked.

"An eighty-five-year-old guy who's convinced his eighty-*two*-year-old wife is cheating on him."

Zach laughed. "You're kidding."

"Nope, and you know *why* he's convinced?"

"Why?"

"Because the woman is *happy*. He says she's been a crabby old bat all their married life and is sure that, since she's happy *now*, she's screwing around on him—with a young whippersnapper. The alleged boyfriend is only seventy-six."

The other three men in the room laughed at this newest information until Sinbad approached Brian again and nudged his hand. He petted the dog absently as he continued.

"I'm meeting with the old guy's wife tomorrow—"

"I'll be damned," Zach interrupted.

"What?" Brian asked. "I'm sure the woman isn't going to hit on me...at least I hope she won't."

"No! The dog. He prompted you to pet him before—and he came back for more."

Chris, too, studied the interaction between man and dog closely. "Try telling him *platz*. And use his name when giving the command."

Brian looked at Chris warily, and then back at the dog. "Sinbad...*platz*."

Without hesitation, the dog dropped to the floor in front of Brian's chair.

"My God, Brian, he actually listened to you!" Caryn

exclaimed as she rounded the fireplace and stopped dead to watch the action.

"He nudged his hand earlier, too, trying to get him to pet him," Zach told her.

She laughed her amazement. "Well, it looks like he's adopted *you* as his new master."

"I'm thinking the same thing," Chris commented.

"Hey, now wait a minute," Brian objected. "I can't afford *fifteen thousand dollars* for a dog, even if I *did* want one…which I don't."

"I wouldn't charge you for him, Brian," the trainer assured him. "His aversion to loud noises makes it impossible for me to resell him. He needs a good home, though, and he *is* a working dog. No offense to you and Caryn, Zach, but I'd much rather place Sinbad with someone who can utilize his capabilities."

"I couldn't agree more," Zach returned. His gaze shifted to his friend. "Face it, Bri, he might come in handy. You may not be a cop anymore, but I'm sure as time goes on, you'll face some pretty dangerous characters in your P.I. business, too. Hell, you're already dealing with this Lanaski guy. You'd probably feel a little more confident if Sinbad was at your side."

"I have my gun, Zach. It's all I need."

"And if you're a former cop," Chris stepped in, "then you know that in order to avoid arrest a person will face *and fight* a uniformed officer who's armed to the hilt—but when the K-9 unit shows up, it somehow defuses the whole situation. Everyone has an opinion about dogs, usually based on an earlier life experience; either they love them or they hate them. One thing everyone will pretty much agree on, though, is that they respect them and don't want to get bitten."

"You sound like you speak from experience on that topic, too," Brian observed.

Chris nodded. "I was sheriff of Fairfield County, Connecticut, for ten years. And, as Zach said, with Sinbad as your partner, you'll feel a lot more confident when facing a criminal—even if you *are* armed."

"With Sinbad as my *partner?*" Brian repeated skeptically.

Chris shrugged. "That's what he would be. That's what *any* police dog is. He's as much his handler's partner as a human cop would be."

"Damn, you guys are really determined to talk me into this, aren't you?"

"We're not only thinking of the dog, Brian," Caryn spoke up again. "We're thinking of *you*. Sinbad could save your life."

"Yeah, right, until a train goes by or we get caught in a thunderstorm. Then he'd turn tail and run! That could *cost* me my life."

"Granted, those are issues you'd have to deal with," Chris acknowledged, "but the one loud noise Sinbad *isn't* afraid of is gunfire. If you were caught in a real bad situation, where you were under fire, he'd come through."

"Right." Brian's gaze dropped to the dog, where he still lay docilely at his feet. "And be killed, just like the *other* Mika was."

"That's a risk the dog would take, just like you did every day when you were a cop." Surprisingly, it was C.J. who intervened this time. "That little girl you're trying to protect...would you abandon an opportunity to help her if this Lanaski guy was armed?"

"Of course not, but that's different—"

"No, it's not," the agitator argued. "Sinbad would willingly give his life to save a victim, just like you would. And he also wouldn't hesitate to save *your* ass. That's what he does. That's what he was *trained* to do...and he'll love every minute of it."

"Look, none of this is for certain, Brian," Chris jumped in again, drawing the P.I.'s attention back to him. "Sinbad's reaction to you is a good sign, yes, but it by no means shows that he's chosen you as his master. We won't know that until we put *you* through the necessary training. Are you willing to give it a shot?"

Brian's chest lifted in a sigh as his gaze moved from one hopeful face to the next. Lastly, he looked at the dog again. Sinbad returned the perusal, his brown eyes unwavering. It was almost as though he were telling him, *Give me a chance.*

"Okay," he finally relented. "I'll give it a try. I know this *training* takes like three days, though, and I already told you I have an appointment with my new client's wife at 1:00 tomorrow. I can't miss it."

"That's fine," Chris agreed. "We'll work around it." The trainer looked at Caryn. "Well, let's eat, so we can get back to work."

Brian stood, along with all the other men, and fell into step beside Zach as they headed to the kitchen. "I know why you're pawning this off on me, buddy."

Zach grinned. "Why?"

"Because it's frigging fifteen degrees outside! You decided it would be more fun to watch *me* freeze my ass off than you."

Zach's grin turned into a chuckle as he clapped his friend on the shoulder and continued on to the kitchen. Sinbad followed dutifully on Brian's heels.

Brian rechecked the house number on the piece of paper Sherry had given him that morning and, sure he had the right place, ascended to the porch and knocked on the door. The inner portal was opened a few minutes later by a frail-looking woman—in pants—who could very well be eighty-two years old. A glass-enclosed storm door still separated them.

"Mrs. Watson?"

"Yes," she replied uneasily.

"Hi, I'm Brian Koski...a friend of your husband, Henry's."

"You're a friend of Henry's?" She couldn't hide her surprise.

"Yes, I am, ma'am, though I'll admit I just met him yesterday. Henry...is a little concerned about you—"

Her already lined face creased further with confusion. "Concerned about me? Why? Does he think I'm sick?"

"No, he...is afraid that there might be some trouble in your marriage."

"Bah! We've been married sixty-six years. We're both too old to cause trouble."

Brian smiled. "Would it be all right if I come in, ma'am? It's a little chilly out here."

She hesitated, her still alert blue eyes sizing him up. "And you're sure you're really a friend of Henry's?"

"Yes, ma'am."

"Well...then I guess it would be all right."

She stepped back, allowing Brian to open the storm door and step into the almost overly warm kitchen. He closed the inner door behind him and turned to where Rosie now stood beside the small kitchen table. "Thank you, ma'am."

"Can I get you a cup of coffee?" she asked.

"That would be great." After witnessing her slow, shuffling movements, he reconsidered. "But I can get it myself."

"No need, young man. I may be old, but I'm still capable of seeing to my guests."

Another smile curved Brian's lips. "Whatever you say, ma'am."

"You're awful polite," she said over her shoulder as she worked at the counter. "Unusual for young people these days."

"I'm not *that* young," he countered.

"You're young to me," she returned as she started toward the table with two half-full, steaming cups of coffee.

"Henry did mention that you're eighty-two. I'm impressed. I'll have to get your secret for living to such a ripe old age. Henry's, too."

"So, you really *did* talk to my Henry?" Rosie asked as she seated herself opposite her guest.

"To be honest, Mrs. Watson, I'm a private investigator. Henry hired me yesterday. He really is concerned about you."

"You can call me Rosie, number one, and what in the world

does Henry have need of a private investigator for?" Her brow furrowed suddenly. "And just how much did he pay you?"

"Only twenty dollars, ma'am."

"Huh," she responded. "You must have considered it a small job."

"Yes, ma'am."

"So, you said he was worried about some trouble in our marriage?"

"Frankly, Henry's worried because you've been so...*happy* lately. He's afraid that maybe you've lost interest in him—"

"Oh, good heavens! This is about that dreadful Oscar Tibbit, isn't it?"

Brian couldn't hide his surprise at her perceptiveness. "It...could be, yes."

"Henry's always complaining about that upstart...and Oscar Tibbit is nothing but a dirty old man!"

Brian hid his latest smile behind the coffee cup. He took a sip. "So you don't like Oscar Tibbit much, huh?"

"Not at all. He slapped me on the behind the other day at the Senior Center, and it was very offensive. Of course, now *Henry*, he thought I liked it, because I didn't say anything." She shrugged. "It wasn't my place. It was his. *He's* my husband."

"So you were upset when Henry didn't confront Oscar?"

"Not upset, really. Just...disappointed, I reckon. I know Henry's older, too, and his arthritis is getting the best of him, but a woman can't help but hope that her man will defend her honor—even if that woman is eighty-two years old."

"And I'm sure Henry would have been very willing to defend you if he still felt capable." Brian took another sip of coffee before he addressed Henry's main concern again. "So, is there a reason why you've been so happy lately?"

"Didn't realize I had been, actually." Her eyes widened in sudden dawning. "Good Lord, does Henry think I've been carrying on with Oscar Tibbit, and *that's* why I've been so happy?"

Brian knew he took a risk in telling her the truth when he had promised his client that he wouldn't. He felt it was worth the gamble. "Yes, ma'am, he does."

"That foolish old coot! I'm too old to be carrying on with anybody! He should know that."

"Obviously he doesn't think so. In fact, he must still consider you very desirable...even to a man six years younger than you."

Rosie had the exact reaction to his words that Brian hoped for. She blushed with pleasure. "I never realized that Henry still considered me...desirable. I mean, we haven't... had relations in over ten years."

"Not because he doesn't want to, Rosie, I'm sure. He's just no longer physically capable of it."

"And neither am I, and he should know that." Her expression became speculative. "You know, now that I think of it, maybe I have been happier these past weeks, but it has nothing to do with Oscar Tibbit." Surprisingly, she blushed again. "It has to do with Henry."

"How so?" Brian asked.

"We were sitting watching *Jeopardy* a ways back—" she looked at him "—it's our favorite show. That and *Wheel of Fortune*. He was sitting in his chair and I was in mine and, out of the blue, he reached across, squeezed my hand, and told me 'Happy Anniversary.'" Rosie shook her gray head slowly. "Do you have any idea, young man, how long it's been since he remembered our anniversary? I mean, neither of us has even said 'I love you' in years. The fact that he remembered, though, it told me that he still cares. And I realized at the time, too, I guess, that I still love that ornery old cuss myself."

"That would definitely be reason enough to make you happy."

"Yes, it would, young man. Yes, it would."

"Oh, and one other thing. Henry was also concerned

because you've started wearing pants. He said, and I quote, that 'you wouldn't be caught dead in them before.'"

"He's upset because I've started wearing pants?" She rolled her eyes. "That man is headed down the road to the funny farm, I swear. Well, Mr. Koski, you can tell my husband when you see him again that I started wearing pants because winter set in and I was cold! How's that for proof that I'm lollygagging with another man!"

The amusement refused to be quelled this time, and Brian laughed outright. "I'll tell him." He crossed his arms over his chest. "Personally, Rosie, I think you and Henry have a wonderful marriage. In fact, if I ever decide to settle down, I might even pay you another visit and get some advice that will help *my* marriage succeed."

She shook her head again. "I guess the years just kinda got away from us. I mean, what with raising the kids, and then the grandkids coming along. He had his job at the paper mill..." She shook her head again. "I guess the romance just kind of took a back seat, but it didn't mean we stopped loving each other."

Brian drained the last of the coffee in his cup and sat back. Strangely, he had no desire to leave. "So, how many kids do you and Henry have?"

"Six," she responded. "And eighteen grandchildren, forty-three great-grandchildren, and three great-great-grandchildren...so far."

"Wow! Now that really *is* impressive."

"There could have been more, but we lost our second eldest daughter, Nellie, back in 1975. She had two girls at the time, but always wanted to give Donald a son."

"What happened to her?"

A profound sadness, even after thirty-seven years, clouded Rosie's eyes. "She just disappeared one day. Left Donald with the girls, said she was going to the little grocery store a couple blocks away—and never came back. The police tried to say at the time that she ran off." She met Brian's eyes. "Nellie wouldn't have done that. She loved those kids, and her husband, with all her heart. All that girl ever wanted was to be a mama."

"So the police never pursued any other angles?"

"No. They never looked beyond the fact that she was young and pretty, and that Everett Klensing disappeared at the same time. He was Nellie's high school sweetheart. Actually, we all figured it was him she would marry, but she just broke it off with him one day during her senior year. Actually, it was after the night of her senior prom. Never did say why. Then a year or so later, after she graduated, she met Donald. He was so good to her. She would never have left him and her girls."

"So the police just *assumed* that she ran off with Everett?"

Rosie nodded. "Like I said, they didn't know my daughter like I did."

"What do *you* think happened, Rosie?"

"Honestly, Mr. Koski, I try not to think about it. Too painful. I do know that those kids of hers suffered. So did Donald. He never did remarry, and me and Henry pretty much raised the girls. Donald spent years searching for Nellie. Never found a trace of her, and never once did she try to contact her family."

"And that in itself is strange. Usually, if a person purposely runs off, you can find traces of where they've been. If they get a job, you can track them through their Social Security number. People had credit cards even back in 1975, so police could have tracked her movements that way, too—"

"Donald did all that. Nothing."

"And you said she never contacted you after she left?"

"No, and it just didn't make sense. Even if she did run off with Everett, she would have called to check on her children. She knew Henry and I were never judgmental. We wouldn't have scolded her for what she did. We would have just wanted to know why."

"I hate to tell you this, Rosie, but I think there's a strong probability that Nellie is—"

"Dead? Oh, I know. So does Henry. Even Donald finally admitted it years later. No, somebody took her, and somebody killed her. It's the only explanation." Rosie looked at Brian, her eyes widening in sudden recognition. "Wait a minute. Now I know why you looked so familiar to me when you first showed up at the door. You were on the police force at one time, weren't you? I used to see you on the TV news all the time..."

Brian nodded. "I'm no longer with the Cheyenne P.D., though. Like I told you, I'm a private investigator now."

"Well, it's a shame. You seemed very capable when I saw you on the TV news."

"Thank you, ma'am."

Rosie rested her forearms on the table and met his gaze directly. "So, Mr. Koski, what would it cost us—our family— to hire you to look into Nellie's disappearance?"

Brian was speechless for a moment, and then finally found his voice. "Mrs. Watson...Rosie, I wasn't trying to solicit a job—"

"I know that. You were genuinely concerned, even about something that happened thirty-seven years ago. That's why I want to hire you. You were always very determined to solve whatever case they were interviewing you about on TV, and I know you'd approach Nellie's case the same way. I know it's been a long time, but this family has never forgotten her. Her *children* have never forgotten her. Neither has Donald. All of us, we just want to know what happened to her—clear her name, if you will. In the older circles in town, the ones that remember what happened, she's still thought to be a mother who deserted her children to run off with her high school sweetheart. And, don't get me wrong. I have no doubt that Everett Klensing was involved in her disappearance, but it wasn't in the way the police thought back then."

Brian's eyes swept the tiny, but immaculate—and very

old fashioned—kitchen, as well as what he could see of the small living room to their right. The Watsons were not wealthy people...

"I'd love to help you, Rosie; in fact, I would be *honored* to do what I could to get to the bottom of Nellie's disappearance, but I have to be honest in that it would be a very expensive proposition. Number one, it's a thirty-seven-year-old case—a case that the police never pursued as a homicide, which means there won't be *any* evidence for me to examine. Basically, I'd have to start from scratch. I'd start here, of course, where she disappeared, but an investigation could take me all over the country—"

"Just tell me how much it would cost, Mr. Koski. Me and Henry might not have much; but, like I told you, we have a big family, and this is important to all of them. If everybody puts in their fair share, we can come up with the money."

He took a deep breath and expelled it slowly. "I'd have to start with a minimum of ten thousand dollars, Rosie. That would retain my services for six months. If I haven't gotten to the bottom of Nellie's disappearance by then, you'd have to decide if you want me to continue...and that would cost *another* ten thousand for another six months. And that doesn't include my expenses. Like I said, this case could take me all over the country..."

"Sounds fair. I'll talk to my children tonight and get back to you."

CHAPTER SEVEN

Brian's training as Sinbad's handler was going better than anyone ever anticipated—especially him. By the end of the second day, the dog dutifully followed him wherever he went, constantly seeking the attention and praise that the canine now knew he would receive only from the former cop. Brian had also learned all of the necessary commands—in German—and had become quite adept at utilizing them. For him, working with C.J. was the most fun...and the most nerve wracking. In fact, Caryn refused even to watch. She remembered all too well the padded "stick" used to simulate a weapon and had no desire to watch Sinbad be whacked with it as Mika had been. The demonstration did solicit a grimace or two from Brian and Zach, though both men knew it would in no way injure the dog.

"Okay, C.J., take off the suit," Chris said when Sinbad again stood docilely at his side.

His son did as told, and Brian held his breath when Chris heeled the dog right up to the now unprotected agitator. Despite the frigid temperatures, C.J. was soaked to the skin under the heavy bite suit. Father and son exchanged hand-shakes and started for the house. Brian, Zach, and Sinbad fell into step beside them.

"So, is that it for today?" Brian asked, billows of steam leaving his mouth along with the words.

Chris nodded. "Tomorrow we'll get into the final part of the training...the search and rescue and cadaver scenting."

"I wanted to talk to you about that," Brian said. "I've got a friend who works at the Laramie County Morgue. I talked to him last night and, when I told him about Sinbad, he offered to let us bring him there around five-thirty tomorrow afternoon, after his boss leaves for the day. He said he has a perfect corpse that could be used for some real 'hands-on' training. Apparently, the guy died in his sleep of a heart attack and wasn't discovered for three days. He's pretty ripe...which means Sinbad should be able to pick up on his scent. He's actually going to hide the corpse—"

Chris raised a skeptical eyebrow. "He's going to *hide* it?"

Brian chuckled. "Yeah, Mike Young—he's the morgue attendant—is actually a pretty funny guy. You wouldn't believe the stories he's told me about what goes on after hours in that place. The attendants are always playing practical jokes on each other. Of course, when I was a cop, I had to *ignore* the stories, but now—"

Chris held up a hand, cutting the other man short. "We'll just use the putrescine, the chemical I told you about that smells like rotting human remains. No offense, Brian, but going to the morgue and working with a *real* body could have legal ramifications, not to mention moral ones. If you want to take Sinbad there on your own, that's up to you, but C.J. and I won't be taking part in it. In fact, our flight leaves at two o'clock, so we won't even be here at five-thirty."

"Whatever," Brian agreed. "I just thought it would be good experience for the dog—"

"And it would be, but I'm not about to jeopardize my business or my reputation by taking part in it." Chris smiled to ease the bluntness of his words. "Though I have to admit, it would be kind of fun."

The four men had reached the steps to the deck by now,

and Sinbad followed them into the blessedly warm kitchen. Caryn already had steaming cups of coffee sitting on the island counter.

"You, lady, are an angel," Brian told her as he took a seat on one of two stools and wrapped his frigid hands around the warm mug. C.J. took the seat next to him. Zach and Chris stood nearby.

"So, this putrescine," Zach asked. "Is that what you use when you're training cadaver dogs?"

Chris nodded. "We use both ground and air scenting. A lot of trainers are purists and stick to one style or the other. I've found that if we ground scent first, and then let a dog air scent after mastering the ground scenting, we end up with a more reliable and effective dog."

"Sounds logical to me," Brian commented.

"So, do you think he's going to work as Sinbad's handler?" Caryn asked, with a smile toward their friend.

"I think he'll work great," Chris said. "In fact, Sinbad is already responding to Brian better than he did his handler at the NYPD...and for good reason. Sinbad was one of fifty dogs that we supplied to the NYPD. He completed his training with their K-9 unit and was assigned a new handler—and by new, I mean *inexperienced*. At some point, the dog was pushed beyond his comfort level. While a police dog needs to be courageous and has to follow direction without question, those abilities don't come naturally in the first days or even months of service. Just as a soldier or cop will gain confidence with experience, so will a dog. They require encouragement and have to be rewarded for conquering new and stressful events. Without that, the dog will question its own safety. Consequently, it will no longer trust or depend on its handler."

"And that is definitely not a good thing," Caryn observed.

Chris glanced at her. "No it's not. It's an owner's duty to build an unbreakable bond between himself and his dog. You and Zach learned that well with Mika. Many others, though, think that just because they own the dog, it will follow their every direction without question. If you think about it, people are constantly reinforcing relationships with every person we come in contact with: friends, children, spouses, bosses, employees... Why would you expect a dog to be any different?"

"Good point," Brian commented as he reached down to stroke Sinbad's ears, where the dog sat docilely beside him. "So, realistically, how much trouble can I expect to have with him when it comes to loud noises?"

"I have to be honest with you, Brian, in that I really don't know. Sinbad's issues were mostly related to working in the subway tunnels; shaking ground, trains whizzing by, the heat, the odors—and a handler that didn't reassure him when he felt insecure. When we got him back to Stonehill Kennel, we gave him a little time to relax and just be a dog. Once he was settled in, we began to work with him, starting with familiar things—obedience, protection, and search and rescue training—just to see where he was at. He showed no anxiety in those situations, so we moved on by taking him out into the community. He continued to show a growing confidence. A trip to a train station, though, showed the chink in his armor.

"He started to pant and pace—in the vehicle—when we got close to the station. When we got him out of the truck, he pulled at his lead and tried to back away from the arriving train. Obedience builds confidence and, since dogs are naturally compliant creatures, we started putting him through his obedience exercises. He resisted at first, but he finally settled down—because we were in the train station parking lot and nowhere near the platform.

"We continued to work him in the parking lot for the next week, and then gradually moved him *onto* the platform, but only when we were sure no trains would be coming. After another week, it was time to really wear him out—in preparation for the train that we knew would arrive near the end of the session. He was still a little nervous, but was able to work through the distraction."

"So you think he's okay now?" Brian asked.

"Like I said before, I can't say for sure. And, regardless, I would never put a dog back into the ring once he's had a confidence issue. That doesn't change the fact, though, that he would be a great personal protection dog." He smiled at the Rikers again. "That's why I approached Zach and Caryn. I knew they'd give him a good home, and it would negate the need for them to have Mika trained. Of course, Sinbad *does* have a lot of other abilities, too, from the time spent at Stonehill Kennel and in the hands of the NYPD K-9 unit. That's why it was so great when you stepped up to the plate and agreed to be his handler. Like I said before, I'd much rather place Sinbad with someone who can utilize his full capabilities."

"So, if we do encounter a train or something, I should just try to reassure him if he gets nervous?"

Chris nodded. "Pet him, talk to him...*distract* him. He loves to chase a ball. You start tossing one around and he'll forget about the train real quick."

"You hope," Brian returned skeptically.

Chris cast him a wan smile. "Yes, I hope."

Zach disappeared early the next morning...and it was up to Brian and Sinbad to find him. Chris had instructed the fire chief to follow a particular path and make turns at pre-disclosed locations. He also told him to leave a trail, so the trainer would know they were on the right track—a scuff mark in the dirt, a bent branch, a hat or glove lying on the path. It took only a half-hour for Brian and his new partner to find the "missing" man. Consequently, Sinbad's new handler praised the dog enthusiastically, and then spent another fifteen minutes engaging in the canine's favorite pastime—chase the ball.

The cadaver training was a little more interesting—at least for Brian. Though Chris had declined to visit the morgue with him and Sinbad later that day, Brian *was* able to enlist Mike Young's help in another way, one that Chris was much more comfortable with. Rather than using the putrescine, the morgue attendant provided them with some slurry—a mixture of bodily fluids and decomposed flesh soaked in sterile gauze. Chris placed the gauze into a piece of plastic PVC pipe that had been drilled full of holes, with a threaded cap on one end. He and Zach took turns then, hiding the container in various areas in the yard and surrounding woods. The final test came when Chris had his son C.J. place the container of slurry over a mile from the Riker residence. Brian knew only the general location of Sinbad's "prize." It took the dog less than an hour to sniff out the noxious odor and receive his reward.

Two hours later saw a confident Chris and C.J. on their way to the airport, and Brian with a new partner—a Belgian Malinois named Sinbad.

CHAPTER EIGHT

B rian and Sinbad rode the elevator to the basement level of the Cheyenne Regional Medical Center just after five-thirty that afternoon. The former police captain was all too familiar with the location of the Laramie County Morgue, and even more familiar with its employees. The coroner himself, Dr. Adam Kruse, was somewhat of a stuffed shirt, but the people who worked for him were, in Brian's opinion anyway, a hoot. In their line of work, they had to have a sense of humor. In Mike Young's case that sense of humor bordered on the macabre.

"Brian my man, great to see you again!" the scrawny, unkempt Mike Young exclaimed when Brian and Sinbad entered the clinical and very sterile morgue. Three of the four stainless steel dissection tables held bodies covered with crisp white sheets. To the average person, the corpses might have been a bit creepy. To a seasoned detective like Brian, it was just part of the job.

Mike moved to stoop before Sinbad and ruffled the fur on the Belgian Malinois' scruff. "And this big boy must be Sinbad. Ooooh," he cooed, "you're such a good boy!"

Surprisingly, at least to Brian, the dog did not object in the least to the almost overbearing attention.

Mike stood again and faced his friend. "So, you ready to get started?"

"Ready whenever you are."

"Good. John Olson's family is coming to view his body at 7:00 in the morning, before we send it off for cremation. So I gotta get him back here and all spiffed up by no later than 6:00."

"I hope we'll be done a hell of a lot sooner than that," Brian scoffed. "It's only 5:30 now. That's over twelve hours."

"Well, that'll depend on how smart your dog is. I hid this guy really good."

Brian shook his head and a chuckle rumbled in his chest. "You are one sick dude, Mike."

"Trust me, you gotta be to work in this place."

Brian tipped his head to where Sinbad was in the process of sniffing the bodies that lay on different tables in the room. No command had been given. He was just curious. "Well, it looks like he's ready, so let's get to it. I'm assuming the body is *not* in here…"

"I'll concede that much." Mike smirked.

"Okay…" Brian started from the room, and Sinbad dutifully followed. When they reached the hallway, the handler turned to the dog. "Sinbad, *Suk*." Pronounced "sook," the command urged the Malinois to tap into his rigorous training and begin searching for the cadaver.

Sinbad trotted down the hallway, with Brian and Mike in close pursuit. Brian went on the assumption that Mike had hidden the body on the lower level of the hospital, and thus avoided taking the dog into stairwells and simply opened any unlocked doors along their path. Sinbad systematically checked each room until a sudden change in behavior indicated to Brian that they were getting close. They stood outside a closed door, one labeled "Maintenance." Sinbad was excited now; he sniffed the crack under the door vigorously, pawing periodically at the closed portal.

Brian turned to Mike with a self-satisfied smile. "It's in there, isn't it?"

The smaller man returned the smile. "I'll never tell."

Brian just shook his head and reached to open the door. Sinbad bounded inside and continued in hot scent mode among the collection of brooms, mop buckets, and other cleaning paraphernalia while Brian waited in the doorway. The dog paused in an empty corner, again sniffing enthusiastically, and then turned to Brian with what appeared to be a confused look in his dark brown eyes.

The private investigator turned to Mike with a sigh. "Okay, you stumped him. Where is it?"

"What do you mean? It's right there—" The morgue attendant brushed past Brian and stopped dead in his tracks. "What the hell!" He quickly moved to shove buckets, mops, and brooms aside, and then swung back to stare at Brian through eyes that were wide with surprise and more than a small amount of panic. "This is where I put it, I swear!"

"Yeah, well it's not here anymore."

"No shit, Sherlock. Did it take *all* of your trained detective's brain to figure that one out?" The morgue attendant chewed nervously on a jagged fingernail. "God, I am so dead. I am so, *so* totally dead."

"At least you're in the right place..." Brian returned drolly.

Mike swung to face the detective again. "Come on, Brian! This is no time for smart-ass comments. You have to help me here!"

Brian could do nothing but shake his dark head slowly in response. "Okay. Obviously the body didn't get up and walk off by itself." He grinned. "Now, if we were Mulder and Scully..."

"Brian!"

"Come on, Mike. You have to admit that this is at least a *little* bit funny."

The withering glance Brian received from his friend proved the man's opinion to be otherwise.

"Okay, maybe not." Brian finally lifted a dark eyebrow in inquiry and got down to business. "So, anyone with reason to play a practical joke on *you*?"

The panic in Mike's eyes segued into sudden dawning. "Kaprick! That son-of-a-bitch!"

"Who?"

"Paul Kaprick," the morgue attendant spat. "I work with him sometimes. He hung around after his shift ended to help me move the body. Afterward, he told me that I looked like I needed a break. Granted, I was kind of huffin' and puffin' after we got that guy all set up in the closet. He wasn't a lightweight by any means. Topped three hundred pounds. Man, you wouldn't believe the shit we found in his stomach. He ate enough that last night to choke a horse! He had burgers and fries, pizza, spaghetti... It's no wonder the guy had a heart attack—"

"Mike..." Brian steered him back on track.

"Oh yeah, right. So, anyway, Paul told me to go up to the cafeteria and get something to eat. He said he'd *cover* for me. He must have moved the fucking body while I was gone."

"Is he still here?"

"No. He went home just before you got here. His shift actually ended at three." Mike dug the cell phone from the pocket of his lab coat and frantically dialed the other morgue attendant. "Okay, asshole, where'd you put it?"

There was a pause as Mike listened to the other man's reply.

"What do you mean, 'that's for you to know and me to find out'! I could lose my job over this, Paul! That guy's family is going to be here at seven in the morning!" Mike stared at the cell phone in disbelief a moment later. "He hung up on me! The bastard hung up on me!"

"He didn't say anything about where the body was?" Brian asked.

"Nope. Just 'happy hunting' and then he hung up." Mike

closed his eyes and lifted his chin toward the heavens. "Come on, John. Help me out here. Where are you?"

When no ethereal answer was immediately forthcoming, Brian looked at his friend. "We'll find him, Mike. Paul can't have taken the body that far by himself...not if the guy weighed three hundred pounds."

"He could if he put it on a gurney, and Paul is one strong son-of-a-bitch, so he could do it. Hell, he throws bodies around like they were toothpicks. There was this one stiff a while back that topped *six* hundred pounds. We had to take him out a window cuz we couldn't get him through the door, and Paul just kinda *rolled* him out, all by himself— "

"Mike!" Brian tried again to end the man's rambling and get him back on topic.

The beleaguered morgue attendant slumped back against the wall and his head lolled back and forth. "God, I am so totally and unequivocally dead."

"Look, will you just calm down! Sinbad will find the damned body! That's what he's trained to do." Brian took a deep breath, calming his own frayed nerves. "Now, how long ago did you get back from the cafeteria?"

"Less than an hour."

"And was Paul in the morgue when you got back?"

"He was just coming down the hall. Said he ran to the bathroom." Mike shook his head. "Shoulda thought about it then. He was coming from the direction of the elevators. The bathroom is the other way."

"So, he was probably just getting back from hiding the body," Brian stated rather than asked.

"More than likely, the bastard," Mike muttered.

"And if he was coming from the elevators, that means he probably hid it on one of the upper floors."

"Logical, I guess."

"And that was less than an hour ago?" Brian pressed.

Mike nodded.

"Good. Then Sinbad should still be able to pick up the

cadaver's scent." He called the dog out into the hallway again and started toward the elevator. "Sinbad, *Suk.*"

The dog trotted off, his sensitive nose sniffing the air as he went.

"God, this is nothing but a damned wild goose chase!" Mike complained six hours later, when he and the exhausted Brian paused to rest in the fifth floor waiting room. Mike was off duty now, but the man did not dare leave the hospital until they found the body...and it was beginning to look like that would never happen. Sinbad had lost the scent long ago. All they could do now was walk the dog through the building and periodically give him the "seek" command to keep him on track. They had checked virtually every nook and cranny in the seven-story structure, and nothing.

Apparently Sinbad was becoming as bored with the ritual as his handler was. Or maybe he was just tired, too. He was sprawled out on the floor at Brian's feet, sound asleep.

"You don't think there's a possibility that he would have taken it *out* of the hospital, do you?" Brian asked.

"I don't know. I don't think so. There wouldn't have been time. I was up in the cafeteria less than an hour." Mike rubbed his tired eyes as the frustration built again. "If the guy would just answer his damned phone! He's probably sitting at home right now, laughing his ass off, and I'm about to lose my job!"

"Okay, about the only place we haven't checked is the roof—"

"And I told you hours ago that you need a passkey to use the roof elevator. The helipad for the Life Flight chopper is up there, and only authorized personnel have access. Paul would have had to use the stairs, which he couldn't do if the body was on a gurney."

"He could have taken it *off* the gurney. If he's as strong as you say..."

"I suppose."

"It's worth a shot, Mike."

"Whatever."

Brian heaved himself up and nudged Sinbad with his foot. "Sinbad, *heir.*"

The dog opened his eyes and came to his feet with a stretch and a yawn just as a nurse walked past the waiting area. She eyed the dog disapprovingly.

"He's a police dog. We're searching for a suspect," Brian spewed their cover story for the hundredth time that evening. This time, though, his patience was at its limit. "Mess with him, or me, and I'll command him to attack."

The nurse clamped her mouth shut and moved on.

"Boy, you really are out to see me lose my job, aren't you?" Mike grumbled. "She's probably on her way to the Chief of Staff right now to report us."

"No, *I'm* not out to see you lose your job. Your idiot friend Paul is." Brian shook his head. "This was a really stupid idea from the get-go. I should never have agreed to let you hide that body."

"Oh, so now it's my fault?"

"Yes, it's your fault! You *hid* the damned body!"

"And I didn't hear you objecting!"

"Oh...just shut up. Let's go up to the roof."

Once again, Brian led the way toward the elevators. Sinbad and a very perturbed Mike followed. They rode the elevator to the seventh floor, where Mike then took the lead. He paused before a steel door labeled "Roof Access."

The morgue attendant swept an arm before his chest in invitation. "Onward, oh revered private detective who has never done a stupid thing in his life."

Brian rolled his brown eyes and proceeded up the steps. He stepped through the door at the top of the stairwell and on to the roof. Mike and Sinbad followed. A blast of frigid air greeted them.

"Great," Mike moaned. "Now I get to freeze my ass *before* they put it in a sling."

Brian simply rolled his eyes again and gave Sinbad the now familiar command. "Sinbad, *Suk*."

Luckily, the dog was in a more cooperative mood than the disgruntled Mike and trotted off in search of his prize.

It took only a few minutes before Sinbad's demeanor indicated that he was once again in "hot scent." Brian and Mike followed the excited canine to a spot on the far side of the roof, opposite the Life Flight helipad and hidden from casual observation. The recessed area, surrounded by three walls, topped with a roof, and open on one end, held the massive air conditioning unit. Sitting on the roof and propped up against the unit itself were the nude remains of what had recently been an overweight living and breathing human being. A floppy, wide-brimmed straw hat had been placed on his head and a fat cigar protruded from his pale, fleshy lips. The stiff fingers on the cadaver's right hand had been wrapped around a glass that was half-filled with what appeared to be whiskey. On his towel-covered lap, held in place by the fingers on the left hand, was a cardboard sign with a private message just for Mike.

IT'S FIVE O'CLOCK SOMEWHERE, MIKE! NEED A BREAK?

"Asshole," the morgue attendant grumbled. "Wait until I get my hands on him tomorrow. It'll be his black ass in a sling before I'm done with him."

"Don't you think this practical joke shit has gone far enough?" Brian mused. "I think you guys need to declare a truce before somebody really *does* lose his job."

"Whatever," Mike muttered. "I'll go get a gurney, then we'll haul this guy back downstairs."

"Great," Brian muttered. "Just the way I wanted to end my day."

"What in the hell you complaining about? You can go home and sleep. Me? I gotta figure out how I'm gonna get this guy back into the morgue and ready for the visitation in the morning without the night shift guys getting suspicious."

Brian clapped a hand on his friend's shoulder. "Don't worry, old buddy. I have faith in you. You'll come up with something brilliant."

A sudden, self-indulgent smile broke across Mike's thin face. "You know me too well, my friend. You know me *way* too well."

The sudden whirr of an approaching helicopter drew the attention of both men to the opposite end of the roof. A half-mile in the distance, and approaching rapidly, was a Life Flight aerial ambulance. There was no doubt in either man's mind that it was headed for their location.

"Son-of-a-bitch!" Mike exclaimed. "What in the hell else can go wrong!"

"Just calm down," Brian gritted.

"Calm down? We're not even supposed to be up here!"

The answer to Mike's first question came in the form of a suddenly agitated Sinbad. The sound of the helicopter's propellers was deafening now as it neared the landing zone, raising the dog's panic level to the maximum. The canine bolted in the opposite direction—toward the edge of the roof. Brian, in turn, lunged to grab his partner. He lifted the terrified dog into his arms and against his chest. The sheer weight of the animal, combined with its frenzied movements, was enough to upset Brian's center of gravity and send him stumbling backward—into the enclosure and onto the lap of the recently deceased John Olson. Mike was quick to join him when the elevator door opposite the helipad slid opened and a trauma team rushed out with a gurney in tow. The morgue attendant, though, chose a more dignified position next to the three-hundred-pound cadaver. He hissed at his cohort.

"Keep that damned dog quiet! What's his problem, anyway?"

"He doesn't like loud noises," Brian explained as he struggled to control the still distressed Sinbad. "Easy, boy," he murmured near the dog's ear. "Easy."

The calming words had the desired effect and, gradually, Sinbad settled across his handler's lap, though his frightened eyes continued to dart toward the right wall of the enclosure, in the direction of the chopper that had landed unseen only fifty feet away.

"You've got a police dog that's afraid of loud noises?" Mike laughed uproariously, the sound of his mirth muffled by the still churning blades of the helicopter. "He'll be real useful if someone starts shooting at you." He tipped his head toward John Olson's lifeless form. "Luckily, you don't have to worry about this guy."

Brian glanced over his shoulder and, for the first time, realized where he sat. He promptly shoved Sinbad off his lap and bounded to his feet. Once again, he lunged for the dog, his quick actions keeping the canine from bounding from the enclosure just as the chopper blades slowed and came to a stop.

"Sinbad, *Bleib!*" Brian whispered. The canine reacted immediately to the "stay" command and plopped down on his haunches just behind the wall.

An exchange of voices between the Life Flight crew and the trauma team relayed the incoming patient's condition for the next few minutes then, much to Brian and Mike's relief, the roof was again emptied of humans and only the helicopter remained.

"We'd better get the hell out of here before that Life Flight crew comes back up to restock the chopper," Mike advised. He nodded toward John Olson. "You want to take his feet or his shoulders?"

"Neither would be my preference," Brian muttered, "but if I have to choose, I'll take the feet." He, too, looked at the cadaver. "But, God, please get a sheet or something to cover him. I don't want to look at his naked pecker and balls as we're bouncing him down the stairs."

Mike laughed. "Better down than up. That's the only satisfying part about all this. Paul had to haul him *up* all by himself, and it must have been a bitch." He patted his friend on the shoulder. "I'll go get the sheet—and a gurney. Be back in a jiffy."

The morgue attendant disappeared through the door leading to the stairwell, leaving Brian and Sinbad to watch over their "charge" until his return.

The P.I. looked at his now docile partner and a wan grin curved his lips. "Guess we add helicopters to the list of things that scare the shit out of you, huh, fella?" He stooped before the dog and reached out to ruffle the fur around his ears, doing his best to ignore the soulful brown eyes that mirrored trust as they looked up at him. "I get the feeling you're going to cause me a hell of a lot of trouble. Hopefully it won't be more than you're worth."

CHAPTER NINE

"Brian?" Sherry's voice accompanied a quiet knock just before the door to his office opened a few inches. He looked up from the file on his desk that contained Collin Lanaski's military records.

"Yeah?"

"Henry and Rosie Watson are here to see you."

Brian closed the file as he came to his feet. "Show them in, Sherry." He rounded the desk just as Sherry stepped aside and the elderly couple entered the office. He held out a hand to Henry. "Nice to see you again, Henry." He tipped his head respectfully toward the man's wife. "Rosie."

"Nice to see you, too, son," Henry returned as he gripped the other man's hand.

Rosie stopped dead in her tracks when she saw Sinbad lying on a rug in the corner of the office. "Oh my, that is a *big* dog."

"He's my new partner...and, trust me, he's harmless." He winked. "Unless you try to attack me, of course."

"He a police dog?" Henry asked.

"A *former* police dog. Now, he's just a friend." He indicated the chairs before the desk. "Please, have a seat." Brian returned to his own chair behind the desk and waited until the slow-moving Watsons were also seated. "Enjoying the nice weather?" he asked amiably.

"Typical January thaw," Henry returned. "It won't last."

Brian smiled at the man's characteristic bluntness. "So, what can I do for the two of you?"

"My Rosie here said that you were willing to look into our Nellie's disappearance all those years ago. Well, she's been talking with our other kids, and they all think it's a good idea. Me, I ain't sure it's worth the money, but they all seem to think it is."

"They all pitched in what they could," Rosie picked up the diatribe. She reached into her large purse and pulled out a thick white, legal-sized envelope. She laid it on the desk. "Donald put in the most. He was Nellie's husband. He still misses her dearly, and has been determined all these years to prove that she didn't just run off with Everett Klensing." She patted the envelope with her age-spotted left hand. "It's all there. Ten thousand dollars, like you said you would need to take on the case—in cash."

Brian reached across the desk and slid the envelope toward him. "A check would have been fine, Rosie."

"Oh, my, I've never written a check anywhere near that big. I don't think these old hands could've handled it. They'd've been shaking too bad." She reached out to pat the back of Brian's hand, where it still lay on top of the envelope. "And I wouldn't want you worrying about whether or not it would bounce."

Brian laughed. "Well, thank you for your thoughtfulness, Rosie."

"That's a hell of a lot of money, son, for someone who only charges twenty dollars an hour," Henry stated. "You must be plannin' on puttin' in a lot of time on this case—"

"And I told you, he was just being nice when he charged you only twenty dollars," Rosie countered. "I'm sure a private detective's fee is a lot more than that, especially in these difficult times."

"Henry is right, though, Rosie," Brian spoke up. "It *is* a lot of money. Are you all sure you really want to do this? I already told you that there's a possibility I won't find any trace of her."

"And that's a risk we're willing to take. Donald spent years trying to find Nellie. He spent thousands of dollars, even back then, and he was just her husband. You're a professional, Brian, and we all have faith that if anybody can find out what happened to our Nellie, it's you."

The detective tipped his dark head in a slow nod. "Okay. As long as you understand the risks." He looked at Henry. "And I can guarantee you, Henry, that I'll earn every dime of this ten thousand. I'll leave no stone unturned in the search for your daughter."

"And you'll keep us posted on what you find, right?" the old man asked.

"Of course. In fact, you'll get a monthly report that will detail everything I've done."

"Donald also said that he would take care of your expenses," Rosie put in, "since you said the ten thousand wouldn't cover that."

Brian nodded. "And I'll do my best to keep the expenses to a minimum. As I mentioned at your house that day, for the most part, I'll only incur expenses if I have to travel outside of Cheyenne to follow up on a lead."

Henry returned the nod. "That sounds fair."

"Now, the first order of business, I think, would be for me to speak to Donald. I'll have some difficult questions for him regarding the status of his marriage to Nellie, and as to their family life in general." The phone on Brian's desk rang. He ignored it as he continued. "I'll also want to speak to their children. Even though you told me, Rosie, that Nellie would never have left her family willingly, I need to confirm that in my own mind before I look into the possibility of foul play."

"We don't only watch *Jeopardy* and *Wheel of Fortune*, son,"

Henry spoke up again. "We watch our share of cop shows, too. We especially like the reruns of *Matlock* and *Murder She Wrote*. We know that the cops always look at the family first."

"Only as a means of clearing them, Henry," Brian assured the old man. "And I'll be totally respectful...unless Donald gives me reason not to be."

"That'll never happen," Rosie interjected. "Donald is a good man. He was always good to our Nellie and to the children."

"Then he won't have anything to worry about."

Another knock sounded on the door and, once again, Sherry poked her head into the room. "I'm sorry to interrupt, Brian, but Melody Patten is on the phone. She says it's urgent."

Brian looked at the two people before him again. "I apologize, Henry, Rosie, but I have to take this call." Brian picked up the receiver on his desk phone. "Melody, it's Brian. What can I do for you?"

"He's here, Brian! He's at the house!"

"Who? Collin Lanaski?"

"Yes! Jeff is out front with him, and I'm afraid they're going to come to blows! He's spouting something about Jeff hurting Angela!"

"Okay, just calm down. I'll be there in a few minutes."

"All right, and please hurry!"

"I'm on my way." Brian hung up the phone and, in one movement, stood and reached for the shoulder holster, complete with a .40 caliber Glock, that hung on the coat rack in the corner of his office. "I'm sorry, Henry, Rosie, but I have to go. Leave Donald's phone number with Sherry. I'll get ahold of you in a couple of days with my plan of action." His eyes shot toward his partner. "Sinbad, *heir!*"

With that, Brian flew out the door, Sinbad close on his heels.

Brian didn't bother rounding the building to get his truck, but just sprinted down the slush-covered sidewalk toward the small, fenced-in, ranch-style house that sat at the end of the next block. He had heard the loud voices just after exiting the office—loud voices that had also drawn the attention of a multitude of neighbors on both sides of the street. The angry words came to him clearly now as he and Sinbad approached the dwelling.

"And I have told you a dozen times that she is not your daughter! Why can't you just accept that!" Jeff Patten yelled.

"I'll never accept it. You stole her the night of the accident, and somehow I'm going to prove it!"

"God, you are such a lunatic! Do you realize how crazy that sounds? Angela is *our* child, and we have the birth certificate to prove it!"

"I can show it to you, if that will help—" This was a female voice that Brian recognized as Melody's.

"And birth certificates can be *faked*! It doesn't prove anything! And her name isn't Angela. It's Courtney, and I'm not going to let you continue to hurt her!"

The scene playing out for all to see was enough to make Brian's blood run cold as he passed the tall pine trees that hid the Pattens' front door from view. It wasn't until he pushed his way through the front gate that he saw the players—and the lunacy in Collin Lanaski's eyes. What bothered him most, however, was the sight of Angela's tear-streaked face as she clung to her mother in the open doorway to the house.

"Get her inside. Now!" Brian ordered as he stormed up the walk, with Sinbad at his side. Melody quickly did as told and the door slammed closed as Brian swung to face Lanaski. "You, out on the sidewalk! The Pattens now have a restraining order, and your ass is going to be sitting in jail if you don't get off their property right now!"

"I don't give a damn about their stupid restraining order!" Collin Lanaski spouted. His now wary eyes darted continually toward the Belgian Malinois. Though the dog stood obediently at Brian's side, it was threatening nonetheless. "Nothing, and I repeat, *nothing* is going to keep me away from my daughter!"

"And *I* repeat, she is not your daughter."

"Yes, she is, and I have proof!"

"What? Car seats and dog tags? I'm afraid not. Now—" Brian's arm shot out toward the street "—out on the sidewalk!"

"No!"

Brian grabbed the much taller man's arm and attempted to shove him toward the gate, but Lanaski jerked free. A warning bark from Sinbad was enough to make the man take a step back.

"Get your fucking hands off me! I'm not going to leave until *he*—" he glared at Jeff "—admits that he's been hurting Courtney and they put *him* in jail!"

Brian's chest heaved in a sigh. He didn't want to have to call the police for help—and he *really* didn't want to have to draw his weapon or utilize Sinbad's restraint capabilities. "What are you talking about?"

"Ask him." Collin's glower shot toward Jeff again. "Ask him why they had to take Courtney to the hospital last night!"

It was Brian's turn to look at Jeff. "You took her to the hospital?"

The other man rolled his eyes in exasperation. "She had a bladder infection. She gets them all the time—"

"Yes, because you've been molesting her!" Collin Lanaski yelled.

"I have not been molesting my daughter!"

"Okay, that's enough," Brian ordered. "This has gone far enough." He looked at Jeff. "You, go in the house." He turned his gaze to Collin. "You, out on the damned sidewalk!"

"Okay, fine," Lanaski ground out. He, too, looked at Jeff again. "But, so help me God, if you so much as lay a finger on her again—"

Brian's arm shot out toward the street again. "Go!"

Lanaski clamped his mouth shut and stomped toward the gate.

Brian took a deep breath, then laid a hand on Jeff's shoulder. "Go inside. If I can't get rid of him in the next five minutes, call the police."

"Good luck. The guy is crazy, Brian, I swear. Now I didn't only steal his daughter, but I'm molesting her, too."

Brian shook his head at what he, too, realized was the absurdity of the whole situation. "It might be a good idea for you to get Angela out of here for a while. If he's this worked up, then your fears about him trying to kidnap her might be justified. Is there anywhere you can take her?"

"I guess we could take her to my sister's in Evanston. She's the only family we have. Melody was an only child, and both our parents are dead."

Brian nodded. "That would be good. It's what, about 350 miles?"

"Give or take."

"That should be far enough. And do it soon. I don't trust this guy as far as I can throw him."

"You're not the only one," Jeff muttered.

Brian patted his client on the shoulder reassuringly. "It'll be okay, Jeff. I'm not quite sure how, but I'll find a way to convince this guy that Angela is not his daughter."

"Yeah, well good luck with that one." Jeff tipped his head toward Sinbad. "By the way, nice dog."

Brian smiled. "My new partner."

"Well, I think he scared the hell out of Lanaski, which is good. The problem was, when you first walked in here, he scared the hell out of me, too." Jeff turned then, and went into the house.

Brian watched until the other man was safely inside then, taking a deep breath, turned and headed down the sidewalk to where Collin Lanaski's agitated pace took him from one edge of the Pattens' small yard to the other. Once again, Sinbad followed. "So, have you calmed down now?" Brian asked, but he already knew the answer.

"No, and I won't until that little girl, *my* little girl, is safe and sound with *me*."

"That's not going to happen, Collin."

Lanaski looked at Brian with determination etched into his ruddy features. "That's what you think."

Brian ignored the resolve in the other man's words. "So, how did you hear that they took Angela to the hospital last night?" He lifted a dark eyebrow in inquiry. "Were you watching their house?"

"No, I wasn't *watching their house*. My sister is a nurse in the ER at the Medical Center. She's one of the few people who *doesn't* think I'm crazy. Obviously, she knew Courtney and she sees the resemblance—"

"She's seen Angela?"

"Only in pictures, until last night."

Brian couldn't help but laugh. "You have *pictures* of Angela?"

Lanaski bristled. "And why shouldn't I take pictures of her?"

"Because she is *not* your daughter, that's why! You have no right—"

"I have every right!"

A low growl in Sinbad's chest issued a warning and, once again, Lanaski stepped back. Brian rewarded the dog with a quick ruffle of his ears before looking at his adversary again. "So, I take it your sister was working last night when the Pattens brought Angela into the ER?"

"Yes. She tended her. According to her chart, *Courtney* has been treated for *twelve* bladder infections in the past two years—like that asshole said. Kylie also noticed some swelling in her...private area. She mentioned it to the doctor, but he didn't think it was significant enough to warrant reporting it. *He* figured it was just caused by the infection."

Brian backtracked for a minute. "So, Kylie, that's your sister?"

Collin nodded. "Kylie Madden. To save you the trouble of

looking it up, she lives on Seymour Avenue here in Cheyenne."
He met Brian's eyes. "Now, you tell me, *Mr.* Koski, why would
a child of only seven years old have that many bladder infections—ones severe enough to cause swelling?"

"I don't know, Mr. Lanaski. I'm not a doctor…but your
sister *is* a nurse, and by telling you what happened in that
E.R. last night, she violated the HIPAA regulations…and
that could cost her her job *and* she could do time in prison."

Collin paled. "What?"

"HIPAA is the abbreviation for the Health Insurance
Portability and Accountability Act, Mr. Lanaski. Because
she's a nurse, your sister is bound by that act. In other words,
because *you* are not directly involved in Angela's care, she
had no right to tell you anything. She shouldn't even have
told you that Angela was in the E.R. last night. She violated
Angela's rights as a patient."

"And the only reason Kylie told me is because Patten has
been molesting her!"

"That's an awful strong accusation."

"And it's true. If you'd spend a little less time investi-
gating *me* and concentrate on *them*, you'd find that out for
yourself."

"I have no reason to investigate *them*. They have all the
legal documentation to prove that Angela is their daughter.
You don't."

"Then why won't they submit to a DNA test? I've asked
them several times, but they always refuse. That would prove
one way or the other, unequivocally, whether Angela is my
daughter—and that's why they won't agree."

"Or maybe the Pattens won't agree because they know
she's their child and they don't want to put her through all
the tests."

"All they would do is swab the inside of her cheek."

"And, regardless, the Pattens are in no way obligated to
submit to DNA testing. They already have legal proof that
Angela is their daughter," Brian repeated his stance on the

issue, with finality evident in his tone this time. He allowed his countenance and his voice to take on a menacing persona. "Stay away from Angela, Lanaski. Violate the restraining order again, and you *will* go to jail...or worse."

"What? You going to sic your dog on me?"

Again, Brian laughed, but this time it was filled with bitterness. "God, don't tempt me."

"Fuck you" was Lanaski's only response before he stepped to the curb, got into his car, and drove away.

CHAPTER TEN

Donald Overton proved to be as sincere and likeable as his in-laws portrayed him to be. In fact, Brian liked the sixty-five-year-old man almost as much as he did Henry and Rosie. His daughters, too, Vanessa and Miriam, were kind and gentle souls—a testament to the mother that raised them until she disappeared and the heartbroken father who had tried so hard to find his wife. His devotion to her was still evident today. Even the old two-story house he lived in was *their* house—the house he had shared with a woman who had been missing for thirty-seven years.

The first half-hour was spent in congenial conversation, with each of Nellie's immediate family members relaying details of their current lives: occupations, interests and basic history, such as marriages and children. Finally, Brian got down to business and broached the true reason for his visit.

"Basically," Brian looked at the three people seated on the worn sofa in front of him, "I'm here to pick your brain. You three were the last to see Nellie all those years ago, so the logical place for me to start the investigation is with you." He looked at the two women. "How old were each of you when your mother disappeared?"

"I was eight," Vanessa answered. "Miriam was only six."

Brian jotted the information on a yellow legal pad and continued. "So, the day she disappeared, had anything out of the ordinary happened? Was she angry in any way?"

"No," Donald answered firmly. "It was like any other day. In fact, Nellie had just been elected president of the PTA at the girls' school, so she was really excited and happy. It was all she could talk about when I got home from work that day. She had all kinds of plans about fund-raising events and different things she was going to do to get stuff the school needed."

"It was also close to Halloween," Vanessa spoke up again. "She disappeared on October 29th. She'd spent the entire day working on our costumes, and had finished them just before we got home from school. She had us trying them on…" Even after almost four decades, tears shined in her eyes. "My, how we laughed. I was the cowardly lion, Miriam was Dorothy. Mother joked about how she'd have to dress Dad like a tin man, and how she could be the Scarecrow…" She looked at Brian. "We'd just watched *The Wizard of Oz* on TV a few weeks earlier. In fact, we watched it as a family every year. It was something we all looked forward to. Miriam and I were fascinated by it, so I guess it was logical that we chose to be those characters for Halloween almost every year. Mom even made a little jacket-like-thing for our dog that had 'Toto' embroidered on it, which was funny in itself, because our dog was a Collie." She shrugged. "It was a great day."

Brian smiled. "Sounds like it." He gave the now teary-eyed family a moment to compose themselves before he went on. "So, when she left for the grocery store, she was in a good mood?"

"Nellie was virtually always in a good mood," Donald said. "She always found the bright side in every situation. She was like a ray of sunshine in all our lives. That's why it made no sense to any of us when the police suggested that she had run off with Everett Klensing. That would have been so…atypical of Nellie. She lived for me and the children. To just leave us would have been unfathomable to her. Even Gertrude Holms, the woman who ran the grocery store, commented at the time about how happy Nellie was that day. Nellie had told her about the PTA president thing and the girls' costumes—"

"Wait a minute," Brian jumped in. "She actually made it to the grocery store?"

"Oh, yes. It was after she left there that she disappeared."

"So, did she buy anything? Did she leave *with* the groceries?"

"I asked Gertrude the same thing," Donald returned. "She said she had two bags of groceries when she left. She also ordered a roast for Sunday dinner. It was a Wednesday when she disappeared; the store always got meat in on Friday."

"And did the police find the bags of groceries?"

"No. No sign of them."

"And they didn't find that odd? That she disappeared along with her groceries?"

"They just figured she took them with her. That she used *my* money to buy groceries for her and Everett. They said at the time that, on the other hand, if they'd found the groceries scattered about an alley somewhere, that would have supported my claim that something happened to her. The fact that they *didn't* find them made it look like she left willingly."

"And I can see their point to a certain extent, but why would she have ordered a roast for Sunday dinner if she didn't intend to be there to pick it up on Friday?" Brian mused.

"Not to mention that, when I asked Gertrude exactly what Nellie bought, she said milk, eggs, and some other things—including a box of *Trix* cereal and a bag of penny candy. The girls had *asked* her to get the cereal before she left. It was their favorite. Why would she buy kids' sugar cereal and candy for her and Everett?"

"Good question," Brian commented. "No, I would say it's closer to the truth that if Everett *did* take her, he took the groceries also because he knew that to leave them behind would indicate foul play."

"That's what I thought at the time," Donald said. "But the police would hear none of it. They were convinced from day one that she left with Everett."

"Why was that? What prompted them to check and see if Everett was still in town?"

"They didn't check. Everett's wife reported him missing a few days after Nellie disappeared."

Brian lifted a dark eyebrow in surprise. "Everett was married?"

Donald nodded. "With five children."

Brian added this tidbit to the wealth of information already documented on the yellow legal pad.

"His children used to taunt us at school," Miriam spoke up for the first time. "They blamed our mother for their father's disappearance."

"They blamed your mom?"

Miriam nodded. "They called her all kinds of horrible names. Said that she lured him away from his family. It got to the point where Vanessa and I didn't even want to go to school."

"So...*was* she pursuing Everett?" Brian asked the hard question.

"Actually, it was the other way around," Donald returned without even a hint of anger. "Everett was constantly badgering Nellie: trying to get her to have dinner with him, to meet him at secret places. He called here and stopped by *all the time*—even when I was home. He was obsessed with her. Had been since high school. She wanted nothing to do with him, and she told him so. So did I."

"You actually talked to Everett about his obsession with Nellie?"

Donald tipped his gray head in a nod. "On several occasions. I tried to reason with him. To tell him that he had his own family now, and that he had to forget about Nellie. She was married to me. She was happy. She wanted nothing to do with him after what he did."

"What he did?" Brian repeated.

"Everett...attacked Nellie the night of her senior prom.

IDENTITY CRISIS

He tried to rape her…in the back seat of his car. She managed to get away, thank God, and broke up with him the next day. Everett could never accept it, though. He continued to pursue her, right up until he got married three years later. She hoped it would end then, but it didn't. We dealt with Everett Klensing nearly every day of our married life in one form or another. I can't count the times I'd come home from work and he'd be sitting at the kitchen table having a cup of coffee. Nellie just could never *not* be nice to him, even when she was telling him that it was over between them. It was her way. She was a kind and loving person, and always looked for the best in people. I think more than anything, she felt sorry for Everett."

"And you're sure that's all there was to it? You're sure—"

"Nellie would never have been unfaithful to me," Donald spoke adamantly. "She took her marriage vows very seriously, and so did I."

"Obviously Everett didn't think so if he kept trying," Brian pointed out carefully.

"Everett Klensing was a disturbed man, Mr. Koski. He was obsessed with my wife. She never condoned it, she never encouraged it. That's just the way it was. He never tried to harm her again, so we just accepted that his continued presence was going to be an ongoing part of our lives."

"Until October 29, 1975," Brian pointed out.

"Yes, until October 29, 1975, and, believe me, I have berated myself for thirty-seven years that I didn't put a stop to it when I had the chance."

The pain relayed in the other man's words transferred to his eyes and, once again, Brian gave Donald a moment to regroup.

"So, I take it nothing of Nellie's was missing after she disappeared? Clothes, personal items…"

"No. She didn't walk out of the house with a suitcase, if that's what you're asking. All of her stuff was still here… because she intended to come back. I'm going to repeat this for a final time, Mr. Koski. My wife did *not* leave of her own volition. She was *taken*. If you can't or don't want to believe that, then I just wasted a hell of a lot of money."

"I'm not saying that I don't believe you, Mr. Overton. In fact, the evidence thus far is pointing toward foul play. I *do* have to cover all bases, though, and that includes ruling out the possibility that Nellie left willingly."

"Miriam and I understand that, Mr. Koski," Vanessa was quick to reassure him. She looked at her father. "And Dad does, too, don't you, Dad?"

The older man sighed, revealing the enormous weight he had been carrying on his shoulders all these years. "Yes, dear, I understand. I'm sorry, Mr. Koski."

"No need to apologize. In fact, I'd be a little suspicious if you *didn't* get upset when it was suggested that Nellie left of her own volition. Now, going back for a minute..." The private detective consulted his notes. "Gertrude Holms, the lady who owned the grocery store, is she still living?"

"No. Gertrude was in her seventies when Nellie disappeared. She died years ago."

"And where was this grocery store located?"

"About two blocks from here...on the corner of Bent and West 24th. It's just a house now, though. The store went out of business in the '80s."

"I'd still like to check it out. The location anyway."

"There are probably old photos to be found somewhere," Donald suggested. "Of the store, I mean, the way it looked back in '75."

"Possibly in the police file on the case?" Brian asked.

"I doubt it. The police didn't do much at the time, other than to talk to me and Gertrude. I was there the night they talked to her, and I don't remember them taking any pictures. It's worth checking into, though, I guess."

"And what about Everett's family? His wife, parents, brothers, sisters, children? Are any of them still in the area?"

"His wife is. She's Clara *Johnson* now, though. She remarried at some point. I heard that she had Everett declared legally dead some years after he disappeared, so she could collect on his life insurance. She kept the house and, as far as I know, her and her new husband still live there. It was on Albany Avenue on the east side. Everett was an only child, so he didn't have brothers and sisters. I'm not sure if his children still live around here or not."

"Did you ever have Nellie declared legally dead?" Brian asked the question as gently as possible.

"No, and I never will. She could still be out there somewhere, Mr. Koski, and until I know different, she's still my wife."

Brian stood outside the 6th District Police station with Sinbad at his heel. Henry Watson had been right in his prediction two days earlier. Winter was not through with them yet. In fact, the ominous mid-January sky threatened snow, and Brian pulled the collar of his jacket closer about his neck to ward off the chill. Sinbad seemed unaffected by the cold. He simply waited obediently at his master's side until commanded to do otherwise. Brian had felt no need to bring the dog with him to the Overton house that morning, but for this trip, he figured he might need the support. It was *his* old precinct, the station he had been in charge of for almost five years. He hadn't set foot in the building since he resigned over four months earlier, however, and wasn't sure what kind of reception to expect. It didn't matter, he kept telling himself. He was there on official business, which gave him the right, as with any other private detective in the city, to enter the hallowed halls and be treated with respect.

Brian looked down at the ever attentive Sinbad. "You got my back, buddy?"

The dog wagged his tail excitedly with the attention and offered an energetic bark in response.

"Okay then. Let's do it."

Brian took a deep breath and started up the steps. He pushed the door inward and marched toward the patrol desk with a confidence he did not quite feel. The officer on duty looked up and, immediately, a broad smile creased the man's face.

"Hey, Captain, great to see you!"

Brian smiled and relaxed. "You, too, Mark. Only it's not captain anymore. Just Brian Koski, common citizen." The smile segued into a self-indulgent grin. "And awesome private eye."

"Yeah, I heard you had your own P.I. business now. How's it going?"

"Good," Brian returned. "A little slow at first, but things are picking up."

"Well, I'm sure it didn't help that Stanley put out an order early on that no one was to refer cases to you." The desk sergeant winked. "And you didn't hear that from me."

"My lips are sealed, Mark. I'd figured as much, though. Stanley isn't exactly my biggest fan."

"Hey, you got a raw deal, Brian. We all know that. Most of the guys still have your back, though, so don't hesitate to drop in once in a while and say hi. And don't worry. Stanley virtually never leaves his cushy office to slum it with us lowlifes down here, so the chances of you running into him are pretty slim."

"Thanks for the invite, Mark. I'll admit it was a little unnerving to just walk in here."

The sergeant tipped his head toward Sinbad. "So, who's your friend? A working dog, I hope, or I can't let him be in here."

"Oh, he's definitely a working dog. Former NYPD. He ran into some hard times, and his handler had to give him up. He's my partner now, and worth every penny I *didn't* pay for him."

"Well, can't beat that. Not many P.I.'s can say they have a trained police dog for a partner...and that they got him for free." The cop leaned forward and rested his forearms on the desk. "So, what can I do you for, Captain?"

"I need to get my hands on a case file—a thirty-seven-year-old case file."

"An open case or no?"

"No. It was closed years ago. A missing persons case."

"Then you'd need to see Ben in archives. Shouldn't be a problem, since the case is closed."

"Will do. Can I go on down?"

"Help yourself." The sergeant grinned. "I think you know the way."

Brian headed for the elevator, with Sinbad at his right heel. He rode to the lower level and proceeded down the long hall toward the door at the end with the stenciled words "Records" emblazoned on the glass. He stepped inside and, once again, was greeted enthusiastically by the attendant.

"Captain Koski! Long time no see!"

"Not by choice, Ben, believe me."

"Yeah, well, you're not the only one Stanley put the axe to, trust me. You were just the craziest one...and I'm not talking your personality, which *was* kind of crazy at times. We all know you, Brian, and we also know you would never have put a bullet in an unarmed, *subdued* prisoner. It's bullshit, pure and simple."

Brian paled slightly, though luckily his reaction to the man's words was not noticeable. "Yeah, well it's long over and done with now, Ben."

"And, regardless, it's still bullshit. But Stanley will get his someday. You mark my words."

"I take it he's not real loved within the department?"

"Are you kidding? Everybody hates the guy. He's so far up the mayor's ass that he's covered in shit." The attendant sat back on the high stool behind the desk and crossed his arms before his chest. "So, what's with the dog?"

Brian could not help but smile. It seemed that *everyone*

lately was more interested in Sinbad than in him. "He's my new partner. Retired NYPD."

"Cool. So, what can I do for you, Captain?"

"I need a copy of an old case file from October of 1975. A missing persons case. Unsolved. Name of the victim was Nellie Overton."

"No case number, I suppose."

Brian smiled wanly. "Sorry."

"Okay. Might take me a few hours to find it. Can I call you?"

"Sure." Brian slid a business card across the desk. "The number's on there. And, if it wouldn't be too much trouble, could you find a single report for me, too? This one is more recent. It was a fatal car crash on Hynds Boulevard in December of 2009. Two victims: Lynn Lanaski and her daughter, Courtney."

Ben jotted down that information, also. "Okay. I'll see what I can find."

"Thanks, Ben. I appreciate it."

"Yeah, and that's the difference between you and Stanley. You appreciated everything we did when you were captain. Stanley, he appreciates nothing unless it furthers his career or pads his pockets."

Brian ran from his truck toward the back entrance to the office a few minutes later. Snow was again blanketing the Cheyenne area and, judging from the increasing winds, the day would get worse before it got better.

Sherry looked up from the computer screen on her desk as he and Sinbad entered. A wry smile touched her lips. "A little nasty out there?"

"Yeah, and it's gonna get nastier," Brian grumbled. He took off his jacket and shook it out on the tiled floor as he headed for his office.

"Hey, knock it off! I just scrubbed that floor last night! Until you can afford to hire a cleaning company, I'm it, and *you* are a pig!"

Brian tossed the jacket through the doorway to his office, where it landed haphazardly on the back of one of the chairs before his desk. He turned back to his secretary as Sinbad made his way to the rug in the corner, plopped down, and promptly went to sleep. "Now, is that anyway to talk to your boss?"

"It is when that boss is a pig," she returned easily. "I expect it from Sinbad. He's a dog, though he's smart enough that you should be able to teach him to wipe his feet."

Brian moved to settle a hip on the front edge of her desk. "Hey now, it wasn't even a month ago that you told me I was a *great* boss. How did I go from being great to being a pig in only a month?"

"I was worried about losing my job then. I had to be nice." She tossed him a saucy smile, then went back to typing up Brian's report on the latest incident with Collin Lanaski.

He lifted a dark eyebrow. "And you're not worried about losing your job now?"

"Nope. We have *two* paying clients, and more on the way, I'm sure. You're stuck with me, boss."

"Which also means that *you're* stuck with *me*," he countered. "And it looks to be a long, cold winter."

Sherry turned from the keyboard, leaned back in her chair, and crossed her arms beneath her ample bosom. "Brian Koski, are you flirting with me?"

He grinned. "I'm trying."

She reached across the desk to pat his knee and, consequently, Brian's eyes strayed to where her blouse gaped away from her chest. "Don't bother. I'm on to you."

"*On to me?*"

"You're a typical playboy, Brian. The one-night stand *king*. Trust me, I was warned by several people when I took the job."

The eyebrow went up again. "Oh, really?"

"Yup, and despite my big boobs, I'm looking for more than that. I have a little girl to think of, and that little girl needs a daddy, not a fly-by-night Romeo." She patted the knee again and sat back. "And, besides, I have a boyfriend."

"Since when?"

"Since a few weeks ago...and don't look so annoyed!"

Brian stood. "I'm not annoyed, Sherry...and congratulations," he returned shortly.

She rolled her big, blue eyes. "God, please tell me you're not going to fire me."

"Why in the hell would I fire you?"

"I know why you hired me, Brian. It was the boobs! And now, because I've told you that I'm not available—or interested—you have no reason to keep me on."

"I do, too, Sherry. You're a great secretary...even though apparently I'm *not* a great boss any longer. I'm not going to fire you."

"Thanks."

Brian started for his office, his face the picture of disgruntled manhood.

"And Brian?"

He paused to look over his shoulder. "What?"

"You *are* a great boss."

The front door to the waiting area blew open, negating any need for a response from Brian, and a frantic Jeff Patten burst into the room.

"He took her, Brian! Collin Lanaski took Angela!"

CHAPTER ELEVEN

A suddenly pale Brian turned back into the outer office. "Okay, Jeff, just calm down and tell me what happened."

"He took her! Melody left this morning to take Angela to my sister's in Evanston, like you told us to do. Lanaski must have been watching her. He forced her car off the road, and he took Angela!"

"Where is Melody now?"

"Probably sitting in her car on the highway somewhere, sobbing her eyes out! She called me at work a few minutes ago on her cell. Damn it, Brian, you were supposed to stop this from happening! It's what we hired you for! If we would have just kept Angela at home, everything would be fine. But, no, we do what *you* tell us to do, and he takes her! He was waiting for an opportunity, and you gave it to him!"

Brian covered the ground between himself and the other man and laid a hand on his shoulder. "I'll find her, Jeff. I promise you that. But first, we have to find out where Melody is and get her home. Call her on her cell phone and find out *exactly* where she is so we can go get her."

Jeff fumbled for the cell phone in his jacket pocket and somehow managed to find his wife's number in the directory and push "Talk." He conversed with her for a few seconds, then hung up and looked at Brian again. "She's on I-80, about five miles south of Laramie."

"Okay. Let's go." He glanced toward the office. "Sinbad, *heir!*"

The dog bounded into the outer office and followed Brian and Jeff out the back door. Sherry could do nothing but watch them go.

Brian pulled his black Dodge Ram onto the shoulder behind Melody's 1999 Chevy Lumina forty-five minutes later. Two Cheyenne Highway Patrol squad cars were also on the scene and had already blocked the right lane of traffic and cordoned off a large area with crime scene tape.

Jeff bounded out of the truck and ran through the fast-growing blizzard toward his wife, but his progress was impeded by one of the state troopers. "She's my wife!" he yelled. "Damn it, get out of my way. She's my wife!"

The officer let him pass and turned to Brian, who, in turn, produced his P.I. credentials. He was then allowed to duck under the crime scene tape, also, and approach Melody. Sinbad followed dutifully on his master's heels.

Melody ran into her husband's arms. "He took her, Jeff! Oh, God, he took her! She was crying so hard. She was so scared!"

Jeff looked at a second state trooper who stood nearby. "Can I talk to her alone for a minute?"

The man nodded. "Sure."

Jeff led his wife to the side of the road and into the ever-deepening snow. Brian and Sinbad followed, but stood a respectful distance away. Even with the wind howling around them, however, he could still hear Jeff's words.

"Why in the world did you call the police? This is what we hired Brian for!"

"I...I didn't call them," Melody stammered, whether

from the cold or emotion, Brian wasn't sure. "He saw me parked on the side of the highway and pulled over to see if I was all right. When I told him what had happened, he called it in and the other squad car showed up."

"And you should never have told them what happened! We agreed we weren't going to get the police involved in this!"

"I'm sorry, Jeff! I didn't know what else to do!" She gripped her husband's jacketed arms in a fierce grip. "He *took* her, Jeff! That awful man has Angela!" Melody dissolved into sobs again, and Jeff pulled her close.

Brian walked up to them. "Let's get her inside the car. It's freezing out here."

Jeff nodded and led his distraught wife to the passenger side of her Lumina. His own Toyota Camry was still at the house. He helped her inside the warm vehicle, shut the door, and turned to Brian again. "That dog of yours—" he indicated Sinbad and raised his voice to be heard over the roar of the wind "—isn't he a police dog? I mean, shouldn't he be able to pick up Angela's scent or something?"

"It wouldn't help, Jeff. Lanaski put Angela in a car and drove off. Sinbad would only be able to follow her scent to wherever the car sat."

"But we have to do something! Every minute we stand here, he's getting further away!"

"I'm sure Melody told the officers what kind of car it was. There's probably already been an Amber Alert issued, and that would include the make and model of the car. They'll find him, Jeff."

"And if they don't?"

"Then *I* will. You were right back in my office. You hired me to make sure this exact thing wouldn't happen, yet it did, on my watch. I'll find her, Jeff. If I have to turn over every blade of grass and rock in the state, hell, in the *country*, I will find her! You, on the other hand, need to take care of your wife. Talk to the police. See if you can take her home. If need be, there's a WHP office in Cheyenne. You can go there when you get back and give a statement."

"I don't think Melody's in any shape to give a statement to anybody."

"I know it'll be hard for her, but she has to. I'll want to talk to her, too, when I get back."

"What do you mean? Aren't you going back with us?"

Brian shook his head. "No. I want to hang out here for a while. I've got a police radio in the truck. If the WHP or the Amber Alert turn up anything, I want to be close by. I want to *be* there when they nail his ass. It'll be the next best thing to doing it myself." Brian patted the other man's snow-covered shoulder. "Take your wife home. I'll stop by when I get back, if it's not too late."

"I doubt that any time will be too late. I don't think we'll be sleeping much tonight, not unless they bring Angela home."

It was just after two a.m. when Brian finally made his way back to the Patten residence. As Jeff had stated earlier, the house was still lit up. In fact, not surprisingly, there were several cars parked in the driveway and on the street that did not belong to the family.

"Did you find her?" Melody cried as she yanked open the front door. Jeff was just a step behind her. "Did you find Angela?"

"I'm afraid not, Melody, but the police are still looking. They'll find her." He stepped into the foyer and was immediately approached by a female in professional attire. Two similarly dressed men waited in the living room. Brian recognized the brunette immediately as being from the local FBI office.

"Brian." She smiled. "Nice to see you again."

"You, too, Kathryn. I have to say that I'm not surprised to see you here."

"We figure there's a good chance Lanaski will take Angela across state lines, if he hasn't already. Probably into the mountains. We're just trying to stay a step ahead of him."

"Well, good luck. I've been playing that game for a month, and obviously I wasn't very good at it."

"No one could have seen this coming, Brian. According to the Pattens, he's been to the house many times and never tried to take her. Sending her to her aunt's in Evanston was a good call, especially with the way the situation was escalating. The only *bad* call I would say you made was not notifying the police the other day when he violated the restraining order. If you had done that, they would have picked him up and this whole incident would never have happened. In fact, as a P.I, and a former cop, you could have hauled his ass down to the station yourself and had them book him."

"Yeah, and I thought I could handle it. Obviously, I was wrong."

"Yes, well if you were wrong, so was the Cheyenne P.D. They should have been involved in this a long time ago, and you can be sure that Chief Stanley will be taking heat from the press because he ignored an obviously dangerous situation."

"Well, I can't say I'll be sorry if that happens."

Kathryn smiled. "And I don't blame you. He really nailed you to the cross, Brian, and you didn't deserve it. You were a good cop. One of the best. As you know, my husband was on the SWAT team that infiltrated the Riker house that night, and he still swears that things went down exactly the way you all first said they did."

"Thanks, Kathryn, but that's all water under the bridge. Right now, we have more important things to worry about." He glanced at the Pattens.

"That we do," the agent agreed, following his gaze. "So, you know this Lanaski guy better than we do. Any ideas on what his next move might be?"

"I think he's already made it. I think he's been planning

this for a long time. He probably had a place all set up where he could take Angela, and he's there right now."

"And if that's the case, then it can't be far from here."

"I'd bet on it. He's never left town for any length of time that I can tell, at least not recently. His harassment of the Pattens has been too frequent to allow for any lengthy trips. No, if he was getting a place ready where he could hide out with Angela, then it's nearby. Probably in the mountains, like you said."

"Do you think she's all right, Brian?" Melody battled another rush of tears as she asked the question. "Do you think Angela's all right?"

"I don't think he would hurt her, if that's what you're asking. If Collin really thinks she's his daughter, which obviously he does, then the last thing he would want to do is harm her in any way. In fact, I'd be willing to bet that the place he took her would be any child's dream. He's probably got it stocked with toys and SpaghettiO's." He reached out to wipe a wayward tear from Melody's cheek. "The only thing that little girl is probably missing right now is her Mama and Daddy."

Melody moved into Brian's embrace, and he held her close for a long moment. "Find her for me, Brian. Find my little girl."

"I will, Melody, and that's a promise."

"Kylie Madden?" Brian asked when the extremely tall, platinum blonde opened the door to her apartment the following morning.

"Yes."

"My name's Brian Koski. I'm a private investigator. I'd like to talk to you about your brother, Collin."

"And I'll tell you exactly what I told the police when they

were here last night. I don't know where he is, and I had no idea that he was planning to leave."

"Or that he was planning to kidnap Angela Patten?"

The thirty-something woman muttered a curse under her breath and started to shut the door in Brian's face. His quick hand stopped the movement.

"Are you aware that you violated the HIPAA Regulations when you told your brother about Angela's visit to the E.R.?"

"So you're the one who told Collin that, huh?"

"Yes, I am...and I'm willing to make you a deal."

Her smooth brow furrowed in sudden suspicion. "What kind of *deal*?"

"You tell me everything you know about Angela, what led you to believe she'd been molested, and I don't go to the hospital administrator and tell him that you disclosed a patient's private information to your brother."

She lifted a delicate blonde eyebrow. "Blackmail, Mr. Koski? I would have thought that to be beneath a *reputable* private investigator."

"I do what I feel is necessary to help my clients, Ms. Madden...just as you did what you thought was necessary to help your brother."

"I didn't do it for Collin. I did it for Courtney. Someone needed to help that child, and luckily Collin had the courage to do it. I'm not saying that I think kidnapping her was necessarily the right choice, but obviously he felt there was no other way to protect her."

Brian crossed his arms over his chest. "So, are you willing to talk to me?"

She sighed and stepped back. "Come on in."

Brian entered the spacious apartment. "Nice place."

"No need for the niceties, detective. Just tell me what you want."

"Is it okay if I sit down first?"

Another sigh. "Be my guest."

Brian seated himself at a small table in the corner of

the room. Kylie sat opposite him. "So, Collin told me you're the only one who believes that Angela Patten is actually his daughter, Courtney."

"She's the spitting image of Courtney when she was little, Mr. Koski. She's also the spitting image of Collin and Lynn. Yes, I believe him."

"So, what led you to believe she had been sexually molested?"

"It was obvious—"

"The doctor on call the other night didn't seem to think so."

"He was actually an intern and, though he should have known what to look for, he obviously didn't. I reported him to the Chief of Staff after that incident. That's how strongly I felt that he was wrong in his diagnosis."

"And your feelings had nothing to do with the fact that you believe Angela to be your niece?"

"I've been a registered nurse for ten years, Mr. Koski, and I have treated relatives before. In fact, I *reported* a relative who I believed to be physically abusing his son and, as it turned out, I was right. My cousin hasn't spoken to me in six years because of that incident. I reported Doctor Stone because it was my job, *not* because I believe Angela is Collin's daughter. He misdiagnosed a patient and put a child in further danger."

"So, it doesn't bother you that there's documented proof that Courtney died in the accident?"

"There's documented proof that *a little girl* died in the accident. There is no proof that it was Courtney."

"Okay. Let's go back to the night the Pattens brought Angela into the E.R. What did you see, medically, that convinced you she was being sexually abused?"

"There was, in my opinion, abnormal swelling of both the vulva and the labia. There also appeared to be a tear in her hymen."

"But Doctor Stone disagreed?"

"Yes, he did. Angela also had a history of chronic urinary tract infections. Though this can admittedly be common in children, and especially girls, it can also be an indication of sexual abuse. Angela also complained that her *pee-pee* hurt."

"Ms. Madden, would you be willing to lie for your brother?"

She answered without blinking an eye. "No, Mr. Koski, I wouldn't. I turned in my own husband for his sexual abuse of a neighbor girl three years ago. I wouldn't lie for him, and I won't lie for Collin."

Brian nodded slowly. "Fair enough. I have just a couple more questions, Ms. Madden, regarding your brother. Does he own any other property besides the house in Cheyenne? Like in the mountains maybe?"

"No."

"And you're sure about that?"

"Yes, Mr. Koski, I'm sure."

"How about a favorite vacation spot. Is he an outdoorsy type guy?"

"He enjoys camping, yes, and hunting and fishing. I don't know if he had a favorite *spot* or not." She stood. "Is that all?"

He followed her lead and stood, also. "I guess so. For now anyway."

Kylie's next words were measured. It was obvious that she had grown tired of the questioning. "I already told you, Mr. Koski, I didn't know Collin was leaving, I didn't know he had plans to kidnap Courtney, I haven't heard from him, and I don't know where he is. I already told you everything about the night the Pattens brought Courtney into the E.R., which fulfills my part of the *deal*. So, please, just leave...and don't come back."

CHAPTER TWELVE

Brian's promise to Melody Patten became more and more hollow as the months wore on, yet he continued his search for the little girl in some capacity each day. As winter gave way to spring, and spring to summer, it became easier to widen the search in mountainous areas, but it seemed that of late Brian and Sinbad were the only ones with the motivation to trudge the rocky terrain. Both the Cheyenne P.D. and the Wyoming Highway Patrol had virtually given up the search two months after the kidnapping. The local FBI hung in for another month; then, deciding they could no longer spare the manpower, they too, pulled the plug. Brian was the only one who kept up the vigil, and his other cases were suffering because of it. Sherry had seen it. Henry and Rosie Watson, and Donald and his girls had also seen the lack of progress in their case, but no one had the courage to confront the determined and almost desperate detective. No one, that is, except his best friend.

"You've gotta let this go, Bri," Zach urged. "You've got other cases that have to take priority...paying cases. You admitted yourself just last week that the Pattens weren't paying you anymore. That elderly couple, though, the ones who hired you to look into their daughter's disappearance all those years ago, they *did* pay you—and you've done virtually nothing to help them."

"And I told Henry and Rosie Watson just the other day that I'd extend their contract for another six months, at no additional cost," Brian countered. "They understand, Zach, that finding little Angela Patten has to take priority."

"And that was all fine and good before, but it's been *five* months, Brian. She disappeared on January 18th, and it's almost July. I hate to say this, buddy, but there comes a time when you have to throw in the towel and just move on. It's okay to spend a *little* time searching for her now and then, but not *every day.*"

"He took her on *my* watch, Zach! How am I supposed to just *move on*! I promised her parents that I would keep her safe, and I failed!"

"Yeah, and your business is going to fail, too, if you don't start taking on new cases and working on the one you've got! You made a commitment to another set of parents, too, Brian, to find *their* daughter, or at least to find out what happened to her. Is that commitment any less important than the one you made to the Pattens? Hell, when I stopped in the office to see you last week, Sherry said that there had been five people in, just in the last few days, looking to hire you, but you weren't there! Brian, you've got to pull yourself together and get back to your life! Sherry said the money is running out, the bills are late again, yet she's sticking by you. You owe it to her and her little girl…and to *yourself* to move on!"

Brian bounded to his feet, almost overturning the heavy wooden table on the deck behind the Riker house, and stomped off. By the time he reached the other end of the twenty-foot deck, however, his pace had slowed and his shoulders slumped. He didn't hear Caryn exit the house upon hearing the commotion through the open windows as the next words tumbled from his mouth.

"You know, I'm beginning to wonder if I'm even cut out for this line of work. I couldn't protect Angela Patten, I

didn't find Miranda Bennington until after she was dead...
hell, I couldn't even protect you and Caryn!"

"Knock it off, Brian. None of that was your fault. You
were a good cop—"

He whirled to face Zach and, for the first time, saw Caryn
standing beside her husband. He didn't let her presence
quell his anger, however, or his self-loathing. "A good cop?
Does a *good* cop let an innocent seven-year-old girl, a girl he
was hired to protect, get kidnapped by a lunatic? Does a *good*
cop let a *twelve*-year-old girl be raped and murdered by a sick
bastard who enjoys hurting children? Does a *good* cop let his
best friends be terrorized by a raving maniac? I mean, look
at you, Zach! You can barely walk now, and that is because of
me...because *I* couldn't catch Dan Hamilton. If I had done
my job, if I'd have found that bastard and locked him up like
I should have, he wouldn't have broken into your house on
Christmas Eve and shot you in both legs!"

"And if it had happened that way, both Zach and I would
be dead now because Dan would have found a way to kill us,
even from prison," Caryn returned softly. "We said it that
night, Brian, and I'm saying it now: the only way we were ever
going to be rid of Dan for good was the way it went down that
night. I wasn't sorry for it then, and I'm not sorry for it now.
You *saved* us, Brian...you *saved* your best friends, because you
had the courage to put an end to the terror once and for all."

Caryn crossed the deck to stand before him. "And you
haven't failed little Angela Patten. Not yet. Because you *will*
find her. I have no doubt. And as for Miranda Bennington?
You did everything you could to find that girl. Unlike Angela,
though, she was taken by someone who *wanted* to hurt her,
like you said. Angela, on the other hand, is with a man who
believes her to be his long-lost daughter. You said it yourself,
several times, that she's probably living the life of a prin-
cess...and she will continue to live that life, *unharmed*, until
you're able to find her. In the meantime, though, you have
to go on. Like Zach said, you have to live your life, and your

life is and always will be devoted to helping people. It's what you do, Brian. It's who you are. That's why you became a cop, and that's why *this* job is so important."

Brian stared at her for a long moment as the anger drained from his body, then finally opened his arms and gathered her close. "You do have a way with words, lady."

"That's *my* job," she murmured against his chest. "It's why I became a teacher, because in reality, words are all a teacher has." She raised her chin to look up at him. "And by the way, Zach is doing fine. He may be somewhat gimpy now, but he needed it just to slow him down."

"Right," her husband grumbled from behind them. "Wait until I get you into bed later. I'll show you just how much I've *slowed down*."

Caryn grinned up at Brian. "See what I mean?"

Brian chuckled as he released her. "Okay, now that I'm done with my pity party, I guess I'd better get back to town and get some work done."

"So, I can't talk you into a piece of apple pie? It just came out of the oven."

Brian considered her offer, but just for a moment. "Okay, so maybe work can wait until tomorrow..." He slipped an arm around Caryn's shoulders and Zach followed them into the house.

Sherry waited until the door to the outer room closed behind their newest client before she sauntered into Brian's office, paused to stroke Sinbad's head, and then eased into one of the two chairs before his desk. "So, *another* new client, huh? What's that, three just this week?"

Brian leaned back in his chair, entwined his fingers behind his dark head, and allowed a self-indulgent grin to curve his lips. "Four, but who's counting."

"Man, you are going to be one busy guy."

"And *you* are going to be one busy lady. I've been thinking about having you start doing some leg work for me...and I don't mean via the computer." He stood and moved to perch on the front edge of the desk and let his appreciative eyes drop to his secretary's long, slender legs. "Not that those legs need a workout by any means."

"You never give up, do you?"

"Nope, and when I do, hopefully I'll be six feet under. Seriously, though, how would you feel about taking some of the caseload off my hands? I think you could handle some of the simpler cases, and it wouldn't hurt to put that criminal justice degree to work."

"Are you serious!" Sherry exclaimed excitedly.

"I wouldn't have mentioned it if I wasn't."

"What about all the paperwork, though? There'll be a lot more now that we have more clients. I don't know if I could keep up with both."

Brian lifted his shoulders in a shrug. "I think, with the new clients, that I can afford to hire you an assistant...and give you a raise. It'll be a challenge to get another desk into the outer office, but I think we can manage."

Sherry didn't even hear the last words as she flew out of her chair and flung her arms around Brian's neck. "Thank you, Brian. I won't disappoint you, I promise."

He placed his hands on her upper arms, pushed her back, and deposited a prim kiss on her cheek. "I hate to tell you this, Sherry, but you disappoint me every day."

Upon the questioning lift of her eyebrow, his gaze dropped pointedly to her chest in explanation.

Sherry just rolled her eyes. "Dream on, boss."

"Oh, I do, trust me, and some of them get pretty steamy."

His secretary shook her blonde head slowly. "God, you are such a letch." She turned and flounced back into the outer office just as the outside door opened and the second would-be client that morning entered the room.

"Hi," Sherry greeted the newcomer. "Can I help you?"

"I need to see Mr. Koski, if that's possible," the woman replied.

"Sure. Just a second." Sherry turned her head toward the open door to Brian's office. "Brian, someone here to see you."

Brian came to the door and the sight of his thirty-some-year-old visitor's slender body, olive skin, and shimmering, shoulder-length ebony hair literally took his breath away. He recovered his composure quickly, however, and extended a hand in greeting. "Hi. I'm Brian Koski."

"Katrina Cordova," the woman returned. "I need to speak with you for a moment, if that's okay."

"Well, come on in then, and we'll see what I can do to help you."

He stepped aside and allowed Katrina to precede him into the office, but paused before entering himself when Sherry wagged a finger, indicating for him to come closer. He moved to her desk, and she promptly grabbed a tissue and wiped a pretend droplet from the corner of his mouth.

"Sorry. You were drooling," she whispered.

It was Brian's turn to roll his eyes as he turned and walked into his office and closed the door behind him. Katrina stood in the middle of the room in obvious indecision, her hesitant gaze centered on Sinbad.

"Don't worry. He's harmless," Brian assured her. He took a seat behind the desk as Katrina claimed the chair recently vacated by Sherry. The private detective met her haunting black eyes and, again, had to reel in his emotions.

"So, what can I do for you, Miss Cordova?"

Surprisingly, Katrina just smiled, a rueful show of skepticism that put Brian on guard.

"What?"

"I'm sorry. It's just that I've experienced this same, polite conversation with so many people...until they hear what I have to say. Then they think I'm nuts."

"So, you've sought out other private detectives?"

"No, the police. I even went all the way to the top—
Chief Stanley. He was the last in a long line. He referred me
to you."

Brian couldn't stop the reactive widening of his eyes.
"Chief Stanley referred you to me?"

She nodded. "He said you were working this case and
that my type of information was more suited to someone
like you." Her dark brow wrinkled in bewilderment. "I'm not
quite sure what he meant by that."

Brian's chest rose and fell in a sigh. "I can only imagine. "
He sat back and crossed his arms before his chest. "So what
type of information do you have…and about who?"

"That missing little girl, Angela Patten."

"Wait a minute." Brian sat forward again, his eyes widening in disbelief. "Chief Stanley referred you to *me* regarding
the Angela Patten kidnapping?"

"Yes. He said his department didn't have time to follow
up on my information right now, but that maybe you would."

"Okay…" *Why is Stanley, of all people, tossing me a lead on
Angela Patten?*

Katrina's gaze dropped to her hands. "This is going to
sound really off the wall…"

"Just spit it out, Ms. Cordova."

She met his gaze again. "I…have visions. I have ever
since I was a little girl."

Brian was tempted to close his eyes and groan. He didn't
interrupt, though, as she continued.

"My mother and father had a really hard time dealing
with it—"

"Please. Just tell me what you saw." He tried to keep the
growing irritation out of his voice.

"I already told you…it was about Angela Patten. I think
I know where she is—and I think she's still alive. In fact, I
think she's actually *happy*."

The speechless Brian studied Katrina's somber visage for
a long moment, then she watched the look in his eyes morph

from confusion to rage in an instant. He bounded from the chair. "Did Stanley put you up to this?"

Her dark complexion paled slightly. "What?"

"Martin Stanley, our esteemed Chief of Police. You said it was *him* who told you that I was working on this case. Did he also tell you that I worked the Miranda Bennington case before he booted me off the force? Did he tell you that the outcome of *that* case tore me apart, and that now the Angela Patten case is doing the same thing because I don't want another little girl to die because I couldn't find her?"

"Please, Mr. Koski, I'm only trying to help..."

Brian stalked to the door and yanked it open. "Get out."

"Mr. Koski..., I really don't understand—"

"Yeah, well I do, all too well. Stanley decided to have a little fun at my expense, and he got you to help him." A scathing laugh jumped from his throat. "So, tell me...this *vision*? Was that your idea or Stanley's?"

"I am not lying! That girl is alive!"

"So how much did Stanley pay you to act out this little charade?"

"Nothing!"

"Get out."

"Mr. Koski, please!"

"I said, *get out!*" He grabbed her arm and, none too gently, escorted her past the stunned Sherry and through the reception area to the door.

"Please, you have to listen to me! That little girl—!"

Brian's response was to yank open the outside portal. A blast of the hot July wind hit his already scalding face. He gave Katrina a shove then, and she landed on her hands and knees on the sidewalk.

Brian slammed the door behind her.

"*Visions,*" Brain grumbled aloud as he flopped onto his stomach in the huge, king-sized bed. "And visions about Angela Patten no less!"

A loud crack of thunder, accompanied by a blinding flash of lightning, accented Brian's words. The storm had been going on for more than an hour, but it nowhere near matched the ferocity of the turmoil within Brian's third-floor apartment in downtown Cheyenne.

Katrina Cordova had been on Brian's mind more often than not in the past two days. He liked to tell himself that it was because of guilt over the whole Angela Patten fiasco. Maybe he had given the woman a raw deal. Maybe he should have heard her out...just in case. More likely, though, the reason he couldn't get her off his mind was because she was hot—extremely hot in fact. And she was in cahoots with Martin Stanley. To agree to bring little Angela Patten into the mix, though, was nothing short of cruel. He might have expected it from his former employer, but not from a woman who could put Angelina Jolie to shame in both looks and acting ability.

And that's exactly why Stanley chose her. He knew Brian's weakness. In fact every cop in the city, or in his precinct anyway, knew Brian had the reputation of being a career playboy. He had never been able to resist a beautiful woman, and would probably never marry for that exact reason.

He couldn't help but smile. "Hell, I even hit on Caryn before she started dating Zach." The grin faded quickly. "But it didn't work, did it, Stanley? I didn't fall for her...either her looks or her story."

He rolled onto his back again and a heartfelt sigh lifted his chest. "And maybe I should have. Maybe I should have heard her out. If there's even the remotest chance that she knows where Angela Patten is, I owe it to that little girl to find out."

The phone beside the bed rang, jarring Brian from his self-destructive reverie. Immediately, a frown furrowed his brow. If he were still on the force, a two a.m. call would not have been at all unusual. Now, though, he could think of no one who would be calling him at this time of night...unless something was wrong out at Zach and Caryn's or the Pattens had received word on Angela.

Brian sat up, turned on the light, and checked the caller I.D. It was an unfamiliar number...

He punched the "Talk" button. "Hello?"

"Mr. Koski?"

"Yes."

"This is...Katrina Cordova."

Instant anger flooded Brian's veins. "Man, you just won't give it up, will you?"

"Please, Mr. Koski...Brian. I really need to talk to you. It's important."

"Oh, really? So playing me for a fool the other day wasn't enough? You want to finish the job?"

"I had another vision."

"Really? So, did you see who killed Jon Benet Ramsey this time?"

"What?"

Brian clamped his eyes shut and was tempted to punch himself in the mouth. He at least owed the woman common courtesy...just in case. "Sorry. It's late, and I'm not in the best of moods. So, what did you see in your *vision* this time?"

"I'd really rather not go into it over the phone. Is it possible for you to come over here?"

"Now? It's two in the morning!"

"I know what time it is, Mr. Koski, and I wouldn't have called this late if it wasn't important. I told you I thought Angela Patten was all right, but judging from the vision I had tonight, she might not be for long."

A heavy sigh lifted Brian's chest. "Okay. Give me your address." Brian grabbed a pad of paper and a pen from the bedside table and jotted down the street number. "I'll be there in about fifteen minutes—and so help me God, if this is more of Stanley's bullshit..."

"It's not...and thank you."

Brian hung up the phone, flung back the covers, and stood. Another flash of lightning bathed his naked body in an almost ethereal light as he reached for his trousers. "God, you are such a gullible idiot," he mumbled as he stuffed his legs into the pants and reached for a shirt. "You're letting her get to you—and you're going out on the roads in a raging thunderstorm. Real smart."

Brian pulled on a pair of socks and jammed his feet into his shoes before he paused to look at Sinbad's sleepy countenance.

"I think I can handle this one myself, boy. No point in us both getting soaked."

Brian left the bedroom then, and grabbed his gun on the way out the door.

Brian approached the huge, Victorian-style home at 2133 West Leisher Road just under twenty minutes later. Lights illuminated the lower windows, contrary to the surrounding houses, but the sheer curtains were drawn.

Brian's gaze strayed to the porch. Katrina stood in the open doorway. Her long ebony hair was pulled back from her face in a careless ponytail, and her petite body wrapped in a satiny robe. It took Brian a minute to approach the house. He owed Katrina Cordova an apology, and it wouldn't come easy.

"Please, come in," she said when he reached the foot of the steps.

Brian followed her into the house, and Katrina closed and locked the door behind them. He looked at the deadbolt with a raised eyebrow.

She managed a strained smile. "Sorry. Force of habit. You know, a woman living alone..." Katrina let the statement trail off as she led the way from the foyer into the large living room. Again, Brian followed.

"Nice place," he commented as he took in the fireplace on the far wall, vaulted ceiling, shiny wood floors, and expensive furnishings.

"Thank you. I kind of *inherited* it after the divorce." Katrina moved to sit on a Queen Anne–style sofa and indicated for Brian to sit in the wing-backed chair opposite her.

He took a deep breath and released it slowly. "Look, I think I owe you an apology…"

"You don't owe me anything," she returned coolly. "You said what you thought to be the truth the other day, and I won't hold that against you. You don't know me. You don't have any idea who or what I am, so there's no reason for you to take me at my word. Let's just leave it at that."

"I can't just *leave it at that*, Katrina. I was very rude to you and, apparently, I had no reason to be. The whole Angela Patten thing just struck me the wrong way."

"I know you don't believe me about the visions. I know you don't believe that I might know where that little girl is. So…check it out for yourself." She stood and moved to a roll top desk across the room, jotted something down on a piece of paper, and returned to hand it to him. "This is the street name I saw. It was on a sign, out in the country on a dirt road. I'm not sure if it's around here or not. The trees were bare and there was snow on the ground, so it stands to reason that it was in the winter…the same time of year that she was abducted. The house is a little log cabin. Kind of cute, actually. Much different, anyway, than Angela's parents' home. I saw that on TV after she was abducted. There's an old wooden windmill in the yard, and several outbuildings. She appeared to be in good health, or at least she was when I had the first vision almost three months ago."

"The *first* vision?"

"I told you on the phone, I had another one earlier

tonight. A more disturbing one. All the information I just gave you came from the first vision."

"And that was *three* months ago?"

Katrina nodded. "In April, I think. A few months after she was taken. Like I said the other day, I went to the police over and over again for weeks. In fact, I hounded the heck out of them in the first couple of days, but they wouldn't even give me the time of day."

"Yeah, the Cheyenne Police Department isn't too keen on psychics," Brian returned almost guiltily.

"I gathered that. It was frustrating, to say the least. I don't *choose* to see the things I do. The visions just sort of come to me...and always during thunderstorms. They started years ago after I was struck by lightning. I was only ten years old. I don't know if my body somehow became *charged* or what, but the static electricity during a thunderstorm seems to trigger the visions. Usually, I don't act on them. This time, though, I felt like I had to, because of the little girl."

"And you're sure it was her you saw? Angela, I mean."

"As sure as I can be. Her face was plastered all over the news for days...along with yours. I didn't see the whole report and just assumed you were a police officer. It was you I went to see that first day, but they informed me that you were no longer with the department."

"Yeah, Stanley booted my ass a few months before I took the Angela Patten case," Brian confirmed. *"Not that I probably would have listened to you, either,"* he added silently.

"So, you were actually a police officer at one point then?"

"Yes, I was," Brian returned stiffly. He brushed the familiar irritation aside and looked at Katrina again. "So, you said Angela looked like she was okay?"

"I said she looked *healthy*. Maybe even happy. There was a confusion about her, though, that I didn't understand...a kind of despondency."

"Did she appear scared?"

"Not really. Just...lost."

"Did you see anyone else? Like her abductor maybe?"

"No. I could feel that there was someone else in the room, but I couldn't see the person. Like I said before, though, I didn't sense that she was particularly frightened of him."

"And what about the vision you had tonight? You said it was more disturbing?"

Katrina nodded. "She was lying in bed, surrounded by stuffed animals. A figure loomed over her. I only saw this other person from the back, but it was definitely a man. He told her that 'it was time to play the game again.'" Surprisingly, tears welled in Katrina's dark eyes. "I could still hear her crying even after I woke up."

A frown knitted Brian's brow. It was hard not to believe her. She spoke with such certainty, such conviction, and Brian's heart raced with the possibilities. She hadn't given him generalities, as most so-called *psychics* did: a panoramic view of a location that could be anywhere. She had given him specifics—and if there was even a shred of truth to her claim, the situation for little Angela Patten was getting worse by the minute.

"Is there anything else?"

"Just that, for some reason, she looked a little younger in the second vision. Probably because she was frightened and so vulnerable."

"Makes sense," Brian concurred. "And you said she *didn't* appear frightened in the first vision?"

"Not really. Or at least not the tangible terror that she was feeling tonight."

Brian returned to the office just before noon the following Monday. Sherry sat at her desk, totally engrossed in the computer monitor before her—so engrossed, in fact, that she didn't even hear him enter the building.

"Must be an awfully captivating game of solitaire."

The secretary practically jumped out of her shoes. "God, Brian, don't do that! You scared the heck out of me!"

He laughed. "Sorry." He moved to rest a hip on the edge of her desk. "So, any luck in tracking down that street name?"

She leaned back in the chair. "Yup, and it's a good thing you bought that special map program. Trust me, Google Search didn't give me shit. It's gonna be awhile, though, before I have anything for you. There are 304 Ashley Roads in the U.S."

"304?"

"Hey, just be glad it wasn't *Main* Street. We'd be here until *next* July. I'm about halfway in compiling a list by state. I haven't found any in Wyoming yet, though. In fact, that was the first thing I did—to see if there was an Ashley Road right here in Cheyenne. There's an Ashley *Drive*, but not an Ashley Road."

"It might still be worth checking out. I'll see if I can find it on my GPS. In all actuality, though, I don't know if this road is even *in* Wyoming. Oh, and once you finish the list, start paring it down to just *rural* roads. My source said this road is in the country. That should narrow the field considerably."

"Whatever you say, boss."

He stood. "I know it's gotta be boring as hell, but it could be really important."

"It beats writing reports...or looking for Mrs. Trindle's missing Shih Tzu."

"Hey, that woman is paying us damned good money to find her five thousand dollar dog. And it's a good first case for a budding P.I."

"Whatever. You just didn't want to do it yourself."

Brian grinned. "That, too."

Sherry lifted a perfectly shaped blonde eyebrow. "So, you going to tell me *now* why I'm looking for every Ashley Road in the country?"

Brian resumed his perch on the edge of the desk. "Can you keep a secret?"

She gave him an exasperated look. "Have I ever, in the past eight months, *not* kept a secret?"

"It's just really important that our clients know that whatever they say here *stays* here, Sherry. Guaranteeing confidentiality is a big part of this business."

"And I told you, my lips are sealed. So…what's so important about Ashley Road?"

"I…got a tip that Angela Patten is being held in a house on an Ashley Road."

Sherry's eyes widened in shock. "Are you kidding?"

"Nope. And if we can find *which* Ashley Road, we might just find her."

"But how could the person who gave you the tip not know which town it's in? I mean, they must have seen her, or at least *know* someone who saw her go into that house."

"Actually, the person saw her *in* the house. This person said she appeared healthy, happy, and…confused."

"Confused?"

"I know. That one got me, too."

"So, she is alive?" Sherry breathed.

"She was three months ago when my informant saw her."

"And, I repeat, how can this person *not* know what town she's in, and why didn't he or she call the police?"

"It's not that I don't trust you, Sherry, but I'm really not ready to get into that right now. If and when I find Angela Patten, the whole town will know—and so will you. But—" he stood "—I'm not going to have *any* chance of finding her if we don't narrow down that list."

"Is it okay if I go to lunch first? I'm starving."

"Sure." He rounded the desk. "Show me what you're doing there, and I'll keep working on it while you're gone."

Sherry spent the next few minutes explaining her attack strategy for the long list of Ashley Roads, and then headed out into the hot late July day.

"Bring me back a burger, would you?" Brian called after her. "You got it, boss!"

By the time Sherry got back from lunch, Brian had finished sorting the 304 Ashley Roads. There was at least one in each of the continental United States—and one near Wheatland, Wyoming, just a little over an hour away. It was also located in the country. Experience told Brian not to get too excited, despite the fact that his initial intuition had told him that Lanaski was holding Angela somewhere nearby.

Brian finished his burger, tossed the wrapper in the trashcan beside his desk, and headed for the back door to the outer office. Sinbad followed close behind. "I'm gonna take a drive," he told Sherry as he passed through the reception area.

She cast him a knowing grin. "To Ashley Road in Wheatland?"

He returned the grin. "You got it. I should be back around 4:00—unless I find a certain little girl."

CHAPTER THIRTEEN

Brian and Sinbad returned to the office at 4:10 that afternoon. The Ashley Road outside Wheatland, Wyoming, had been a total bust. There *were* at least a dozen homes on the road, but none of them fit the description Katrina had given him, and none of them had a windmill in the yard.

Brian spent the next day checking out another Ashley Road, this time nearly three hours away near Breckenridge, Colorado. It was another country road and another dead-end. The seasoned cop refused to let frustration mount, however...and he also knew he had to take Zach's advice and put Angela Patten's whereabouts on the back burner, at least for the time being. He had other cases to tackle, ten of them in fact, and he owed a certain elderly couple and their son-in-law the courtesy of giving *their* case priority.

"Clara Johnson?" Brian asked when the sixty-some-year-old woman opened the door at 1014 Albany Avenue on the east side of Cheyenne.

"Yes," she returned cautiously.

"My name is Brian Koski. I'm a private investigator." Brian pulled his P.I. credentials from his wallet and showed them to the woman to verify his identity. "I've been hired by

Henry and Rosie Watson to look into the disappearance of their daughter, Nellie."

"Nellie Overton, you mean?"

"Yes, ma'am."

"She disappeared over thirty years ago."

"Yes, ma'am. Would it be possible for me to come in and talk with you for a bit?"

"I...guess so." The white-haired woman stepped back and allowed Brian to enter the small foyer, then led the way to a much larger living room. An elderly man looked up from his newspaper as they entered the room. "This is my husband, George."

"Nice to meet you, sir."

"This man is looking into the disappearance of Nellie Overton," Clara told her husband.

The other man simply grunted and went back to his reading.

"You can sit down if you want," Clara said, turning to Brian again.

"Thank you." He took a seat in a worn recliner across from where Clara had seated herself on the sofa. "So, Clara... is it okay if I call you Clara?"

"I guess so."

"I understand that you were married to Everett Klensing back in 1975?"

"Yes."

"And I also understand that Everett disappeared about the same time as Nellie?"

"Yes."

"They were high school sweethearts, right?"

"Yes."

Brian groaned inwardly. It was already obvious that getting information from this woman would be like pulling teeth. "The Watsons, and Donald Overton, Nellie's husband, seem to think that Everett might have been involved in Nellie's disappearance. Would you agree with that?"

"Probably."

"So, you, too, think he might have abducted Nellie?"

"Probably."

"And why do you think that?"

"Because she was all Everett could talk about. He was obsessed with her. Used to compare me to her."

"Did you have reason to believe that Everett was romantically involved with Nellie?"

"No, though he wanted to be."

"Why do you say that?"

"Like I said, he was smitten with her, even after she broke it off with him."

"So, if he was so...smitten with Nellie, why did he marry you?"

"I have no idea."

Brian fought a smile. "I understand that you and Everett had five children?"

"Yes."

"Was he a good father?"

"No."

"Why do you say that?"

"Because he was an ornery son-of-a-bitch." This statement came from George. The man set the newspaper aside and looked at Brian. "Everett used to beat the shit out of Clara and her kids."

Brian lifted a dark eyebrow upon this information. He looked at Clara again. "Is that true?"

Her emerald gaze dropped to her lap. "Yes."

"Did you ever report the abuse to the police?"

"No."

"It was a different time back then," George elaborated. "Women felt like they had no choice but to put up with the abuse. The man ruled the roost. In Clara's mind, she had made the bed, and she had no choice but to lie in it."

"I'm sorry to hear that, Clara. No woman should have to go through what you did. No children either."

"She did her best to protect her kids," George defended

his wife. "When Everett would start on them, she'd draw his attention back to her and take the beatings herself. She was a good mother."

"Sounds like it," Brian agreed. "So, Clara, the day Everett left, did he take anything with him? Clothes, personal items, anything?"

"No. He didn't take anything with him."

"Except the quilt and the car," George put in.

Brian looked at him again. "The quilt?"

"Clara's grandmother made it. It was like a family heirloom. She treasured it. Used to keep it on the back of her couch. That day, though, she and Everett had taken one of the boys to the emergency room after he beat him a little too hard and broke his arm. It was cold, so she wrapped the quilt around the boy before she helped him outside. It got left in the car, and Everett *took* that car when he left that night."

"Huh," was Brian's only response.

George looked at his wife. "Tell him about the time Nellie came to see you."

Brian's eyes darted back to Clara. "Nellie came to see you?"

The woman nodded. "She wanted my help. She said Everett was coming to her house all the time. Trying to start something with her. He used to try and get her to meet him... in secret." Surprisingly, the woman's eyes filled with tears. "I wanted to help her. Really, I did, but I didn't dare. If I had said anything to Everett about her, he would have killed me."

"Did you tell all of this to the police back then, Clara? About Nellie's visit, about Everett's obsession with her, about the abuse you suffered?"

"No."

"No?"

"They never asked her," once again it was George who explained. "Clara never had any contact with the police back then, except when she reported Everett missing."

Brian looked at Clara again. "They never questioned you about his involvement in Nellie's disappearance?"

"No. Everybody, including the police, just assumed they had left together. That she went willingly. The whole town was convinced that they were having an affair and took off together." Again, Clara's eyes found her lap. "I know I should have spoken up, but I was just so glad to have him gone…"

"Do you think he killed Nellie, Clara?"

Her eyes teared again. "Yes. I think he took her, and when she wouldn't accept his advances, he killed her."

"Probably in a fit of rage," George put in. "I mean, he was so taken with her that I don't think he would have willingly just killed her. Hell, he finally had what he wanted. She was with him. Maybe not willingly, but she was there. But, like Clara said, if he tried to take her…to have sex with her, and she fought him…" He shrugged. "Who knows? Like I said, Everett was an ornery cuss. I wouldn't put anything past him."

"Did you know Everett personally, Mr. Johnson?"

"Oh, yeah. Went to school with him. He was a jerk even back then. Don't know what Nellie Watson ever saw in him."

Brian looked at Clara again. "I hear that you had Everett declared legally dead. Is that right?"

"I had no choice. He left us with virtually nothing. The kids and I had to go on welfare. I worked two jobs… The only thing he *did* leave was a life insurance policy. By the time he'd been gone seven years, the house was in foreclosure. I had no choice but to declare him dead, so I could get that money."

"Best day of your life, right?" George smiled.

"You can say that again," his wife scoffed. She looked at Brian. "I really hope you find out what happened to Nellie, Mr. Koski…for her family's sake. They deserve to find peace."

"Brian, Henry and Rosie are here," Sherry declared quietly from the doorway to his office the next afternoon.

The detective took a deep breath and pushed himself up from behind his desk. He entered the outer office and immediately moved to shake hands with his two clients.

"You sure you're up to this? Like I said on the phone, I can have Donald do it."

"We *want* to do it, Brian," Henry returned. "It'll be the first concrete thing we've been able to do in thirty-seven years that might help find Nellie."

The private investigator nodded slowly. "Okay. First, though, were you able to come up with anything that might contain some of Nellie's DNA? I know it probably wasn't easy after this many years—"

Rosie dug into her massive purse and produced a silver-handled hair brush. She handed it to Brian. "This was Nellie's. Donald kept it all these years. There are still strands of her hair in it—"

Brian's eyes widened in surprise. "Are you kidding?"

"And, please, take good care of it. It's all we have left of her."

"If," Brian struggled with the next words, "if I send this off to the lab for DNA testing, chances are we won't get it back. I'm sorry."

The slight withering of the old woman's brow was the only indication that his statement was in the least upsetting. "Then I guess I'll just have to be happy with my memories, won't I?"

"And the photos, Rosie," her husband reminded gently. "We've got lots of photos."

"Yes, that we do." The now eighty-three-year-old Rosie's shoulders straightened with determination. "All right. Now, where are these pictures you wanted us to look at?"

"Actually, they're on a computer website. It's called *The Doe Network*. This website has an extensive database of unidentified people that have been found over the years. Virtually all of the listings have a picture of the victim, whether it be a reconstruction from skeletal remains, or a sketch of the actual victim. We can search either by the area where the unidentified person was found, or by the year. I'm thinking we should start searching by area. We'll start with Wyoming, then branch out to neighboring states. It's going to be a long process, though. There are *lots* of pictures to go through."

"We have nothing better to do," Henry returned.

Brian smiled. "Good. Sherry will show you the basics of how to navigate the site. If you find anyone who looks like Nellie, let her know."

"And if we do find someone?" Rosie asked.

"Well, it'll be a start, is all I can say. We can't confirm that it's actually her until I get the DNA results back. I use a private lab, so it won't take as long as it would if I sent the sample to the state, but it'll still be a while."

"So what if we *don't* find a picture that looks like Nellie?" The question came from Henry this time.

"Then we keep looking."

Henry reached out to pat Brian on the shoulder. "Glad to see you're back to your old self, son. You had us worried there for a while."

"Well, I'm sorry for that, and I owe you both a sincere apology."

"It was understandable, Brian," Rosie assured him. "Any word on that missing little girl?"

"I've got some new leads. In fact, I'm going to spend the next couple days working on that case. I also need to get started on a couple new ones. I'm sure it'll probably take you that long to get through the entire database of unidentified persons anyway…unless we get really lucky."

"Well, then let's get to it," Henry urged. He looked at Sherry. "Neither me or Rosie have ever touched a computer in our lives, honey, so I hope you got tons of patience."

Brian smiled as he stepped aside and allowed Sherry to seat the Watsons before the second computer that had been purchased specifically for this purpose. She leaned over between the couple, and Henry turned to wink at Brian as her ample bosom was displayed for his view.

CHAPTER FOURTEEN

Over the next two days, Brian checked and ruled out four more Ashley Roads. He also dove into several new cases: a medical malpractice suit, an identity theft incident, and a wrongful death action. His heart and soul were still dedicated to the Patten case, however, and, though he was no longer being paid by the couple, he still felt it was his duty to report his progress—meager though it was.

Brian's initial knock on the Patten front door received no response and, assuming no one was home, he was halfway down the walk when a quiet voice caused him to turn. The woman who now stood in the open doorway in no way resembled the normally well-dressed, immaculate Melody Patten that he had come to know so well. She wore an old robe and slippers and it appeared that her hair had not seen shampoo or a brush in days. Her always slender body was painfully thin now, hollowing out her pale cheeks. It was the vision of her sunken, lifeless eyes, though, that was so unnerving.

"Melody?"

"Brian?" She was down the steps and inches from him in an instant. "Did you find her? Did you find Angela?"

"I'm...I'm sorry, but no. I just wanted to see how you were doing."

"Well...that was very kind of you. Please, come in and I'll get you a cup of coffee. I also baked a cake..." Her words trailed off into confusion, matching her expression. "No, wait. That was weeks ago. I made a cake for Angela for an after-school snack, but she didn't come home."

He laid a hand on the small of her back. "Come on, Melody. Let's get you inside and out of this heat."

She sniffed. "It is rather warm for March."

Brian paused. "It's August, Melody."

She looked up at him, confusion again marring her emaciated features. "August? Then Angela should have been home long ago."

He took her arm and, again, tried to nudge her toward the house. "Come on. Let's go inside."

She jerked free. "Where is my daughter, Brian?"

"Look, let's just get you inside, and then I'll go look for her. Okay?"

"All right." She paused to look up at him. "Check the playground at the school. She loves it there."

Brian nodded slowly. "I will."

The inside of the Patten house was as unkempt as its mistress. Discarded plates of food, clothing, and general trash littered the interior from the foyer to the living room. Brian swept newspapers and unread mail aside and gently eased Melody down onto one end of the sofa. He brushed an equal amount of litter from the coffee table and seated himself before her.

"Where is Jeff, Melody?"

"At work." She smiled. "He's such a hard worker, my Jeff." She glanced around the room. "Have you seen Angela?"

"Um...no, but I'll go look for her in a minute."

An exaggerated sigh lifted her chest. "That child. She's always hiding. Jeff found her in the closet once. She loves to hide from her daddy."

"Melody, do you know Jeff's number at work?"

"Oh, no! I never call Jeff at work. He doesn't like it. He's very busy blowing up buildings and such." Her brow knitted. "But I did call him once…" Her eyes widened again and flew to Brian. "Oh, my God! He took her! He took Angela! That awful Collin Lanaski, he took her!"

Brian laid calming hands on her shoulders. "I know he took her, Melody, and I'm going to find her. I promise. But right now, we need to get a hold of Jeff. There must be an emergency number where you can reach him. His cell phone maybe. Do you have it written down somewhere?"

"It's in my little book." She stood and brushed past Brian to survey the room. "My, everything is such a mess. How can one little girl make such a mess?"

"Where is the book, Melody," Brian pressed. "The one with Jeff's number in it?"

"It's right here!" she screeched as she flung debris from the end table beside the sofa. "It's always right here! Everything is always in its place. It *has* to be, or Jeff gets mad!"

Brian stilled her flailing arms, holding them to her side. "It's okay, Melody. I'll find it." He forced her down onto the sofa again. "You just sit here, and I'll find the book."

She looked up at him. "What book?"

Brian could do nothing but shake his head as he began to sort through the dozens of items that had previously been on the end table. There was no "book" to be found.

"Have you seen Angela?" Melody asked again.

"No, Melody, I haven't," he replied as he moved his search to the coffee table.

"She died, didn't she?" she sobbed.

Brian looked at the distraught mother. Once again, tears streamed down her cheeks.

"No, Melody. She didn't die, and I *will* find her."

Melody flew off the sofa. "No! She died! Jeff hurt her, and she died! He buried her in the backyard!"

Once again, Brian's hands restrained her. "Angela is *not* dead, Melody. Jeff didn't hurt her, and Collin Lanaski won't hurt her. I promise you that."

142

Her brow furrowed again as she wiped her nose on the sleeve of the robe. "Collin Lanaski? He's Angela's teacher."

Brian pushed her down onto the sofa again. "He *was* her teacher, but he's not anymore."

"That's too bad. He was a nice man."

Brian grunted as he resumed his search for the "book." "Right."

The front door to the house opened and closed, and Brian whirled as Jeff Patten stormed into the room.

"What in the hell are you doing here?"

Brian's chest heaved with relief. "I came to see how you both were doing." His gaze slipped to Melody. "And obviously she's not doing well at all."

"Yes, thanks to you. Now, get out."

Brian stood his ground. "How can you leave her alone when she's like this?"

"That is none of your business. Now, leave!"

Melody bounded to her feet. "Jeff, please, you have to be nice!"

"Shut up!"

Melody plopped down on the sofa again, totally cowed.

Brian looked at Jeff again. "I also wanted to tell you that I'm following a new lead."

The other man's brow furrowed. "What kind of lead?"

"I can't really get into it, but it sounds promising—"

"Yeah, right. I've heard your *promises* before. All you did was take our money and do *nothing*!" Jeff paused. "No, wait. You did something. You got my daughter kidnapped! *That's* what you did."

Melody flew off the sofa again. "Angela was kidnapped?"

Jeff looked at his wife and just rolled his eyes.

"I didn't *get* your daughter kidnapped," Brian gritted. "I did what I could to *help* you. Collin Lanaski was just one step ahead of us—and I *will* find her."

"Yeah, right. Well, go *find* her then. Anything to get you out of my house."

Brian started for the foyer. "I'll be in touch."

"Whatever...and don't let the door hit you in the ass."

He paused, looked at the other man, then just shook his head and left the house.

Brian sprinted from his Dodge Ram and into the office two hours later. The phone call from Sherry a few minutes earlier had added the urgency to his step. He skidded to a stop when he entered the outer office and was confronted by three somber faces.

"You found her?" he asked breathlessly.

"They think so," Sherry said as she looked at Henry and Rosie, where they still sat before the computer.

"It sure looks like her," Henry added as he glanced at the monitor again. "Not *exactly* like her, but it's close."

"Where were the remains found?" Brian asked as he moved to stand behind the elderly couple and squint at the computer screen.

"Colorado," Sherry answered. "In 1991."

"'91? Wow." He laid his hand on Henry's shoulder. "Can I take a look?"

The old man stood and let Brian take his seat. The face on the computer screen seemed to jump out at him. He had seen pictures of Nellie hanging on the Watsons' living room wall. He also had several in her file. The resemblance to the woman on the computer screen was remarkable.

The Doe Network: Case File 921NPER

Reconstructions of Victim; Left by Peter Manifeld

Unidentified White Female

- The victim was discovered on April 23, 1991 in Cañon City, Fremont County, Colorado
  - Estimated Date of Death: Over 5 years prior
    - Skeletal Remains

Crime Scene

- Strands of human hair found clutched in victim's hand. No match found
  - Victim found wrapped in a quilt

Vital Statistics

- **Estimated age**: 20-35 years old
- **Approximate Height and Weight**: 5'4-5'6"
- **Distinguishing Characteristics**: Dark brown hair
- **Cause of Death**: Broken hyoid indicates probable strangulation
- **Dentals**: Available. The victim's tooth # 11 is a diminutive tooth, 2/3 the normal crown dimension. Tooth #18 is rotated to the lingual side. Teeth 20, 21, 22, 23 are slightly crowded. No staining or deposits indicative of tobacco use. Good dental health.

Case History
The victim was found 3 miles northwest of Cañon City, CO in an overgrown field off of State Hwy 50.

Investigators
If you have any information about this case please contact:
Mark Collier
Fremont County Chief Medical Examiner.

One particular detail listed under the *Crime Scene* header was of particular interest to Brian. He kept it to himself for now as he scanned the remainder of the listing. "Well, the age and height match. So does the hair color. And you're right. It sure does look like her."

"And Nellie didn't smoke," Rosie put in. "It says that her teeth weren't stained. I never noticed that any of her teeth were crowded, like it says, but they could have been."

Brian looked at his clients. "We need to get Donald over here."

"I already called him," Sherry informed her boss. "He's on his way. So are his daughters."

The private detective reached over to squeeze Rosie's hand. "You done good, Rosie. I know it must have been hard, but you done good."

The old woman's eyes teared, and she voiced the question that had been sitting on her lips since they first discovered the picture. "So, this means that Nellie *is* dead?"

Brian squeezed her hand a little harder. "We won't know that for sure until the DNA results come back, but it's looking that way. I'm sorry."

"Don't be," Henry spoke up as he moved to lay a hand on his wife's shoulder. "We figured it all along. And, actually, it's nice to know. Brings some closure. It's hard, but at least it's finally over."

Rosie turned her hand under Brian's and wrapped her gnarled fingers around his palm. "I always hoped I'd know what happened to my Nellie before I died, and now I do. Thank you, Brian."

An hour later saw the entire Watson/Overton clan crowded into the outer office. Even Vanessa and Miriam's husbands and children were present. So were Henry and Rosie's remaining children.

"So, you all concur that the woman in that reconstruction

picture is probably Nellie?" Brian asked no one in particular from where he again perched on the edge of Sherry's desk.

The family nodded as one. Several of them wiped at tears.

"So, it looks like the bastard strangled her, huh?" Donald asked.

"It appears so. I'll know more after I talk to the Fremont County Coroner. It's too late to call him today, but I will first thing in the morning."

"The hair that was found clutched in her hand," Vanessa asked softly. "Can that be tied to Everett?"

"Possibly, if I can come up with a sample of his DNA. If not, I can see if his children would be willing to submit samples for testing. Their DNA would contain some genes that match their father's. I'll work on that one, too. It's still possible, though, that his wife might have something of Everett's that would contain his DNA." He looked at Nellie's husband. "Donald did, even after all these years."

"I doubt it," Henry spoke up. "Not if she was as glad to see him gone as you said. She probably burned all his stuff the day after he left, and then threw a party."

Brian smiled. "That's possible, I guess, but I'll still talk to her." Brian scanned all the stoic faces in the room. "There's one other thing that I wanted to tell you. I haven't even told Henry and Rosie this yet, but it's more proof that it was Everett who killed Nellie."

"What's that?" Donald asked.

"When I talked to Clara Johnson, Everett's wife—or at least she was his wife back then—she mentioned something about a quilt that went missing after Everett left. It was a family heirloom—"

"The listing mentioned that she was wrapped in a quilt!" Miriam exclaimed.

Brian nodded. "Exactly. If I can get my hands on that quilt, and I will, and Clara Johnson can identify it, we've pretty much got Everett dead to rights. If we can match the hair to him, too, that's just icing on the cake."

"But why would he take the quilt?" Donald asked. "I mean, we're *assuming* that he was watching Nellie or something and saw her go into the grocery store, then confronted her when she came out. He wouldn't have had reason to bring a *quilt* with him."

Brian pushed himself up and wandered the room, difficult though it was with close to twenty people in attendance. "Actually, the quilt was in his car. They had taken one of their kids to the emergency room earlier that day, and Clara wrapped him in the quilt. It got left in the car. Everett used *that* car later that same night when he abducted Nellie."

"So, he grabbed her outside, threw her into his car— along with the groceries—and drove off," Donald deduced.

"Sounds like it," Brian agreed. "Then either he killed her here and drove across the state line to dump the body, or he drove to Colorado and *then* killed her. That, we'll probably never know."

"But why kill her?" Vanessa's husband asked. "I mean, he was obsessed with her, and he finally had what he wanted. He had *her*. It doesn't make sense that he would rob himself of the thing he wanted most."

"Actually, Clara Johnson's husband had a theory about that, and I think he's probably right. Everett, as George Johnson put it, was an ornery cuss. He had a temper. So bad a temper that he beat his wife and children on a regular basis. If he tried to rape Nellie in high school, it stands to reason that he wouldn't hesitate to do the same thing after he kidnapped her. More than likely she fought him and, in a fit of rage, he killed her."

"Do you think he could still be alive?" Vanessa asked.

"It's very possible," Brian returned. "He'd only be in his sixties. And I can try to find him and bring him to justice if you want, but I have to tell you that it wouldn't be a cheap proposition. He could be anywhere in the country after thirty-seven years."

"No," Rosie answered firmly, and apparently none of her

family members were going to argue with her. "We found Nellie, and that's all that's important. Everett Klensing will pay for what he did when he meets his Maker." She looked at Brian. "I want to bring my daughter home, Brian. She deserves a proper burial."

"I'll talk to the coroner in Colorado about it, Rosie, but chances are they won't release the remains until the DNA results come back and they have a positive I.D."

Henry reached out to squeeze his wife's hand where they sat side-by-side in the two chairs before the computer—a computer that still had Nellie's face displayed on the monitor. "We've waited thirty-seven years to bring her home, Rosie. I think we can wait a while longer."

Rosie's eyes misted, but she nodded her agreement.

"It's just too bad we didn't know about this *Doe Network* before now," Miriam commented. "We could have had Mom home years ago."

Donald moved to lay an arm around his daughter's shoulders. "Well, we know where she is now, and we know what happened to her. We'll have her home soon. And all that is thanks to Brian."

"And modern technology," the detective added.

Donald moved to stand before the P.I. and held out a hand. "Somehow saying thank you just doesn't seem like enough."

"You paid me a hell of a lot of money, too, Donald. All of you did. So, trust me, thank you will suffice."

"Yeah, well, money doesn't mean much when it comes to family," the other man replied. "I'd of spent every dime I had to find out what happened to Nellie. We all would have."

Henry heaved himself up to clap a hand on Brian's shoulder. "Thinkin' you should have charged more, son?"

"Any other family but the Watsons and maybe," he joked. "In all seriousness, though, it was an honor to help you find Nellie and I, too, am just glad we can finally bring her home."

CHAPTER FIFTEEN

An early August thunderstorm rolled through Cheyenne, and Brian couldn't help but think of Katrina Cordova. Granted, her visions had brought him no closer to finding Angela Patten, despite the fact that he and Sinbad had now checked over a dozen Ashley Roads. Still, he couldn't help but feel the woman was sincere in her belief that the visions were proof positive that the little girl was alive and well, and that realization made Brian rest easier, too.

"Her *first* vision showed her to be alive and well," Brian edited his thoughts. "The second vision? Not so much."

He plopped down on the sofa in his living room and his head found his hands. "Damn it, Angela, where are you?"

The ringing of the phone on the table beside him interrupted his musings.

"Hello?"

"Brian? It's Katrina Cordova."

He couldn't help but laugh. "Man, you really *are* psychic, aren't you? I was just thinking about you."

"Really," she stated rather than asked.

"Yup. Thunderstorms, you...they kind of go hand-in-hand."

"Yes, they do...and I just had another vision."

"Why am I not surprised?"

"Can you come over?"

Brian sighed. "I'm on my way."

Once again, Katrina met Brian at the door of the Victorian mansion and, once again, his body reacted very physically to her almost overly seductive persona. She ushered him into the parlor.

"Can I get you a drink?"

"Sure. Why not," he said as he moved to sit in the same wing-backed chair that he had more than a month earlier.

"Scotch okay? It's all I've got, unless you prefer a beer."

"The Scotch is fine."

The sound of ice clinking as it landed in the bottom of two glasses was the only sound in the room for the next few minutes, other than the howling wind. Finally, Katrina crossed the parlor and handed him one of the two drinks. It did not take a detective's mind to notice that she was shaking.

"You okay?"

"No, I'm not. This vision..." Her voice trailed off.

"So tell me about it. Is Angela okay?"

"This vision wasn't about Angela."

Brian sat back. "Then why did you call me?"

"I don't know, honestly. I guess because you're one of the few people who kind of believes me."

He lifted an eyebrow. "Kind of?"

"I'm not stupid, Brian. I know you're still skeptical."

"Yeah, well maybe I need to come over the next time a storm is predicted so I can see you in action. I might be a little more convinced."

A flash of lightning followed by a loud crack of thunder caused the lights in the room to flicker. "Yes, well it doesn't appear that *this* storm is over yet, so you might get lucky."

"Yeah, the wind was really picking up when I was driving

over, so it's just getting started." He sat forward again and rolled the glass of Scotch between his hands. "So, you can have more than one vision per storm?"

Katrina rolled her dark eyes. "Yes, I can have more than one."

"Hey, just asking. I'm new to all this...paranormal stuff."

"And sometimes three or four storms can come and go and nothing. It's just...random."

"So, can you like...target your visions? I mean, can you pick what they're about?"

"Usually I have to be exposed to something or someone in particular, like if I've just seen a news report—that's what happened with Angela. And, once I've had that first vision, it like...opens the floodgates or something, and then I will sometimes see more. Again, like with Angela."

"So the second vision wasn't prompted by a news report?"

"No. I *was* thinking about her at the time, though. So I guess maybe I could *target* a vision, like you said. Honestly, I've never tried."

"Huh. Interesting." He sat back again. "So, what was your vision about earlier tonight?"

The shakiness in Katrina's hand increased again as she brought her own glass of whiskey to her lips. She took a generous swallow.

"Man, this one really has you rattled, doesn't it?"

She stood suddenly and crossed to stand before the massive marble fireplace on the outside wall. Brian couldn't keep his eyes from straying to her pert, jean-covered behind as she retreated. "Yes, it does."

He stood and moved to stand behind her. "So tell me about it."

Katrina turned and was immediately uncomfortable with his nearness. She quickly sidestepped and crossed the few feet to the tall, multi-paned window beside the fireplace. "There...was an explosion. A *massive* explosion. People were screaming." She whirled. "They were *dying*, Brian! Hundreds, maybe thousands of people!"

His brow furrowed. "Where was this?"

"I don't know! All I saw was the explosion, and blood and…limbs flying everywhere."

"Limbs? Do you mean, like, human limbs? As in body parts?"

"Yes, human limbs!" To Brian's amazement, her black eyes filled with tears as she continued. "I've never had a vision like this before. Usually they're rather…benign, but this one… There was so much blood. So much *dying!*"

"And you have no idea where or when this is going to happen? You weren't watching the news before you had the vision?"

"No. I mean, the TV was on…a baseball game, I think. I do that a lot, just to have noise in the house. But there was nothing about an explosion." She wiped at her tears, a quick jerk of the hand, as if the show of weakness angered her. "The only thing I know for sure, Brian, is that it *is* going to happen."

"And you're sure you weren't seeing something in the past, like the Boston Marathon bombing? Or Oklahoma City?"

"No. It definitely hasn't happened yet."

"How do you know?"

"I just do."

"Okay…" It was Brian's turn to stand before the cold fireplace. "Look, Katrina, I really don't know what you expect me to do about this. I mean, if you don't know when or where it's going to happen…"

"I just needed to tell somebody, okay? Somebody who wouldn't think I was crazy." She took a cautious step toward him. "You don't think I'm crazy, do you?"

He turned. "Honestly, I don't know what to think, Katrina. I mean…I hardly know you. And so far, you don't have a great track record, at least not with me. The 'Ashley Road' thing has turned up nothing and, believe me, I've checked a lot of them. I'm no closer to finding Angela Patten than I was seven months ago."

"I'm sorry," she murmured. "I wish I could give you more."

"So do I." He moved to stand before her. "Look, why don't we sit down, enjoy our drinks, and just try to relax."

"Yeah, right. You don't have visions of bombs going off filling your head."

He reached out to caress her cheek. "So, maybe you should let me do something to make the visions go away. I mean, you *did* invite me over..."

Her eyes widened suddenly and she stumbled back. "Is *that* why you think I asked you to come over here? So I could offer you some horizontal refreshment?"

He smiled. "I've never heard it put that way, but, hey, the night could end in worse ways."

"Not in my book." She marched to stand before him and promptly took the glass of half-finished Scotch from his hand. "I'll take this. You're leaving."

Another blast of thunder roared through the house, and its accompanying flash of lightning was reflected in Katrina's glittering onyx eyes. Brian had to quell a shudder. She looked every bit the part of a stereotypical witch at that moment, and it took him a second to realize that the sudden blackness that enveloped the room was due to a power outage and not some cauldron-stirring spell.

"Uh...I'd be glad to leave, Katrina...if I could find the door."

"Son-of-a-bitch," he heard her mutter in the darkness.

"Actually, my mother was a pretty nice lady."

"Will you just shut up!"

He heard her turn and, a moment later, a loud thump. "Son-of-a-bitch!" She yelled the expletive this time.

"You really need to broaden your vocabulary, Katrina."

"Just be quiet!" she hissed. "I ran into the table."

"Want my help? I can feel my way until I find you."

"God, you're such a letch!"

"You know, my secretary called me that once."

"Gee, I wonder why."

Another thump. "Ouch! Where in the heck is the damned fireplace! There are candles on the mantle."

"It was on the far wall the last time I checked."

"Thanks."

"Glad to help."

Another flash of lightning lit the room, and Brian was able to make out her shapely form silhouetted ten feet away. To his amazement, she crumpled to the floor just before the room was again encased in darkness.

"Katrina?" he called. No answer. "Katrina!"

Brian stumbled forward and his shin promptly collided with the same end table she had encountered only minutes earlier. "Son-of-a-bitch!" he gritted.

He took a few more cautious steps until his foot nudged her prone body. He dropped to one knee. "Katrina?" He shook her and received only a moan in response. "Damn it!"

He stepped carefully over her body and felt his way the last few feet to the fireplace. His seeking hands found the tall candle and, thankfully, the box of matches that sat next to it. He struck one against the flint on the side of the box and lit the wick. Gradually, a dim light filled the area around him. He turned back to Katrina.

Strangely, her eyes were open. Brian was unable to stop the shudder that wracked his body this time. She was looking right at him, but it was obvious that she didn't see. He gathered his courage and moved to stoop beside her, then laid his fingers against the side of her neck. The pulse was there and, surprisingly, it raced.

"What in the heck?" He laid his hand on her shoulder and shook her again. "Katrina?"

Still no response. He dug in his pocket for his cell phone then, and pushed the "Talk" button to bring it to life. An even brighter light filled the room. "Christ, why didn't I think of this before?" He pushed 911 on the keypad and brought the phone to his ear.

"911. What's the address of your emergency?" came a female voice a moment later.

"I'm at 2133 West Leisher Road. I need an ambulance. There's a woman passed out."

"*What's your name, sir?*"

"Brian Koski."

"*And what happened to the woman?*"

"I have no idea. She just collapsed."

"*Is she breathing?*"

"Yes."

"*I have an ambulance on the way, Mr. Koski.*"

"Good. Let them know that the power is out in the house, so to bring flashlights."

"*I'll let them know. We have reports of several power outages in that area.*"

Brian jumped nearly a foot off the floor when Katrina inhaled deeply, the life returned to her eyes, and she bolted to a sitting position.

"What the hell...!"

"*Is everything all right, Mr. Koski?*"

"Yeah, she just woke up."

"Who are you talking to?" Katrina asked, her voice weak and a trifle confused.

"911," he answered. "You collapsed."

She brushed off his concern as she came slowly to her feet with his help. "I don't need an ambulance. I'm fine."

"You're sure?"

"Yes, Brian. I'm sure."

"Okay..." He put the phone to his ear again. "I guess she's okay. You can cancel the ambulance."

"*All right. Just let us know if you need anything else.*"

"I will." He pushed "End" on the keypad, then turned to look at Katrina with wide eyes. "What in the hell happened?"

She sat on the Queen Anne sofa now, her forehead resting on her palms. "I had another vision."

"Is that what happens when you have a vision? You pass out?"

"Yes, and believe me, I have the bumps and bruises to prove it."

"But your eyes were open!"

She lifted her head. "Yes, Brian, my eyes stay open and it's like I'm looking right through you. I know. It used to freak my parents out, too, and my husband."

He moved to sit beside her and set the candle on the table before them. "So, does it always happen when there's a flash of lightning? There was one just before you went down."

"Yes. Like I said earlier, it's like the lightning triggers it."

"Weird."

"Tell me about it."

The room lit with yet another burst of nature's fury, and Brian's eyes darted to her.

Katrina smiled. "I'm fine. It doesn't happen every time."

There was a long moment of silence as Brian pondered whether he even wanted to ask the next question, and Katrina feared that he would.

"So...was it the same vision?"

She nodded slowly. "Exactly." She looked at him. "It's going to happen, Brian. There's going to be an explosion, people are going to die, and I have no idea how to stop it."

CHAPTER SIXTEEN

B rian took some much needed time off a week later. The beautiful late summer weather was pushing eighty degrees, and he considered it the perfect opportunity to take his newest conquest, a thirty-two-year-old voluptuous red-head named Veronica, on a two-day road trip to Jackson, Wyoming, more than six hours from Cheyenne. They checked into a motel, then purchased a picnic lunch from a local deli, complete with a bottle of wine and vase of roses, and headed south to State Highway 22, better known to the locals as the Teton Pass. Brian's plan was to wine and dine his date into submission. It wouldn't be hard, he knew, not if the two steamy nights they had spent together earlier in the week were any indication.

"I can't believe you brought your dog," Veronica complained as they walked the short distance from his truck to the meadow nestled high in the Rockies, with Sinbad tagging dutifully behind. A stream trickled nearby, completing the romantic setting. Even Brian was impressed with the locale he had heard about from a friend and former co-worker just a few nights earlier.

"Don't worry. He's well-trained. He'll look the other way

when we—" he reached out to squeeze her shapely behind "—start our horizontal refreshment."

Veronica tossed him a saucy look over her shoulder. "Horizontal refreshment, huh? That's a new one."

"Yeah, well what can I say? I'm a funny guy."

Veronica paused in the middle of the meadow, about fifteen feet from the creek. "Here okay?"

"Looks good to me."

She spread the blanket she had carried up the hill and plopped down in the middle of it as Brian set the picnic basket aside and joined her. Veronica glanced wryly at the shoulder holster adorning Brian's left side. "I also can't believe you brought your gun."

"Hey, I need to be prepared to protect you. There are wild animals in them thar hills." He indicated the Rockies that surrounded them before he leaned over to nuzzle her neck.

Veronica pushed him away. "Somehow I think it's *you* that I'll need to be protected from."

"You never complained before," he commented easily.

"Yes, and now it's the middle of the afternoon and we are *outside.* Anyone could come along." She reached up to pat his cheek. "Don't worry. I'll take care of your amorous side later when we get back to the motel. And, besides—" she reached for the picnic basket "—I am starving!"

"So am I," Brian countered as he dove for her neck again.

Once again, Veronica stalled his advances. "You know, for a forty-four-year-old man, you're incredibly horny."

"I'm just storing it up for all the time I'll lose in my seventies."

"Seriously, Brian, I'm hungry," she whined. "Can we eat?"

He sat back. "Whatever."

The cold fried chicken, potato salad, and baked beans were consumed a half-hour later. The now stocking-footed couple sipped on wine as they let the meal settle. An equally sated Sinbad lay on the grass a short distance away. Brian's shoulder holster and gun lay beside him. Brian quickly grew tired of the subsequent small talk, where he lay on his side on the blanket, with Veronica perched on her knees before him. He reached up to toy with the laces that held the bodice of her peasant-type blouse together.

"It's getting kind of warm. What do you say we get rid of some of these clothes?"

"We are *outside*, Brian."

"So all the more reason to commune with nature."

He slid his hand inside the shirt and caressed the mounded flesh beneath.

"Brian..." she protested again, though the objection was considerably less heartfelt.

His hand left its amorous duty to pull her head closer to his, then slid downward over a rounded hip and snaked between her jean-clad thighs. A guttural groan left Veronica's throat as she hungrily claimed his mouth.

"Watch it," he mumbled against her lips. "We're still outside."

"Shut up." She pushed him onto his back, moved to straddle him, and pulled the shirt over her head in one liquid movement. Brian yanked her down on top of him and her mouth attacked his neck as his hands moved to the closure on the back of her bra. He freed the clasp and eased the straps over her shoulders.

He paused. His line of vision had changed with their frenzied movements. Off to the northwest and now visible above the tree line in his prone position was an old wooden windmill. Its steel blades churned slowly in the gentle breeze.

Brian flew to a sitting position, unseating Veronica and sending her sprawling onto her back on the blanket beside him. Her bra now lay on his lap.

"What in the heck...!" she spouted.

Brian reached for his tennis shoes, stuffed his stocking feet inside, and secured the laces.

"What in the heck are you doing!"

He bounded to his feet and crossed the few feet to where his shoulder holster lay in the grass. He slipped it on as he turned to Veronica. "I have to go check something out. I'll be right back."

"What?!" she cried, her disbelief obvious in her wide eyes and slack jaw. "Where are you going?"

"I said, I'll be right back. Just stay here." Brian sprinted down the hill, calling for Sinbad over his shoulder. "Sinbad, *heir*!"

Veronica scrambled to her feet, her naked breasts heaving with agitation as she screamed after him. "Brian!...Brian, you can't just leave me here! Brian!"

He was already in the truck and headed west.

Brian continued west on the Teton Pass Highway, doing his best to keep the old wooden windmill in view off to his right. It was getting larger now, which meant he was getting closer. He hadn't driven more than a few miles when he slammed on the brakes and brought the Dodge Ram to an abrupt halt. He gaped through the front window of the truck in wide-eyed disbelief. He had to be seeing things, but knew he was not.

No more than five feet away, an old, faded road sign stared back at him. The words "Ash Road" had been stenciled on the sign, but of more interest to Brian were the three tiny letters that had been hand-painted after the first part of the name. Those letters, "ley," completed a puzzle that he had been trying to solve for seven long months. He could only guess. Maybe a child, or a teenager, had lived on the road at one time—a child named Ashley—and had stood on a ladder and painted the sign to match her name. It would explain why this particular Ashley Road wasn't in any of the databases Sherry had painstakingly searched; the road wasn't named Ashley, but Ash, and somewhere along the way someone had changed it so a psychic would one day see it in a vision and help save a little girl.

Brian took a deep breath to calm his pounding heart. This was only the second piece of the puzzle. The third would be a small log cabin, and the last a child named Angela.

Brian turned the Dodge Ram onto the dirt road.

Brian's heart almost thundered out of his chest a few minutes later when a small log cabin came into view on his left. Behind the cabin stood the weather-beaten windmill he had seen from more than two miles away. He slowed the Ram, but did not stop. The cabin was surrounded by trees, and several outbuildings dotted the landscape...just as Katrina Cordova had also seen in her vision. There was no car parked outside, however; another reason why it had taken so long to find them. The Amber Alert when Angela was kidnapped had listed both the car and the license plate. Lanaski had been smart enough to get rid of both.

Brian continued on a few hundred feet past the cabin, then pulled the truck onto another dirt road, turned it around, and threw the gear shift into park. He could still see the house, but would remain unobserved.

He pondered whether or not to call the local police for backup, but decided to wait. He had to be sure. Five minutes later, he was. The door to the cabin opened, and Collin Lanaski exited with a steel bucket and crossed the yard to an old hand pump. He worked the handle for a few minutes until water spilled from the spigot and into the bucket. Brian's attention was again drawn to the house when a Golden Retriever puppy bounded through the open doorway and pranced out into the yard. Immediately on its heels was a little, blonde-haired girl...a little girl named Angela.

He had found her.

"Well, I guess he got her her puppy. Or rather, he got *Courtney* her puppy."

Angela sprinted after the puppy and scooped it up into her arms, then ran to join Collin at the pump. He smiled, tousled the sandy locks atop her head, and bent to drop a kiss on her cheek before he headed back to the house with the bucket of water. Angela tagged along behind.

Brian reached for his cell phone, powered it up, and dialed 911.

Nothing.

He checked the display and muttered a curse. He had no signal. Not surprising, since he was high in the mountains. It took him only an instant to make a decision. He would be a fool to tackle the situation with only Sinbad at his side, and Brian was no fool. Lanaski could be armed and Angela could end up the victim. It was obvious that Collin Lanaski wasn't going anywhere. He had found his hideaway and, after seven months, he felt safe.

No. Brian would head back to Jackson and enlist the aid of the local police. He could be back within a couple of hours…after he picked up Veronica.

"Shit!" he exclaimed. "She's gonna kill me."

He slammed the Dodge Ram into drive and headed back down Ashley Road.

"I don't give a flying fuck if you found King Tut's tomb! You left me in that stupid meadow, and you are *not* going to leave me here!" Veronica railed as her flailing arm encompassed the large motel room, complete with a hot tub in the corner.

"I'm sorry, Veronica," Brian gritted, "but I've been searching for this little girl for a long time. I'm not going to just leave her there. I shouldn't be gone more than a few hours."

"*A few hours*! And what in the hell am I supposed to do? Mingle with the locals and knit an afghan?"

Brian's temper was at its limit after listening to her

complain all the way back to town, and for the fifteen minutes they had been at the motel. "Frankly, Veronica, I don't
give a shit what you do. Hell, go down to the corner bar for
all I care and find someone to come back here and fuck your
brains out…on me."

He turned then, and left the room, ignoring the sound of
a clock radio smashing against the portal.

Brian had joined forces with the Teton County Sheriff's
Department an hour later. Angela Patten's kidnapping was
big news all over Wyoming, and the local sheriff was not
above realizing that helping to secure her safe release would
be a feather in his cap and that of his department. Since
Collin Lanaski had not taken Angela out of state after all,
it was mutually decided that there was no need to contact
the FBI. They did, however, notify the Wyoming Highway
Patrol, since they were first on the scene when the kidnapping took place. Consequently, it was nearly four hours after
Brian first discovered the location of Collin Lanaski before
the team was in place and the cabin surrounded.

"Collin Lanaski! This is Sheriff Michael Porter of the
Teton County Sheriff's Department," the man called through
the intercom installed in his cruiser. "We have the cabin surrounded. I want you to put down any weapons and exit the
cabin through the front door with your hands in the air."

Surprisingly, it was only a few minutes before the front
door of the cabin swung inward and the six-foot-four Collin
Lanaski bent to step through the opening. His hands were
extended palms forward in front of him. "Don't shoot!" he
yelled. "There's a child in here!"

"Nobody's going to shoot anybody, Mr. Lanaski. Now,
just step forward…slowly, and get down on the ground."

Again, Lanaski did as told without argument and, immediately, a dozen officers closed in to subdue him.

"Daddy!" the now eight-year-old Angela bounded from the cabin and was scooped up by a nearby sheriff's deputy before she came within ten feet of her kidnapper. "Daddy!" she screeched again as she struggled fiercely in the officer's arms. Tears saturated her rosy cheeks.

Brian hurried up to them. "Can I take her?"

The officer was only too grateful to relinquish the wild little girl into Brian's arms. He carried her a short distance away and set her feet on the ground. He stooped before her. "Do you remember me, Angela? I talked to you at your mommy and daddy's house one day a long time ago."

"My name isn't Angela. It's Courtney!" Her arm shot out toward Collin as two police officers escorted him to a squad car. "*He's* my daddy, and my mommy is in heaven!"

"You have to calm down, Angela..."

"Where are they taking him?"

"They're taking him to jail, honey. He isn't your daddy. He just told you he was. He's a very bad man."

"No he's not! Please, I want my daddy!"

"Look, honey, I know you probably don't remember, because it's been a long time, but Jeff and Melody Patten are your mama and daddy. Collin took you from your mom. Don't you remember? He made your mom pull her car over on the highway, and he took you from her."

"No! She's not my mama, and he isn't my daddy. Please, don't make me go back there!" Angela struggled against Brian's hold on her arms. "Let me go! I want my daddy!"

A female police officer approached them. "I'll take her. We need to get her to the hospital and have her checked out."

Brian nodded before he looked at Angela again. "I'll talk to you again tomorrow, okay? You'll probably have to spend a little while in the hospital, and then we're going to take you home."

"This *is* my home!" The female officer took the distraught

little girl's hand and started to lead her toward a second squad car. "Please, I want my daddy! *I want my daddy!*"

Sheriff Porter approached Brian with a slow shake of the head. "It's amazing how they can brainwash them, isn't it? It's like she doesn't even remember her real parents, and it's only been seven months."

"Oh, she remembers them," Brian countered. "He's just got her convinced that *they're* the bad guys."

"Well, she'll settle back in quick enough once she gets home. Then hopefully, with a little counseling, she'll be able to forget about *him*." The sheriff removed his wide brimmed hat, smoothed his hair, and then returned the hat to his head. "At least she looks in good shape. It doesn't look like he hurt her."

The memory of Katrina's second vision bombarded Brian's brain. "Not in any way that's visible anyway."

"Well, if he did do something to her, they'll find out when she gets to the hospital. And, for Lanaski's sake, I hope he didn't. The kidnapping charge is bad enough. Add child molestation to it, and he's going up for life."

"Or to a mental institution," Brian elaborated. "The guy's a real whack job."

"Yeah, well, I'm just glad he didn't put up a fight. This could have ended a lot worse."

"Yup, it could have and, to be honest, I'm surprised it didn't."

Veronica, along with her suitcase, was gone when Brian and Sinbad got back to the motel at around midnight. He had no idea where she'd gone or how she'd gotten there and, at this point, he didn't care. He'd stopped by the hospital on his way, but Angela was sleeping. The nurse informed him that they had to sedate the little girl just to get her to calm down.

"Man, I hope she'll be all right. That's all Jeff Patten

needs is a combative daughter. He's already got a wacky wife to deal with." Brian flopped onto his back on the bed. "And hopefully that *wacky wife* will get a grip on herself when she gets her daughter back."

Brian had wanted to make that call himself, but had finally relented and allowed Sheriff Porter to take the glory, both with Angela's parents and with the bevy of reporters who were now staking out the hospital.

"More power to him," he grumbled as he rolled onto his side. "I'll get to see Angela's parents when I bring her home... and he's more than welcome to take on the reporters."

That was one point Brian had not caved on. He had spent more time than anyone looking for Angela Patten, and he would damn well be the one to return her to her parents. The doctors figured she would spend no more than two days in the hospital, time enough for them to run a battery of tests, so the sheriff had encouraged the Pattens to wait for Brian to bring their daughter to them.

"And surprisingly, they went for it," Brian told the empty room as a prolonged yawn escaped his mouth. "If it was my kid, there's no way I'd have waited. I'd have been on my way to that hospital as soon as I hung up the phone." He grinned ruefully. "Not that I'll ever have kids, but whatever."

It still amazed Brian that the whole thing went down as smoothly as it did. He had expected at least *some* resistance from Collin Lanaski...but nothing. The man had actually reacted like he was somewhat sane. Why? Why fight so hard to get Angela, and then give her up so easily? Had the man finally come to his senses and realized that his own daughter *was* actually dead? He *did* refer to Angela as just "a child" when the sheriff called him out, and not his daughter.

"Hell, maybe he was ready to bring her back and we just beat him to the punch," Brian mused aloud.

The thought nagged at him. Why? Why had Lanaski been so cooperative? Why had he not even *tried* to run?

Brian had to know...and there was only one way to find

out. He swung his feet over the edge of the bed and, leaving Sinbad to continue his nap in the corner, left the room.

Luckily, Sheriff Porter was still at the office when Brian arrived a few minutes later. It took some doing, but the former police captain managed to get the sheriff to agree to put him in an interrogation room with Collin Lanaski, rather than making him talk with the prisoner over a phone line with bulletproof glass separating them, as would have been the case in the normal visitors area. The sheriff did insist that there be an officer present in the room also, and that Brian leave his sidearm at the front desk.

Brian opened the door to the interrogation room and spent a long moment standing in the doorway, relishing the sight of Collin Lanaski clad in an orange jumpsuit, hand-cuffs, and leg irons. The prisoner refused to even look up, though he obviously knew who had just entered the room and taken a seat opposite him.

"So, you were the one who found us, huh? I should have known."

"Why is that?" Brian asked.

"Because you were one stubborn son-of-a-bitch."

Brian smiled. "I guess it comes with the territory. I was a cop before I became a P.I."

Collin finally raised his head. "You were a cop?"

"Yup. Right in Cheyenne, for over twenty years."

"What made you quit?"

"Let's just say that I was...misunderstood."

A short laugh jumped from Collin's chest, but it held no humor. "I know the feeling."

Brian leaned forward in the chair and rested his forearms on the table. He clasped his hands before him. "I always thought you were a pretty stubborn guy, too, Collin, and determined. A little confused, but determined. So why did all that change tonight?"

"What do you mean?"

Brian sat back again and shrugged. "I don't know. I guess I expected more of a fight from you. I mean, we did come there to take Angela...a child you considered to be yours."

"Right. I'm surrounded by a dozen cops—cops with guns—and I'm unarmed. My daughter is with me. I may be stubborn, Mr. Koski, but I'm not stupid."

Brian's brow creased slightly in bewilderment. "So that's why you gave up so easily? Because Angela was there?"

"Because *Courtney* was there, yes. I wasn't going to take the chance that she might get hurt."

Brian shook his head slowly. "Still sticking with that story, huh? That Angela is your long-lost dead daughter?"

Collin's jaw hardened, however imperceptibly. "She *is* my daughter. Even she remembers now."

"Yeah, right, with a little prompting from you." Brian crossed his arms before his chest. "They call it *brainwashing*, Lanaski."

"No," he gritted. "The stuff she remembered, she remembered on her own."

"Like what?"

"Like my tattoo." Even with his clasped hands, he managed to pull up his left shirtsleeve enough so Brian could see the tattoo of a mermaid. "Courtney's favorite movie when she was little was *My Little Mermaid*. I always used to call her *my* little mermaid and, at one point while I was deployed, I got the tattoo. You can't see it, because I can't get the sleeve up high enough, but it has her name at the top. We used to play this game where she would point to the mermaid on my arm and ask, 'Is she your little mermaid, Daddy?' and I would tickle her and say, 'No, *you're* my little mermaid!'." He looked at Brian again. "She remembered that, Mr. Koski. She remembered the game...with no prompting from me."

"That's easy for you to say now, when there's no way to prove otherwise."

Collin flung himself against the back of his chair. "God, why do I even bother? Of all the people involved in this whole fiasco, I thought maybe you were the one person who would weigh both sides and actually try to come up with the truth. But you won't listen to reason either."

"And how am I supposed to do that when you haven't said even *one* reasonable thing?"

Collin flew forward again, and the cop on patrol near the door stepped forward in warning. The prisoner sat back slightly before he continued. "And you might not feel that way if you would at least *try* to look at this thing from my angle. You're looking through rose-colored glasses provided by the Pattens. You're seeing and hearing only what they want you to. Have you even asked to see *Angela's* birth certificate? Have you asked them what hospital she was born in, have you checked to see if her eye color matches theirs, have you questioned why she's so tall for her age when they're both short? Have you done any legwork at all to prove that she actually *is* their daughter?"

"There's no reason for me to do any of that, Collin—because there is no reason for me *not* to believe she's their daughter. You, on the other hand—"

"Do it, Mr. Koski. Please! For God's sake, you're going to send her back to them. Is it too much to ask that you spend a few hours checking out their story to make sure they're who they say they are?"

It was Brian's turn to sit back in his chair and consider the other man's words. "I'll think about it, Collin. That's all I can promise."

"Which means that you aren't going to do a damn thing, right? You're just going to let them take her back so he can continue molesting her."

"There's no proof that Jeff Patten has been molesting his daughter, Collin."

"Courtney, *Angela*, is the proof! All you have to do is talk to her!"

"Oh, so now I suppose you're going to tell me that she said her father was molesting her."

"Yes!"

"Even if that were true, which I highly doubt, it would never hold up in court. The Pattens would just say that *you* had been coaching her for the past seven months."

Collin flung himself against the chair again and let his head fall back. "So she's screwed then. He can do whatever he wants to her, without consequence, because I'm stuck in here and can't do a damned thing about it."

"Angela will be fine, Collin, and if it'll make you feel better, I'll check on her periodically to make sure she is."

His head came up again. There was no anger in his eyes now. Just pain. "Yeah, you do that. Just try to *check on her* before he goes too far one day and kills her."

CHAPTER SEVENTEEN

Brian picked up Angela at the hospital at around three the following afternoon and began the six-hour drive back to Cheyenne. The doctors had pronounced her to be in good health, physically anyway. They did recommend that she undergo extensive psychological counseling, which Brian would pass on to the Pattens. Only then would they find out if there had been any type of sexual abuse, since there were no obvious physical signs. There were bound to be repercussions just from the kidnapping, however, that would need the attention of a therapist. The fact that she insisted Collin was her father now was just one example of the brainwashing that had taken place over the past seven months.

"So, are you happy to be out of the hospital?" Brian asked the little girl belted in on the passenger seat beside him as he steered the Dodge Ram onto US 191. Sinbad would ride in the back of the pickup for the duration of the trip. Angela's puppy, though, had been rewarded with a seat on her lap. Sheriff Porter had taken the animal the night of the arrest and given it to Brian the following day. He was more than happy to be taking the Golden Retriever to its new home, too. One night stuck in a motel room with the rambunctious, untrained puppy was about all he and Sinbad could handle.

She nodded. "I don't like hospitals."

Brian smiled. "I don't know many people who do."

Angela looked at him. "Where's my Daddy?"

"I'm taking you to see them. *Both* your mommy and daddy."

"I mean my *real* Daddy. Collin. Where is he?"

"Collin is in jail, honey, and he's not your daddy. He just told you he was. You'll remember when you see Jeff and Melody. *They* are your real Mommy and Daddy."

"No, they're not!" Tears filled her eyes and rolled down her cheeks. She hugged the puppy to her. "I don't want to go back there!"

"You have to, honey, and you'll feel better once you see them." Brian tipped his head toward the Golden Retriever that was being held in a death grip by the little girl. Surprisingly, the puppy didn't seem to mind. "What's his name?"

"He's a girl, and her name is Blondie," Angela returned as she wiped her nose with the back of a hand. "My daddy got her for me, just like he promised he would."

Brian decided it would be wise not to argue with her at this point. At least she wasn't crying anymore.

"Well, she's a very nice puppy. Sinbad and I had a lot of fun with her at the motel last night," he lied.

"Is Sinbad your dog?"

"Yup."

"He's a really *big* dog."

"Yeah, well, Blondie will be a big dog, too, when she grows up. Sinbad is a police dog, though. He's my partner. He helps me catch bad guys."

The little girl giggled—the first sign of happiness Brian had seen in her. "A dog can't be a policeman's partner. Only a person can be."

"That's not true. There are lots of policemen who have dogs for partners."

"Really?"

"Yup. Really."

"Are you a policeman?"

"Not anymore, but I used to be."

"You act like a policeman. You ask lots of questions."

Brian laughed. "I guess I do. I'm still *kind of* a policeman, though. I'm a private detective. I still help people. I just don't do it for the police anymore."

"Can you help my daddy? He's in big trouble."

"Yes, he is, honey. Or *Collin* is. Jeff Patten is your daddy."

"No, he's not."

"Yes, he is, Angela."

"My name is Courtney, and no he's not! He's mean. He hurts me."

Brian sighed. "He doesn't hurt you, Angela."

"Yes he does! I have to hide in my closet so he doesn't find me." Her chin drooped. "But he still does."

Brian glanced at the eight-year-old girl as his mind returned to Melody Patten's statement weeks earlier—a statement he *thought* had been made in madness. *Jeff found her in the closet once. She loves to hide from her daddy.* He also remembered something Katrina had said about her second vision...how Angela had somehow seemed *younger* when the figure was looming over her. If she was younger in the vision, then it was not Collin Lanaski who threatened her. The doctors also said there were no signs of physical or sexual abuse when they examined Angela, so that meant that *Collin* had not been molesting her. Could his sister have been right? *Were* all the bladder infections, the swelling in her private area, due to sexual abuse...at the hands of Jeff Patten?

"Angela, how does your daddy...how does *Jeff* hurt you?"

She hugged Blondie closer to her chest. "He...makes me play a game."

Again, Katrina's words about the second vision jumped into Brian's mind. *He told her that "it was time to play the game again."*

He swallowed convulsively. "What kind of game?"

Tears rolled down her cheeks again. "I don't like to talk about it. It hurts me."

"It's okay, honey. You don't have to talk about it." He reached over to pat her leg and, to his amazement, a suddenly frightened Angela sidled out of his reach...as far as the seatbelt would allow.

Brian's brow furrowed in growing concern. He was well aware of the fact that a child who had been physically or sexually abused might shy away from touch or flinch at sudden movements. Something else Katrina had seen in the second vision came to the fore of his mind.

"Angela, did you sleep with lots of stuffed animals on your bed at Collin's house?"

"No. I did at my other house, though. My other daddy used to buy me new ones all the time, but only if I would play the game."

"Jeff, you mean?"

She nodded.

That fucking son-of-a-bitch, Brian's mind railed. *Collin was right. Jeff Patten has been molesting her.* But he had to be sure.

"Angela, I know it's hard, but I need you to tell me about the game you and Jeff used to play."

"I don't want to." The tears were instantaneous.

"I know, honey, but if I'm going to help you, you have to tell me."

"So if I tell you, you won't bring me back there?"

Brian could already feel the hot water he was getting himself into rising. "No, honey. I won't bring you back there."

"Okay. He used to put his fingers in my pee-pee, and he would kiss me there to make the owie go away."

Brian pulled the Dodge Ram to the side of the road. He couldn't drive. Not now. It took him a moment to recover enough to ask the next question. "Did he...do anything else?"

"He used to make me kiss his snake. It would get bigger when I did, and then I had to touch it." The tears rolled down her cheeks now, and she hugged Blondie even tighter.

The puppy yelped and struggled to get free. "One time, just before I went to live with my real Daddy, he tried to put his snake into my pee-pee, and it hurt a lot. I had to go to the hospital the next day, and I don't like going there."

Brian leaned against the headrest behind him and closed his eyes against the pain that was almost overwhelming. There was one final question he had to ask, however, for his own peace of mind. "Angela, did Collin tell you to say this about your daddy? About Jeff?"

"No. He didn't even like to talk about the game. It made him cry."

His head rolled toward her. "So, how about your mommy... Melody. Did she know about the...game your daddy played with you?"

"Uh-huh. She was the one who wanted to take me to the hospital when my pee-pee was bleeding, but Daddy wouldn't take me till the next day. She yelled at him, and she cried, too, but he hit her and told her to shut up."

Brian sat forward again. "Angela, would it be okay if I give you a hug? I won't hurt you. I promise."

She thought about his request for a moment, and then her blonde head bobbed. "Okay."

Brian undid his seatbelt and leaned over to gather the little girl into his arms. Blondie jumped onto the floor. "I am so sorry this happened to you. No little girl should have to go through what you did. But I'm going to make sure it doesn't happen anymore, okay?"

Angela nodded as she sat back and buckled her seatbelt again. "Okay."

Brian pulled the truck back onto the highway and continued toward Cheyenne. "So," he looked at Angela again, "how would you like to spend a few days with Mrs. Riker?"

"My teacher?"

"Yup, although she won't be your teacher anymore. In fact, you probably have to go to a new school when we get back."

"Really?"

"Yup. Lebhart only has kindergarten, first and second graders. And *you*—" he reached over to touch the tip of her nose "—are a big third grader now."

Angela giggled. "I didn't get to go to school when I lived with my daddy. My *Collin* daddy. But he used to make me read and do my arithmetic every day."

"Well, that's good. You *might* still have to go to second grade again, though, after you get home. We'll just have to wait and see."

"Mr. Koski?"

"Yes, honey."

"When I grow up, will I have to let my husband put his snake in my pee-pee?"

Brian almost drove off the road. He waited until he had control of the vehicle again before he looked at Angela. "Why would you ask something like that?"

"Because that's what my daddy told me."

"Collin or Jeff?"

"Jeff."

God, I'm going to wring that bastard's neck, if I don't kill him first! "I...think that that's something you should ask Mrs. Riker when we get there."

"Okay. Mrs. Riker has a little boy. His name is Evan. He's adopted."

Brian smiled at her. "Did Mrs. Riker tell you that?"

"Uh-huh. I think I would like to be adopted."

"Why is that?"

"Because Mrs. Riker said they got to pick Evan to be their little boy. He was never in her tummy. She said they just loved him so much that they wanted him to be their little boy, so he was. If a mommy and daddy love their little boy or girl that much, they won't hurt them, right?"

"No, honey. Or at least they're not supposed to."

"Like my daddy hurt me? Jeff, not Collin."

"Yes, honey. Like your daddy hurt you."

Blondie climbed onto Angela's lap and began to lick her face. "Mr. Koski?"

He grinned. "How about if you call me Brian."

"Okay. Brian?"

"Yes," he asked through a chuckle.

"I think Blondie has to pee...and so do I."

"Okay. There should be a rest stop soon. We'll stop there. If not, we'll just stop on the side of the road."

"I can't pee on the side of the road! Someone might see!"

"Not if you pee behind the truck."

"Promise you won't peek?"

"I promise," he returned solemnly.

"Okay."

Brian looked at the adorable little girl beside him again, and one thought was now foremost in his mind.

Maybe it wouldn't be so bad to be a father after all.

Angela was sound asleep by the time Brian pulled the truck up before Zach and Caryn's garage. He carried her into the house and tucked her into one of the beds in the loft, with Blondie at her side, then joined his friends in the great room before the massive stone fireplace. He had called ahead an hour earlier, while Angela was napping, to tell them they were coming, but didn't elaborate on the reasons why... until now.

"So what in the heck is going on?" Zach asked. "Why didn't you take her home? Her parents must be going crazy."

"Yeah, and they can continue to go crazy for the rest of their lives as far as I'm concerned. In fact, Melody Patten is already there."

Brian spent the next few minutes telling Zach and Caryn about the sexual abuse of Angela at the hands of her father.

He spared no detail, including the question Angela was likely to have for Caryn when she woke up.

"Thanks a lot," she muttered, then simply shook her copper-topped head. "My God, that poor little girl."

"So what are you going to do?" Zach asked. "Obviously, Angela can't just stay here. Her parents are bound to go to the police, and that's going to put *you* in trouble."

"Not after they hear her story. I'll call one of the female detectives from the sex crimes unit at my old precinct in the morning and have her come talk to Angela. The Pattens are in that district anyway. They'll go a lot easier on me than any other of the city precincts would. And, luckily, tomorrow is Saturday, so you guys can be here when the detective gets here."

"Which is all fine and good, Brian, until Chief Stanley gets wind of all this. He'll hang you out to dry," Zach worried.

"I was only doing what was best for Angela. Even he can't argue with that."

"And he'll say you should have taken her to the police, not here. You'll be lucky if he doesn't charge *you* with kidnapping."

"Yeah, well, Angela knows Caryn, and I knew she'd feel safe here. If Stanley wants to argue that point, let him. That little girl has been through enough. She doesn't need to be stuck in some foster home where nobody gives a shit about her. If we're lucky, they'll just let her stay here until this whole thing is settled."

"Hey, now wait a minute," Zach objected. "We didn't say she could stay here."

"Can she?"

The Cheyenne Fire Chief rolled his eyes. "Of course, she can, but it would've been nice of you to ask instead of just volunteering us."

"I haven't volunteered you." Brian grinned. "Yet."

Zach could do nothing but shake his sandy head.

"So, are you going to go see the Pattens?" Caryn asked. "They must be wondering why you're not there yet."

"Yeah, they're my next stop, and Jeff Patten will be lucky if I don't throttle him."

"Watch yourself, Brian. There are bound to be reporters at the house. They don't need to hear any of this...not until the police decide to tell them."

"Okay, so I won't throttle him until we're *inside* the house." He heaved himself up with a heartfelt sigh. "And, speaking of which, I'd better get going. Like you said, they have to be wondering what happened to me...and Angela."

"So, are they going to bring Collin Lanaski back here for trial?" Zach asked as he and Caryn walked Brian to the door.

"Yeah. There's no need to go through extradition proceedings, since he never left Wyoming, so they should be bringing him back here in a few days."

"Do you think there's any chance that he could be telling the truth?" Caryn asked. "That Angela actually *is* his daughter?"

"I don't know how she could be when his daughter died in that crash. I mean, *that* is documented. No, I still think Lanaski is delusional, although I will admit that he treated Angela a hell of a lot better than her own parents did. It's hard to say what will happen to her now, though. More than likely, Jeff is going to find his ass in prison for molesting her. Maybe Melody, too, because she knew about the abuse and did nothing. And even if they don't arrest her, I don't know that Melody is mentally capable of raising Angela alone."

"Sounds like Evan's case all over again, or at least his sister's case," Zach murmured.

Brian grunted. "Yeah, it sure does, except that Evan's sister died. I wanted to make sure that *didn't* happen to Angela, and that's why I brought her here."

The block surrounding the Patten home looked like the White House on Election Day. News vans from every major network, as well as a bevy of local reporters, crowded the street, making it nearly impossible for Brian to weave the Dodge Ram through the throng and into the Patten driveway. Cheyenne police were also on scene, mainly for crowd control, and Brian suffered a moment of trepidation when he exited the truck without a certain little blonde-haired girl. To his increasing dismay, when the front door to the house opened and Jeff and Melody stepped out onto the stoop, Chief Martin Stanley accompanied them.

"Great," he muttered. He turned back to the truck. "Sinbad, *heir*. I might need you to save my neck."

The Belgian Malinois bounded from the cab, and Brian slammed the door behind him.

"Mr. Koski, where is Angela?" one reporter called.

The single question was followed by a dozen others, all related to the missing little girl. Brian ignored the reporters and made his way through the gate in the fence that surrounded the yard and walked up to the house.

"Where is Angela?" a frantic, if much more normal looking, Melody asked. "Brian, where is my daughter!"

"Let's go inside." He made a motion to usher them into the house, but Martin Stanley stepped forward, blocking his advance.

"Where is the child, Brian?"

"That's none of your business, Stanley," the detective gritted.

"A missing child, who is a citizen of Cheyenne, is definitely my business. Now, where is she?"

"She's somewhere safe."

"What do you mean, she's *somewhere safe*?" Melody screeched. "What place can be safer than her own home?"

"Please, can we take this inside?"

"Where is my daughter, Brian?" Jeff Patten asked. This time, it was he who blocked the other man's path.

"Trust me, Jeff, you don't want me to get into that in front of all these reporters. Now, let's go inside."

The man finally relented and turned to guide his distraught wife into the house. Brian laid a hand on Martin Stanley's chest as he made a move to follow. "This is between me and my clients, Martin. There is such a thing as confidentiality. If they want to call you in after I've talked to them, that's their choice, but for now, I have to ask you to remain outside."

The Police Chief lifted his chin in a show of superiority. "You have no right, Brian…"

"I have every right. They're *my* clients. What I have to say to them is for their ears alone until they decide otherwise."

The Chief's jaw hardened, but he stepped aside. Brian continued into the house, with Sinbad at his heels, and closed the door behind them. Jeff and Melody stood in the much neater foyer. "Let's go sit down," he told them.

"Where is Angela, Brian?" Jeff spat out.

"I told you outside, she's safe, and right now that's all that matters."

"Like hell that's all that matters! You were supposed to bring her home!"

"I'll get into the reasons for my decision as soon as we sit down."

Jeff muttered a curse under his breath, but took his wife's arm and led the way into the orderly living room. The Pattens seated themselves on the sofa and looked at Brian expectantly.

"First of all, I want to assure you, as I did on the phone, that Angela is fine. Collin Lanaski didn't hurt her in any way."

"Then why isn't she here!" Jeff railed. "Do you have any idea what my wife is going through? What *we* have been going through? We've been waiting for two days for you to bring her home! In fact, we've been waiting almost eight months!"

Brian ignored the other man's tirade and took a seat in

the chair at a right angle to them. Sinbad plopped down on his haunches beside him.

"Why in the hell did you bring that dog in here?" Jeff started again.

"Because after you hear what I have to say, I might need him."

"What in the hell is that supposed to mean?"

"Angela...told me some things on the drive back from Jackson. Some very disturbing things."

"About Collin?"

"No. About you."

Jeff's expression became guarded. "What do you mean?"

"She told me about the *game*, Jeff."

"Oh, Lord," Melody moaned.

Jeff tossed a glare in his wife's direction. "Shut up." He looked at Brian again. "I don't know what you're talking about."

"Oh, I think you do, Jeff. In fact, I think you know all too well. Collin Lanaski was right, on that point anyway. You *have* been molesting your daughter."

"I haven't been doing anything of the kind!"

"That's not what Angela says."

"And she is lying! Lanaski put her up to this! Hell, he's had her for eight months. He could have convinced her of just about anything in that time. I suppose the next thing you're going to tell me is that she thinks *he* is her father now, too."

"Yes, she does. That I'll admit was just brainwashing on Collin's part. But as for the other accusations, the things you did to her, there was just too much detail...things an eight-year-old child's mind couldn't come up with on its own."

"It could if someone told her to say those things... someone like Lanaski!"

"It's more than just what she said, Jeff. There are other things that corroborate her claims."

"Like what?"

"Like the fact that Angela told me she used to hide in the

closet to get away from you." He glanced at Melody. "The same thing your wife told me."

Her eyes widened in horror as they flew to her husband. "Jeff, I never said anything. I swear!"

"Yes, you did, Melody. You probably don't remember, because you...weren't yourself the last time I saw you, but you did tell me."

"The fact that Angela used to hide in her closet means nothing. It was just something she did. It was a game," Jeff spouted.

"Like *your* game was just a game? The game where you shoved your finger inside her, kissed her vagina, and made *her* kiss your *snake* before you *raped* her?"

Jeff flew off the sofa. "This is bullshit!"

Sinbad was on his feet in an instant, and the low, threatening growl that rumbled from his throat was enough to make Jeff freeze in his current position.

Brian smiled. "I'd sit back down if I were you. He doesn't like loud noises."

Jeff's jaw hardened as he resumed his seat.

"There was one other thing that corroborated Angela's story. I've been working with a local psychic on this case—"

"A *psychic*? You've got to be kidding."

"No, I'm not. In fact, it was because of her that I was able to find Angela. She had a vision of the place Lanaski was keeping her...and it was spot on. When I finally located that place, I located her. This woman also had a *second* vision about Angela. In that vision, a figure of a man loomed over her when she was lying in bed. He told her it was time to play the *game* again." Jeff paled as Brian went on. "Angela was surrounded by stuffed animals in the vision. There were no stuffed animals in the cabin where I found her, but she told me *you* had purchased lots of them for her...as rewards for playing the game."

Jeff swallowed convulsively. "This is crazy. No one is going to believe a psychic."

"Care to show me Angela's room? I'm willing to bet it's just like she left it...including all the stuffed animals on her bed."

"I don't have to show you anything anymore. You no longer work for us."

"Actually, I haven't been working for *you* for almost two months, since your retainer ran out and you quit paying me. I've been working for Angela and, I hate to tell you this, Jeff, but *she* won't be coming home."

"You can't prove any of this."

"I don't have to. That will be the police's job. A sex crimes detective will be talking to Angela in the morning. And I think I can be safe in saying that they'll have a few questions for you once they're done talking to her." Brian looked at Melody. "They'll want to talk to you, too. They'll want to know why you did virtually *nothing* to protect your daughter."

Melody's face blanched to a sickly pallor.

Brian stood. "Well, now that I kept my part of the bargain and told you why I didn't bring your daughter back, I think I'll be on my way." He started for the door, with Sinbad at his side, but turned back. "Oh, and I'll send Chief Stanley in so you can explain to him why I chose not to bring Angela home. Hell, he might just believe you when you tell him it's all lies. He's kind of an asshole himself."

"You won't get away with this, Brian," Jeff called after him. "I'll get my daughter back."

"I wouldn't count on it. The courts have this thing about turning children over to child molesters...even if that molester *is* her father."

"You son-of-a-bitch!" Jeff practically leapt across the room, his hands poised to grip Brian's throat.

The alert Sinbad used his powerful back legs to launch himself off the floor and tackle his master's would-be attacker to the floor. His equally powerful jaws closed around Jeff's throat, but didn't bite down. Melody screamed.

The front door to the house burst open and Martin

Stanley bounded inside. He took one look at the subdued
Jeff, and his gaze flew to Brian.

"What in the hell is going on in here!"

"Ask him," Brian growled. "Sinbad, *aus!*"

The dog immediately relinquished his prize and returned
to Brian's side, then followed him out the door.

CHAPTER EIGHTEEN

Brian pulled up before Katrina Cordova's Victorian mansion fifteen minutes after leaving the Patten house. Though it was nearing midnight, the downstairs lights were still on, so Brian felt safe in ringing the bell. It was a few moments before he saw her pull back the sheer curtain on the window beside the door and look out. The portal opened a moment later.

"Brian? What in the world are you doing here?"

"Sorry to stop by so late. Hope I didn't wake you." Obviously, he hadn't. Her hair was pulled back in its usual pony tail and she wore jeans and a lightweight burgundy sweater that came almost to her knees.

"No. I was still up. Come on in."

He stepped into the large foyer, and Katrina closed the door behind him.

"I found Angela," he informed her before she had even turned back into the room.

She smiled. "I know. I saw it on the news. Congratulations."

"It was largely due to you."

She lifted a dark, perfectly-shaped eyebrow. "Oh?"

"I took a...friend up into the mountains near Jackson, Wyoming, a couple days ago. We were having a picnic lunch when I noticed a windmill in the distance. I checked it out and, lo and behold, it was in a yard on an Ashley Road...a yard surrounding a log cabin."

Katrina's eyes widened. "Really?"

"Yup. Actually, the road was named *Ash* Road, but somewhere along the way someone had added the letters *ley* between the two words. Probably a kid who lived on the road at one time."

"So that explains why it didn't show up in any of the databases you checked."

"Exactly. I found it by pure luck."

"And more than a small amount of determination," she added.

"Yeah, that, too, I guess."

She moved past him and started down the hall before them. "I was just about to make myself a snack. You hungry?"

"Actually, I'm starving. I haven't had anything to eat since Angela and I stopped for dinner at around six."

"Well, follow me and we'll fatten you up."

Brian followed her down the hallway and into a massive kitchen. A huge island dominated the room, long enough to accommodate five stools. He seated himself on the center chair. The remainder of the open and airy room had been left true to the Victorian style with what appeared to be the original tall, white, glass-inlaid cupboards and long, sash-type windows. Immaculate butcher block countertops completed the effect.

"The more I see of your house, the more impressed I am," Brian commented. "This room is really nice."

"Well, you can thank my ex-husband, not me. He's an architect. Actually, a craftsman is more true to fact. He has a real gift. He restored the whole place himself." She smiled as she set a frying pan on the cooktop built into the island in front of him. "You should have seen it when we first bought it. It was pretty scary. It took him five years to get it looking like this." She held up the frying pan. "I'm just going to do grilled cheese sandwiches. That okay with you?"

"Sounds great. I'd settle for raw hamburger about now." He nodded to the half-full coffee maker on the opposite counter. "Okay if I help myself to a cup of coffee?"

"Sure. The cups are to the right of the sink."

Brian retrieved a cup, filled it to the brim, and returned to the island. "Your ex must have been real thrilled when you got the house in the divorce, seeing as how he put so much time and money into it."

"Actually, he offered to let me have it," Katrina said as she set the bread, butter, and a package of sliced cheese on the counter. "We're still really good friends. He comes over to fix stuff for me all the time. He bought another place right after the divorce—another Victorian. He's been working on that for the last three years."

"It's not too often that a couple remains friends after a divorce."

"Steven is a really good guy. We just couldn't live together. Mostly he couldn't handle my visions."

Brian nodded slowly. "Steven Cordova. Okay. I didn't make the connection before. It's no wonder he could afford not one, but *two* Victorian mansions. His architectural firm is the largest in Cheyenne, I think."

"Pretty close. They do a good business, that's for sure." Katrina finished buttering the bread, and then started to lay out the cheese slices as she continued. "So, I suppose the Pattens were pretty ecstatic when you brought Angela home, huh? They were on the four o'clock news and were very anxiously awaiting your arrival."

"I...didn't bring Angela home. I left her with some friends of mine, for the night anyway. We'll see what happens in the morning."

Katrina paused in making the sandwiches to look at him. "Why didn't you bring her home?"

The next few minutes were spent with Brian relaying the

details of Angela's abuse, and of his subsequent visit to see her parents. "So, basically, both of your visions were right on the mark," he concluded.

The grilled cheese sandwiches were done now, and Katrina moved to sit beside him at the counter. "I can't believe it was her father I saw in the vision. I was sure it was Collin Lanaski."

"So was I, until Angela told me different. What her mom told me about her hiding in the closet, and what *you* told me about all the stuffed animals on the bed she was in just confirmed it."

Katrina shook her head slowly. "That poor little girl."

"I think she'll be okay, as long as she doesn't have to go back to them. But, that'll be up to the police and Child Protective Services. I'm sure they'll be at Zach and Caryn's to see her tomorrow, too. I'm just hoping they'll let her stay there. They're a great couple, and they adopted a little boy a couple years ago who was also abused, so they'll know how to handle her."

"Well, that's good anyway." Katrina took a bite of her sandwich and swallowed before she asked her next question. "So, what will happen to Collin Lanaski now?"

"He'll be brought back here to stand trial for the kidnapping. The fact that he treated Angela so well should go in his favor. I'm sure they'll also put him through a battery of psychological tests. If he gets a good attorney, he might even be able to beat the rap."

"I almost feel sorry for him. I mean, to lose his wife and daughter the way he did, it could send anybody over the edge."

"He wants me to check out the Pattens," Brian said as he bit into his own sandwich.

"Why?"

He chewed and swallowed. "To prove whether or not Angela is really their daughter. Obviously, he's hoping I'll find something to strengthen *his* claim."

"Such as?"

"I have no idea."

"So, are you going to do it? Check out the Pattens, I mean."

"I don't know. I didn't see any point in wasting my time before, but that was before I knew Jeff Patten had been molesting Angela. I'd love to prove she isn't really his daughter. Somehow it would make what he did less...sick."

"I think you should. Check them out, I mean."

"Why?"

"I don't know. Just a feeling."

Brian smiled. "Is that your psychic side talking, or simple woman's intuition?"

"Maybe a little bit of both."

They spent the next few minutes finishing their sandwiches, then Katrina stood to clean up the kitchen.

"So, any more visions about the bombing?"

She looked at him over her shoulder as she moved toward the dishwasher. "Have *you* noticed any thunderstorms since you were here last?" She bent to put their dirty dishes in the dishwasher, failing to notice Brian's eyes stray to her shapely behind. She stood again, and turned. "No. No more visions."

Katrina leaned her hips against the counter before the sink and looked pointedly at Brian. "It almost seems as though you believe me now...about the visions, I mean."

"I don't have much choice. The 'Ashley Road' thing was enough to convince me. Hell, you could have knocked me over with a feather when I saw that sign. Not to mention the windmill and the log cabin."

"Thank you," she murmured.

"No. Thank *you*." He stood and moved to stand before her. "So, any chance that you hate me less now than you did the other night?"

"Enough to offer you some horizontal refreshment, you mean?" she asked astutely.

He grinned. "That would be a start."

She reached up to caress his stubbled cheek, and Brian

held his breath. The caress, however, ended in a gentle slap. "Not on your life."

She sidled out of his reach and moved back to sit at the island. She propped her elbows on the counter, and rested her chin on her hands.

Brian groaned as he turned. "You're killing me, Katrina."

"No, I haven't seen a vision of *that* yet."

It was his turn to lean against the sink. He crossed his arms. "Come on. You can't tell me you haven't had any boyfriends since your divorce."

"I never said that."

"So why are you being so difficult?"

"I would say that the fact I hardly know you would be number one on that list."

"So..." He moved to lean his forearms on the counter in front of her and leaned in to within inches of her face. "...get to know me better."

"You didn't let me tell you what would be number *two* on that list."

"What?"

She reached up to pat his cheek. "You're a playboy, Brian. I don't go for one-night stands."

"Trust me. With you, I could handle a hell of a lot more than one night."

She sat back and crossed her arms beneath her breasts. "Tell you what. I'll make you a deal."

Brian straightened, and his brow furrowed with suspicion. "What?"

"You go six months with *me* being your only date, and I'll...consider sleeping with you."

Brian looked at her as though she had just asked him to jump off the dome of the Wyoming State Capitol. "You've got to be kidding."

"Nope. That's my offer. Take it or leave it."

"I'll leave it, thank you." He started for the door to the hallway. "Goodnight."

Katrina let her head fall to the side. "Goodnight, Brian."

Brian arrived at the Riker house just after eight the following morning. He had called his old precinct before leaving the apartment, and Detective Maria Parenteau of the sex crimes unit would meet him at the house at nine. The woman specialized in child sexual abuse. She also informed him that she was required to call CPS and that, more than likely, a caseworker from that office would show up at some point, too.

Brian walked in the back door and entered the kitchen. Sinbad followed him in. The entire Riker family sat at the dining room table, eating breakfast.

Angela jumped down from her chair and ran to meet him. Surprisingly, she wrapped her arms around his waist and gave him a big hug. "Hi, Brian!"

"Hi, honey. Did you sleep good?"

"Uh-huh. And Mrs. Riker made pancakes. Do you want some?"

"Hey, I never pass up Mrs. Riker's cooking."

Caryn smiled as she stood. "I'll get another plate."

Brian took a seat at the table, next to Evan. He ruffled the hair on the boy's head. "Hey there, squirt. How you doing?"

"Good," he mumbled through a mouthful of pancakes.

Caryn returned with another plate, silverware, and a cup. She placed them in front of Brian, then resumed her own seat.

Brian looked at Angela, where she was now seated across from him. "Angela, a nice lady is going to come here soon to talk to you. She's a police officer who's specially trained to help kids. Do you think you can tell her what you told me about the game your daddy used to make you play?"

The little girl's eyes found her plate of half-eaten pancakes. "I guess so."

Caryn reached over to squeeze her hand. "It'll be okay, honey. You just have to tell the truth."

"I always tell the truth, because it's not nice to lie."

"That's right," her former teacher returned. "And do you know what?"

"What?"

"After you've told the nice police woman about everything your daddy did, then *we* are going to bake some cookies!"

"Yippee!" she yelled, then dove into her pancakes.

"I also talked to Judge Reinhardt this morning," Brian spoke up again. "The one who handled Evan's adoption. He said he saw no reason why Angela couldn't stay here until the investigation is completed." He smiled at the little girl, then looked at both Caryn and Zach. "If that's okay with the two of you."

"We already said it was, Brian," Zach returned.

"Good. He was going to call Detective Parenteau before she comes out here, so there shouldn't be a problem. With her or CPS."

"So they'll be coming today, too?" Caryn asked.

"At some point, yes."

"So, how'd it go with you-know-who last night?" Zach asked.

"Not good," Brian returned. He glanced at Angela. "I'll tell you about it later."

The family and their guests finished breakfast, and the table had not even been cleared when a knock sounded on the back door. Brian moved to answer it.

"Hi, Maria," he said as he admitted the sex crimes detective.

"Nice to see you again, Captain."

Brian smiled. "It's not *Captain* anymore. Just Brian." He rounded the fireplace to where Angela and Evan watched cartoons on TV. Blondie was curled up on Angela's lap. "Angela?"

She scooted off the couch and, with Blondie in her arms, moved to Brian's side. He laid his hand on her shoulder. "This is Detective Parenteau, honey. I told you she would be coming to talk to you. Is that still okay?"

The little girl, hesitant though she obviously was, nodded her head.

The petite Maria stooped before the child. "Hi there, Angela. My name is Maria, and *you* are an awfully pretty little girl."

Angela managed a small smile.

"So, did you get breakfast this morning, Angela?"

"Uh-huh. We had pancakes."

"Oooh, yum. They're my favorite, too," Maria told her. The brunette reached out to pet Blondie. "And who is this?"

"She's Blondie. My other daddy, Collin, gave her to me."

"Well that was awfully nice of him. I'll bet you and Blondie have lots of fun together."

"Uh-huh. She likes to play with a rope and play tug-of-war and she likes to chase me around the yard."

"Well, that sounds like lots of fun. You know, I'll bet the Rikers have a room where we could go visit. Is that okay?"

"Can Brian come with us?"

"Well, I'd really like to talk to you alone, but if it gets too hard for you to tell me your story, then I'll call Brian. How does that sound?"

"Okay."

Maria reached out to pet Blondie again. "But Blondie can come with us if you want her to."

"Okay."

Maria stood and looked at the Rikers expectantly.

"I'll show you where the game room is," Zach volunteered. "That would probably be the best place."

"Sounds good," Maria returned cheerfully. She laid her hand against Angela's back and she and Blondie followed Zach back around the fireplace.

Brian watched after them with a worried expression. "I hope she'll be okay."

Caryn moved to slip an arm around his waist. "She'll be fine."

Brian's arm, in turn, went around her shoulders. "You know, all of a sudden I don't have such an aversion to having kids. That little girl really got under my skin."

Caryn looked up at him with a wry smile. "You'd need a wife first, Brian."

"Yeah, and that's the problem." He pressed a kiss to her temple. "You're already taken."

The next two hours were the longest of Brian's life. The CPS social worker, Connie Boden, arrived only minutes after Maria Parenteau began her interview with Angela, and Caryn had shown her to the privacy of the game room, where she introduced the woman to Angela. It was a well-known fact among sex crime interviewers that, when talking to children, it was best to keep the interviews to a minimum. Introducing Connie to the mix now would negate the need for a second interview later.

"God, what in the heck can be taking so long?" Brian railed as he bounded off the sofa. "It only took her five minutes to tell me the story!"

"And they're probably having her go into a lot more detail, Brian," Caryn assured him. "They have to be sure about this. They'll use anatomically correct dolls, puppets, they might have her draw pictures..."

"I know, Caryn. I was a cop, remember?"

She moved to lay a hand on his arm. "Angela is fine, Brian. Maria told me she was doing great when I brought the social worker in. She was coloring pictures and eating cookies that Maria brought with her."

"Yeah, well I still wish they'd just finish up."

Brian's wish came true fifteen minutes later when the two women and Angela rounded the fireplace and entered the great room. Their voices were heard long before they were actually seen.

"Oh, now I don't know about that. I think Spiderman is better than Superman," Maria's voice drifted to their ears.

"But Superman can fly!" Angela argued. "And he's really strong."

"And Spiderman can climb walls and catch things in his web," Maria countered.

"Personally, I like Batman," Connie joined the conversation. "He's got a really cool car."

Angela bounced around the fireplace and ran up to Brian. "Who do you think is better, Brian? Superman, Spiderman, or Batman?"

He stooped before the little girl. "I like Superman, because he has x-ray vision!"

"Surprise, surprise," Zach muttered, and received a grin from his friend.

Angela turned to Maria and the caseworker. "See!"

Maria waved her hand, brushing off Brian's opinion. "Ah, whatever. Spiderman is still better."

Angela turned to Caryn. "Can we bake cookies now?"

Her teacher laughed. "Yes, honey. We can bake cookies now."

The little girl looked at Maria and Connie. "Do you want to help?"

Maria stooped before her again. "I have to go back to work, honey, and so does Connie, but first I want to talk to Brian for a minute. Is that okay?"

"Okay."

Caryn took Angela's hand and led her into the kitchen.

"Bye, Maria! Bye, Connie!" the child called over her shoulder.

"Bye, Angela," the two women returned in unison.

Zach shook his head. "You two are amazing," he said softly. "It's like she just returned from a trip to the zoo, instead of a meeting where she had to talk about being molested by her father."

"She's a great little girl," Connie Boden returned. She looked at Brian. "And she did wonderfully."

"She sure did," Maria agreed.

"So, what did you want to talk to me about?" he asked.

The petite brunette took Brian's arm and led him toward the front door, and further away from Angela. "I called the precinct and told them to send a couple of squad cars over to pick up Jeff and Melody Patten. Judge Reinhardt already signed a warrant. When the squads got to the house, though, the Pattens were gone."

"What!"

"The officers on scene talked to the reporters that were still there, and they said the Pattens left early this morning. They didn't say a word to them—just smiled and waved, like everything was still peachy. They got in their Camry and drove off. Their other car, the Lumina, was still in the driveway. We've issued an APB for the Camry, but—"

Brian ran a suddenly shaky hand through his dark hair. "Son-of-a-bitch!" he muttered. "They must have seen this coming."

"The two squad cars are still on scene. We're not totally convinced that they aren't coming back. The reporters said they had nothing with them when they left...no suitcases, nothing."

"Yeah, because they're not stupid!" Brian hissed. "They knew if they left with suitcases in hand, the *reporters* would be calling the cops...or following them. Those reporters might not have known exactly what was going on, but they knew something was up when I went there last night *without* Angela."

"Yeah, well the Pattens won't get far, if that is the case,"

Maria assured him. "Every cop in the state will be looking for them."

"Yeah, and every cop in the state was looking for Collin Lanaski, too, when he took Angela, and they didn't find him...and the Pattens have a hell of a lot longer headstart than he did."

"Well, I just wanted to let you know. I have to get back to the office and file my report. Judge Reinhardt is waiting for it. Then I'm going to head over to the Patten place and take a look around. I've already got a forensics team headed over there. Oh, and by the way, they brought Collin Lanaski in from Jackson this morning. He's cooling his heels downtown in the county jail."

Brian nodded. "Thanks, Maria."

The detective and the caseworker headed for the kitchen and, a few moments later, exited the house.

Zach's uneven gait brought him to his friend. "What's up?"

"Jeff and Melody Patten flew the coop."

"You're kidding."

"Nope, and luckily they have no idea where Angela is, or we could have another Dan Hamilton situation on our hands."

A frown rippled Zach's brow. "You really think the Pattens are that dangerous?"

"Melody, no. Jeff, a definite yes. That little girl can put him away for life and, trust me, he's an explosion waiting to happen."

Brian waited in one of the attorneys' visitor rooms at the Laramie County Jail an hour later. Once again, the jail attendants knew and respected him, and he had encountered little trouble in securing a face-to-face meeting with Collin

Lanaski. The prisoner was led in a few minutes later, his feet and hands again secured with handcuffs and leg irons.

Brian looked at the restraints, then at the guard. "Don't you think that's carrying it a bit far, Jim? The guy's not a serial killer."

"Sorry, Brian. Orders."

He just shook his head as Lanaski eased himself down into the chair opposite the detective. The jailer took up a post near the door.

"Glad to be closer to home?" Brian asked.

"Not really. I'm still locked up, and I still can't see Courtney." Lanaski sat back in the chair. "So, are you here to torment me with more comments about how *crazy* I am?"

"No, I'm here to tell you that you were right."

"About what?"

"About the abuse. Angela told me on the way home from Jackson about the *game* her father used to make her play."

Collin's blue eyes widened. "She *told* you?"

"Yup. She definitely did not want to go back to the Pattens, and she finally told me why."

The prisoner closed his eyes and tipped his chin toward the heavens. "Thank God." He looked at Brian again. "Is she okay?"

"She's fine, and she's in a safe place. A detective from the sex crimes unit at my old precinct talked to her this morning. So did someone from Child Protective Services. They believed her, Collin."

"So they won't let her go back to the Pattens?"

"No, she'll stay where she is until the investigation is over, then we'll go from there."

"The Pattens will go to court. They'll try to get her back. You do know that."

"I don't think so."

Collin's brow furrowed. "Why is that?"

"Because they're gone."

"They're *gone*?"

"Yup. Left early this morning. Waved to the reporters in the yard, got in the car, and left. No suitcases, nothing."

"Probably because they knew it would look suspicious if they took anything with them."

"Precisely," Brian agreed. "The police have issued an APB for their car and a warrant for their arrest. They won't get far."

Collin could do little else other than shake his head. "Incredible." He looked at Brian again. "Thank you, Mr. Koski. Thank you for looking after Courtney."

"*Angela* is and always has been my main concern in all this, Collin. And she will continue to be."

The inmate nodded. "Good. I'll feel better just knowing someone is looking out for her." Collin sat forward and rested his arms on the table. "So, are you going to check them out now, like I asked?"

"Trust me, Collin, there will be a lot of people *checking them out* now. If there's anything suspicious about their parentage of Angela, it will come out."

"I'd still feel better if you did a little digging yourself. You've got a vested interest in this case now. You said so yourself. You might find things that others would miss."

"The sex crimes unit from the 6th District precinct is good, Collin. They won't miss anything."

He nodded slowly. "So, Courtney, she'll get the help she needs, right? Even if I stay locked up in here...or if they send me to prison?"

"You are *not* her father, Collin. Even if they were to let you out on some technicality, which you shouldn't hope for by the way, it wouldn't be up to you to see that she gets into counseling. But, yes, *Angela* will get the help she needs. *That* I will see to."

"Thank you."

Brian stood. "Well, I have to get going. I just wanted to let you know about the Pattens."

Brian started for the door and the jailer, in turn, took

a step toward Collin. Both men paused when the prisoner spoke up again.

"One last thing, Mr. Koski. I forgot to tell you this when I saw you in Jackson."

Brian turned. "What?"

"I...uh...took Courtney to the medical clinic in Jackson a couple months ago. They took swabs from both of us to do a paternity test—"

Brian's eyes widened. "You did what!"

"I had to prove it, okay! I had to prove that she is my daughter!"

"You had no right to do that without her parents' consent, Collin."

"And I *asked* the Pattens a dozen times to have a DNA test done, and they refused...*because* they knew she wasn't really their daughter! I had no choice, Mr. Koski. I had no choice but to tell the doctor she was legally my child."

"So you lied."

"I didn't lie. Courtney *is* my daughter."

"And the doctor didn't question it? He didn't ask for proof that you were her legal father?"

He shrugged. "I had her birth certificate. That was enough."

"You mean you had *Courtney's* birth certificate."

"Yes."

Brian just shook his head. "Whatever." He turned to leave again and, again, Collin's words stopped him on a dime.

"The results of the paternity test will be delivered to your office."

Brian turned back slowly. "What?"

Another matter-of-fact shrug lifted Collin's shoulders. "I couldn't very well have them sent to me...at either of my addresses. I wasn't in Cheyenne, and I had no address in Jackson. I knew you were working this case, so I figured you were the logical one to have the results sent to."

"Great."

Collin sat back again. "I'll be waiting for another visit

when you get the results...the results that confirm unequivocally that Courtney, *Angela*, is my daughter."

Brian stared at the other man for a long moment. The level of certainty in his eyes was almost unnerving. "Whatever," he repeated and left the room.

The reporters were gone when Brian pulled into the Patten driveway. There were several squad cars in attendance, however, and other unmarked cars that he knew belonged to the local police.

Brian approached the open front door and stepped into the foyer. A uniformed cop immediately approached him. "Hey, Captain Koski. What are you doing here?"

"Hi, Mike. I was hoping you guys might be willing to let me take a look around."

"If it were up to me, no problem. I know you've been working this case. But Detective Parenteau is in charge. I'd have to clear it through her."

"Can you do that?"

"Sure." The young officer turned and went into the living room. Maria Parenteau entered the foyer a moment later.

"Boy, Brian, you're really making me stick my neck out here. If Stanley gets wind of the fact that I let you check out a crime scene, he'll have *my* neck."

"I won't stay long, Maria." He held up three fingers on his right hand. "Scout's honor."

"Okay, but if you find anything, you turn it over to me. Deal?"

"Deal."

He fell into step beside Maria as she turned to reenter the living room.

"Any chance that you came across Angela's birth certificate?"

"As a matter-of-fact, yes, we did. It was in that desk," she said as she nodded to a small computer desk in the corner, "along with a bunch of other important papers." The Pattens' personal computer had already been dismantled and, Brian could only assume, loaded for transport to the station.

"Okay if I take a look at it?"

Maria sighed. "Sure." She moved to an evidence box that sat on the sofa and rifled through the papers inside until she found what she sought. "Nothing unusual about it, though. The Pattens are listed as her parents, all nice and legal."

"I'd like to look at it anyway, if I could."

She handed him the piece of parchment. Brian scanned the entries: Date of birth, child's full name, parents' full names, the hospital where she was born, attending doctor, height, weight, hair color, eye color...

"Wait a minute. Doesn't Angela have blue eyes?"

Maria nodded. "I can check my report to be sure, but I'm almost positive that she does. Why?"

"Because it says here that she has *brown* eyes *and* brown hair."

Maria moved to look at the document over his shoulder. "A typographical error maybe?"

"Maybe. It's weird, though, that they would get both her eye and hair color wrong. And, now that I think about it, I'm almost sure that both her parents have brown eyes. I *know* they both have brown hair. How did she end up with *blue* eyes and *blonde* hair?"

Maria shrugged. "Could be a throwback to a grandparent or something." The detective moved back to the box and dug some more until she found Jeff and Melody's birth certificates. She turned back to Brian. "You're right. The Pattens do both have brown eyes."

"I've also thought it was kind of strange that Angela is so tall for her age, when both her parents are under six foot. I don't think even Jeff is much over 5'8". I know he's a few inches shorter than me, and I'm 6'1"."

"Again, a throwback to a family member?"

"Kind of pushing it, don't you think? I mean, usually a kid will inherit at least *some* of their parents' physical characteristics. Angela got *none* of them." *But she* does *resemble Collin Lanaski. Right down to the blonde hair, blue eyes, and 6'4" height.*

Brian handed the birth certificate back to Maria and moved to study the pictures of Angela that hung on the wall next to the front window. They ranged in age from birth to present time. Once again, the discrepancies became readily apparent—now that he was looking for them. "Maria, come look at these pictures."

She moved to his side.

"See anything strange?"

"Not really...wait a minute. When she was a baby, she had the brown eyes and hair, then—"

Brian nodded and finished the statement. "After about two or three years old, she's blonde and blue eyed."

"It's like the pictures are of two different children," Maria observed.

"Yeah, it sure is. Even their features are different." Brian shook his head. "Damn, why didn't I see this before? I've been in this house close to a dozen times in the past year, and I've looked at these *pictures* before."

"You didn't see it because you weren't looking for it."

"But I should have been, Maria. Collin Lanaski has been saying from day one that Angela was not really the Pattens' child. I mean, hell, she resembles *him* not *them*. Why didn't I see that?"

"Again, because you had no reason to. There was no reason until now *not* to believe the Pattens."

"But if she isn't their child, whose is she? Collin Lanaski's daughter *died* in that car accident."

"I don't know, Brian, but it definitely bears some checking into. There is tons of stuff around this house with the Pattens' DNA on it. I'd say the first order of business is to have some tests run to see if Angela *is* actually their child."

"I'll let you handle that. I'm going to keep checking and

see if we can come up with anything else. Any place you haven't checked yet?"

"Just the garage. I sent a couple guys out there just before you came in."

"I'll go give them a hand."

Maria nodded. "Sounds good. Let me know if you find anything."

Brian headed for the garage. The two officers were in the process of pulling stuff down from the rafters. He quickened his step and moved past the workbench and rack of small, plastic containers to help them with an old mattress.

"Thanks, Captain," one of the officers said as they leaned the mattress against the wall of the garage.

"No problem. Find anything out here yet?"

"Nothing but a bunch of junk. I don't think these people ever got rid of anything."

"Well, keep looking. You never know." Brian's attention was drawn to a bit of color on an object that had been stuffed into a corner, along with a lot of other miscellaneous possessions, he assumed, by the officers. He pushed other paraphernalia aside and uncovered a car seat—a booster-type car seat...a *Dora the Explorer* car seat. Brian's heart practically beat out of his chest.

"Did you guys find this?"

"Yeah. It was up in the rafters, along with all this other stuff."

The officers went back to their search as Brian dropped to one knee on the cement floor and more closely inspected the car seat. It looked almost new, despite the fact that it was covered in a thick layer of dust. *New because it was put in the car only six months before there was a horrible accident where a woman and her child supposedly died?* Brian wondered. Or was it just a coincidence that both the Pattens and the Lanaskis had purchased the same car seat for their daughters—the same *limited edition* car seat? The odds were astronomical.

Brian searched further and discovered an elasticized pocket on the left side of the chair. From it he pulled several small toys—and a 5X7 photograph. The picture was of two little girls, both two to three years old, sitting on Santa's lap. The time stamp on the back of the picture was December 16, 2009—the same day as the Lanaski accident. The stamped information also indicated that the photo was taken at Wal-Mart.

Brian couldn't be sure, of course—call it a hunch—but he was willing to bet that one of the two little girls in the photo was Courtney Lanaski. But how had her car seat ended up in the Patten garage? And who was the second little girl? *Angela?* One of the children in the picture did have blonde hair and blue eyes, and the other brown. Was it possible that the Pattens and the Lanaskis knew each other even at the time of the accident and that, for some reason, neither of them had mentioned the fact? Could they even be related?

There was only one way to find out.

Brian quickly shoved the photo in his pocket and stood. He turned to the two officers, who still pulled stuff from the rafters. "I really don't think we're going to find anything out here. It's just a waste of time. Why don't you guys head back in and see if Detective Parenteau has anything else she wants you to do. I'll straighten up out here and close and lock the door."

"You sure, Captain?"

"Yup. I'm sure."

"Okay."

The two officers headed back inside. Brian waited until they had closed the adjoining door behind them before he snatched up the car seat and sprinted to his truck.

"Back so soon?" Collin Lanaski asked as the jailer ushered him into the attorneys' visiting room for the second time in the past two hours. "Boy, you really must be calling in some favors for them to let you see me twice in one day."

Brian didn't answer, but just waited until the prisoner was seated and the guard had closed the door and taken up his position next to it. He moved then, to pick up the car seat where it had been sitting behind the open portal and slammed it down on the table before Collin.

"Recognize this?"

The other man's eyes widened instantly. "That's Angela's car seat. The one we bought just before I left for Iraq! Where in the hell did you find it?"

"In the Pattens' garage."

"What?" Collin exclaimed.

Brian ignored the man's question as he sat down opposite the inmate. "Are you sure it's the same one?"

"As sure as I can be, I guess. It looks like it."

The detective reached into his inside jacket pocket then, and pulled out the photograph. He pushed the car seat aside and laid the picture on the table before Collin. "Do you recognize these two little girls?"

Collin picked up the picture with his handcuffed hands and, again, his gaze widened. "They're Courtney and Danielle. Where did you get this?"

Brian ignored this question, too, and asked for confirmation on the identity of the second child. "Danielle?"

"Danielle Carrington. My niece. Lynn's sister's little girl." Collin looked at the P.I. again. "Brian, what is going on?"

"I'm not sure. It says on the back of the picture that it was taken on December 16, 2009, at Wal-Mart."

Collin flipped the picture over and read the stamped words, then looked at Brian again. "The day of the accident?"

Brian nodded. "From the look of it, your wife took the two girls to Wal-Mart to have their picture taken with Santa and had the accident on her way home. I stopped at the office before I came here and called the manager at Wal-Mart. They have a Santa in the store from four to nine p.m. every day starting the 1st of December. The accident happened just after six."

Collin swallowed convulsively and fought back tears. "So it was actually *Danielle* who died in the accident? She didn't go missing?"

"What do you mean, go missing?"

"When I came home from Iraq after the accident, Lynn's sister came to see how I was doing. Becky told me that her ex-husband had taken Danielle—on the day of the accident—and disappeared with her. She filed a missing persons report, but Danielle was never found..."

"But if she was sure her ex took her—"

"That's just it. She *wasn't* sure. She just assumed he had, because he was always threatening to take her. Becky was an alcoholic and drug abuser back then. She used to pass out all the time, and Danielle would be left unattended, sometimes for hours. She was only two years old at the time, just a few months younger than Courtney. Hell, even Lynn used to drive to Laramie and take Danielle...." Collin's eyes widened again, this time with excitement. "My God, Brian, that must have been what happened! Lynn probably tried to call Becky, and when she couldn't reach her, she drove to Laramie. She found her passed out again, and she *took* Danielle with her. It was *Danielle* who died in that car crash. *Not* Angela!"

"Let's not jump to conclusions here. Wouldn't Becky have known that your wife took Danielle? I mean, wouldn't Lynn have told her before she left?"

"Not if she was passed out! Becky probably had no recollection of Lynn taking her. It used to happen *all the time*. Lynn would just go there and take Danielle, then she would call Becky the next day and, if she was sober, she'd bring Danielle back. Becky *never* remembered Lynn taking her, and she probably did it a dozen times."

Brian sat back in the chair, and his mind raced with the implications of what he had just discovered.

"It all makes sense now, Brian. Don't you see? Lynn took the girls to Wal-Mart. She got their picture taken, then took Hynds Boulevard, like she always did when she went to Wal-Mart, to go home. The place Jeff Patten works, K.C. Demolitions, is *on* Hynds Boulevard. He would have had to pass the spot where the accident happened on his way home. It was a real lonely, isolated stretch of road. Patten must have seen the accident. Maybe he stopped to help, I don't know. Whatever his reasons, he took Courtney out of that car before it blew up and, instead of reporting it to the police, he took her home!"

"That doesn't make any sense, Collin. We *found* Angela's birth certificate. It checks out. The Patten's *do* have a daughter named Angela...a legal daughter. I also had my secretary check on that when I stopped at the office. The hospital *confirmed* that a child by that name was born to Jeff and Melody Patten on April 23, 2007—Angela's birthday."

"Look, I can't explain it any better than you can, Brian, but I know for certain now that Courtney did *not* die in that accident. She is alive and going by the name Angela Patten. Jeff Patten *took* her out of that car, still in her car seat, and that's why the car seat ended up at their house."

Brian admitted, if only to himself, that it *did* make sense. It would explain all the discrepancies. The difference in Angela's eye and hair color, her above average height, and—most important of all, as Collin had pointed out—the car seat.

"By the way, where did you find that picture?" Collin asked.

"In a pocket in the car seat," Brian returned absently.

"Then that's even more proof that this *is* Courtney's car seat! Brian, you have to listen to me! You have to *believe* me! Please!"

He looked at the other man's desperate face for a long moment before he answered. "I do, Collin. I do." He couldn't help but smile. "You're a pretty determined guy, aren't you? Even when everybody thought you were crazy, you just wouldn't give up."

"I'm not a determined *guy*, Brian. I'm a determined *father*. Hell, even *I* thought I was going crazy at first. I mean, like you said, it just didn't make sense. Courtney was dead. I had accepted that. And then I started noticing all the things about Angela. Her comment—a very *detailed* comment, by the way—about my dog tags, the scar on her shin, the fact that she was really tall for her age, when her parents were both short. Hell, she even *looked* like me and Lynn. And then there were the discrepancies about the accident. The fact that Courtney was not wearing her dog tag, the wrong car seat being in the car, the fact that it was on the wrong *side* of the car. I couldn't just ignore all that. I knew in my heart that my daughter didn't die that day, and I knew that Angela Patten was *her*."

"You do realize that we can't prove any of this...because the Pattens are gone."

"We can prove it when the DNA test results come back."

"Okay, so we can prove that Angela *is* actually Courtney Lanaski...maybe. But we *can't* prove that Jeff took her from the car that night. There were no witnesses to the accident. And if he did take her, and has been raising her for the last four years as *his* daughter, then what happened to his *real* daughter?"

"I don't know and, to be honest, I don't care. I'm just glad that someone finally believes me, other than Kylie. And I'm especially glad that someone is you, because *you* actually have the means to prove that everything I've been saying for the last year is true."

"You think so, huh?"

"Yes, I do, and if you're willing to take the case, I want to hire you to do it."

Brian shook his head. "You don't have to hire me, Collin. I want to get to the bottom of this now as much as you do. Which brings us back to square one. I have to find Jeff and Melody Patten."

CHAPTER NINETEEN

Brian sat at his desk the following morning studying the accident report from the day Lynn Lanaski died. He was no longer willing to say that both Lynn and Courtney Lanaski succumbed to their injuries that day, but he wasn't ready to admit that the victims were Lynn Lanaski and Danielle Carrington, either.

Brian's eyes paused on one section of the report. He then reread it to make sure he had read it right the first time. "Son-of-a-bitch!" he muttered. "There was a witness!"

"Can I help you?" came Sherry's voice from the outer office.

"No, but *he* can."

Brian looked up as Detective Maria Parenteau marched into his office. "Okay, where's the car seat?" she demanded.

"Hi to you, too, Maria."

"Damn it, Brian, I told you to tell me if you found anything at the Patten house, and I certainly *didn't* tell you it was okay to just take whatever you found! Luckily, the two officers remembered pulling the car seat out of the rafters in the garage. They also remembered your interest in it and they also noticed it was gone! Now, where is it?"

Brian indicated with a thumb over the shoulder motion

to where the car seat sat against the wall behind his desk. Maria stomped to retrieve it, then returned to stand before the desk.

"You do realize that you broke the law here, don't you, Brian? You tampered with evidence. Do you expect me just to ignore that?"

"It would be nice," he said with a smile.

Maria just shook her head and started toward the door to the office with the *Dora the Explorer* car seat in hand.

Brian sat back in his chair. "Did you know that there was a witness at the Lanaski accident scene?"

Maria turned. "No, and I really don't care."

"Would you be more interested if I told you that this witness saw a car pull away from the scene just after Lynn's car exploded? A blue Toyota Camry."

She paused. "As in the *Pattens'* blue Toyota Camry?"

"That would be my guess."

"Okay, I'll bite. And *why* would that be your guess, Brian?"

"I think you'd better sit down, Maria. This could take a while."

"So you're telling me that Angela Patten *is* actually Collin Lanaski's daughter?"

"It's sure beginning to look like it."

"And you think that Jeff Patten stole her from the car on the night of the accident."

"Yup."

"In *this* car seat," she said, indicating the carrier beside her.

"It would explain why I found it in his garage."

Maria sat back. "That's crazy, Brian. We found Angela's birth certificate. She is legally the Pattens' daughter."

"And the Medical Center confirms that Jeff and Melody had a baby on the date listed on the birth certificate, so it *is* legit." He smiled. "I checked. That's what good P.I.'s do. We like to be thorough."

"Okay," Maria said as she crossed her arms beneath her petite breasts. "Give me the punch line."

"I talked to Melody Patten awhile back. It was five or six months after Angela disappeared. Let's just say she was not herself. In fact, she was certifiable. You know." He drew a circle next to his ear. "Wacko. She didn't make a whole lot of sense, but there *was* one thing she said that day that has gotten me to thinking."

"And that would be?" Maria was tempted to grit out the words.

"She said, 'Angela is dead, isn't she?' I, of course, assured her that Angela was fine. That Collin Lanaski wouldn't hurt her. *She*, on the other hand, started screeching at me that it wasn't true, that Jeff had *hurt* her and she was dead—and that he had buried her in the backyard."

Maria's eyes rounded. "Are you serious?"

"Yup. I chalked it all up to madness at the time, but now I'm not so sure. It would explain a hell of a lot."

"Like why Angela had brown eyes and hair in her baby pictures, and blonde hair and blue eyes when she got older?"

"Yup. And why her birth certificate was legit, but not accurate. It would also explain why Jeff Patten would see fit to abduct *another* little girl about the same age from the scene of an accident."

"And take her home to his distraught wife to *replace* the daughter he had killed."

Brian pointed a finger at her. "Bingo."

Maria stood. "So, want to come help me dig up the Pattens' backyard?"

"Honey, I wouldn't miss it for the world."

The skeletal remains of a child's body were discovered in the Pattens' backyard four hours later. It would take DNA testing to determine if she was, indeed, Jeff and Melody's daughter, but to Brian's state of mind, that would be just a technicality. The private detective could feel no satisfaction, however, in a job well done. A little girl was dead—a little girl named Angela Patten—and that left no reason to celebrate.

"So, you going to go to Judge Reinhardt and get Collin Lanaski released from jail, or am I?" Brian asked Maria, where the two of them stood in the Patten driveway watching the coroner's van pull away from the scene.

"We still have no concrete proof that he's Angela's—or rather, Courtney's—father," Maria said. "I think it would be a little premature to release him now. And he *did* kidnap her. That's still a felony."

"Oh, come on, Maria! The guy was only trying to protect his daughter, and with good reason. Jeff Patten was *molesting* Angela—Courtney." *That* was going to take some getting used to. "Just as he was probably molesting his own daughter and, if you haven't figured it out yet, which I'm sure you have, that's probably what killed her. She was only two-and-a-half years old, Maria. More than likely, he raped her, she hemorrhaged, and she died. Luckily, he learned his lesson, though...to a certain extent. He didn't rape *Courtney* until she was five years old."

"Yeah, a real compassionate guy."

"So, you gonna spring Collin or not?"

"It's not up to me, Brian." He lifted a skeptical eyebrow, and she sighed. "But I will go talk to Judge Reinhardt *and* the D.A. With any luck, Lanaski will be free by morning."

"Thank you, Maria."

"Don't mention it. And, by the way, *where* is that picture...the one you *also* stole from a crime scene? I'll need it to include in evidence when I do my report."

Brian reached inside his jacket and removed the photo

from the pocket. "Take good care of it. That's the last picture Danielle's mother will have of her."

"We haven't proven *that* yet, either," the detective pointed out, "and I don't know that we ever will. They couldn't identify the remains as Courtney's four years ago, so I doubt that they could identify them as Danielle's now."

"Who knows? They've come a long way with DNA testing in the last four years."

Maria shrugged. "I guess it's possible." The sex crimes detective leaned back against her car and looked at the man before her. "So, I *know* you're going to make it your life's work now to find the Pattens...and so am I. Can we work as a *team* on this one, instead of you going off half-cocked and hoarding evidence?"

"Oh, I might think about it." An easy grin curved his lips. "Provided that you'll have dinner with me tomorrow night."

Maria reached up to straighten the lapels on his jacket. "Captain, I thought you'd never ask."

Brian knocked on the Watsons' kitchen door early in the afternoon three days later. Henry answered the summons.

"Brian, didn't expect to see you. Come on in."

Rosie, too, had appeared in the doorway of the kitchen by now and, as usual, was an efficient hostess. "Can I get you a cup of coffee, Brian?"

He smiled at the elderly woman. "Sounds great, Rosie."

Brian took a seat at the kitchen table. Henry sat opposite him.

"So, what brings you out here, son?"

"I...got the DNA results this morning on the hair sample from Nellie's brush," he began slowly as Rosie crossed the kitchen with two half-full cups of coffee. Brian waited until she had placed the cups on the table before himself and Henry, and then seated herself next to her husband before he continued. "It was a match. The DNA positively identifies the remains found in Cañon City in 1991 as Nellie's."

Henry just sat back in his chair and slowly shook his gray head. Rosie released a shaky sigh. "So, it's for sure then," the former said. "She's dead."

"I'm afraid so," Brian returned gently.

"We were expecting it," Rosie added. "I mean, it comes as no great surprise, but it's still hard to hear—even after almost thirty-eight years."

Henry reached over to pat her gnarled hand. "At least we can finally bring her home now, dear." He looked at Brian. "Right?"

He nodded. "I'll check with the Fremont County Coroner to be sure, but he should have received a copy of the DNA results, too. There shouldn't be a problem."

"Well, good," Henry returned. "Then it's over."

"And in more ways than one," Brian informed them. At the questioning look in both the Watsons' eyes, he continued. "I told you that Everett Klensing's children also agreed to have DNA swabs done shortly after you found Nellie on *The Doe Network*."

Both Henry and Rosie nodded.

"I got those results, too, a few days ago. I didn't see the point in saying anything until Nellie had been positively identified, but those tests, too, confirm that there's a strong probability that the hair clutched in Nellie's hand *was* Everett's."

"So it *was* him who killed her," Rosie interpreted softly.

"It sure looks like it. And one more thing: I also managed to convince the coroner to loan me the quilt that the remains were wrapped in. I showed it to Clara this morning, and she identified it as the one she left in the car on the day Nellie disappeared. The Jackson police can't make a definite determination on any of this, though, without DNA from

Everett himself and, as it turns out, it looks like we got lucky on that score, too."

"How so?" Henry asked.

"I did some checking in the last few days. Actually I had Sherry run Everett's name through a couple of databases just for the heck of it, and she got a hit. Apparently, Everett met another woman at some point after he killed Nellie, a woman from Idaho. According to the police report Sherry found, he was beating this woman, too. She didn't take the abuse like his wife did. She shot and killed him back in 2003."

Henry's eyes widened, matching his wife's expression.

"Everett is dead?" the former exclaimed.

"It looks like it. I can't be sure it's him, of course, until I get the DNA sample I requested from the sheriff in Boise and match it to the hair found in Nellie's case. I mean, it *is* possible that there was another Everett Klensing who beat his woman friend."

"Possible, but not likely, right?" Henry asked.

"That's my opinion, yes."

"Well, if he *is* dead," Rosie spoke up, "at the risk of sounding un-Christian-like, it was a fitting end for him after what he did to Nellie."

"Yes, Rosie, it was."

"So, it really *is* over then," Henry repeated. "We know Everett killed Nellie, and we also know he paid for it. Maybe not as a direct result of murdering our daughter, but he paid for it just the same."

"Yes he did, Henry, and now Nellie can *truly* rest in peace."

CHAPTER TWENTY

September 1st found Brian stuck in the office. Sherry was out sick, and with their growing number of new clients, he didn't dare leave the office unattended. Admittedly, he had procrastinated in hiring her an assistant, but decided today would be a good day to conduct interviews. He spent the first hour calling to set up appointments with potential new employees. Those he couldn't reach were simply out of luck.

"Kathy?" he asked the pretty twenty-four-year-old brunette who entered the office for his ten-thirty appointment.

She nodded.

"Hi. I'm Brian." He shook her hand, then indicated the chair before Sherry's desk. "Have a seat."

"Thank you."

He glanced at her application and résumé. "So, I see you've waited tables in several restaurants, but never held an office position?"

"No, I haven't, but I'm really good with people, and I'm a quick learner."

He nodded. "Well, that's good. How about schooling?" he asked as he looked at the résumé again. "High school graduate. No college?"

"No." Her gaze dropped. "I just haven't been able to afford

it. I really want to go back to school, but the finances just won't allow it."

"Are you working now?"

"Yes. I'm hostessing at Applebee's. I got that job just a few weeks ago, after I sent you my résumé."

"Are you happy there?"

She smiled wryly. "Not really. I'm looking for something a little more challenging. Something where I can advance."

Brian smiled. "And something that pays enough to allow you to go back to school?"

She returned the smile. "That, too."

The phone on Sherry's desk rang. Brian looked at Kathy. "Why don't you answer that for me?"

Her eyes widened. "Are you sure?"

"Yup."

She stood and reached for the phone. "B.K. Investigations. This is Kathy. How can I help you?" She listened for a moment, then put her hand over the mouthpiece and looked at Brian. "It's a Detective Parenteau. She would like to speak to you. She says it's urgent."

"I'll take it in my office. Can you wait around for a minute?"

"Sure."

Brian went into the office and closed the door behind him. He picked up the phone. "You can hang it up now, Kathy."

He heard a soft click on the line a moment later.

"Hey, sexy. What's up?"

"We've got 'em."

The beat of Brian's heart increased. "The Pattens, you mean?"

"Yup. Their car was just spotted by a couple of hikers outside a mountain cabin near Colorado Springs. Apparently, one of the guys saw a report on the news and recognized the vehicle. He also wrote down the license number. It's definitely them."

"Colorado Springs is two-and-a-half hours away. You honestly think they'll still be there when we get there?"

"The local P.D. has the place surrounded. They're not going anywhere. Hell, everything could go down before we ever get there. So, want to go along for the ride?"

He glanced at the closed door to the outer office and took only a moment to make his decision. "Yeah. I'll take my own vehicle, though, since I've got the dog. Where should I meet you?"

"Out front of the station in ten minutes."

"On my way."

"Oh, and Brian?"

"Yeah?"

"The Colorado Springs P.D. was also looking for the vehicle...in connection with the kidnapping of an eight-year-old girl two days ago."

Brian sank down into the chair behind his desk. "Son-of-a-bitch."

"The third Angela, you think?"

"I'd bet on it."

"Okay. See you in a few."

"Yeah."

Brian hung up the phone, leaned back in his chair, and closed his eyes. "Damn!" he moaned. "Why can't this guy just accept that his daughter is dead and quit trying to find replacements?" A wry grin curved his lips. Strange. He had said the same thing about Collin Lanaski.

He slapped his hands down on the arms of the chair, pushed himself up, and turned to bark at Sinbad. "Sinbad, *heir.*"

The dog was up in an instant and followed him into the outer office. Kathy immediately took a step back, her eyes wide with sudden fear.

"He's fine," Brian assured her. "He won't hurt you. So, are you willing to take the job?"

"What?" she exclaimed.

"Are you willing to take the job? But only if you can start right now."

"Yes! Of course!" she said. "No problem."

"Fifteen an hour work?"

"Yes, that's great."

"Good. There'll be other applicants showing up," Brian rattled off orders as he headed for the door. "Just tell them the job is taken. If anybody calls, take detailed messages and tell them I'll get back to them as soon as possible. Don't do *anything* else. Play Solitaire on the computer or something. Lock up at five. There's a key in Sherry's top drawer. If I'm not back, she should be here in the morning. She'll put you to work."

"Okay!" Kathy called after him as he and Sinbad blew out the back door.

Brian, Sinbad, and the four Cheyenne detectives arrived at the Colorado Springs scene just over two hours later. A dozen local police cars already jammed the winding mountain road approach. The new arrivals ditched the cars and traveled another half-mile on foot before coming within site of the Patten hideout. The small house nestled in a grove of pine, elm, and oak trees reminded Brian of another scene, and another cabin—minus only a few outbuildings and an old wooden windmill.

Maria took the lead upon their arrival and sought out the Colorado Springs detective she had spoken to on the phone.

"Detective Parenteau?" the tall, slightly overweight man asked as he approached the group.

She nodded. "Detective Barnes?"

"Nice to meet you," he acknowledged with a handshake. "Let me bring you up to speed. Patten and his wife are holed up inside the cabin with the Marloe girl. So far, we've had very little contact with him, and that's not for lack of trying. He's been pretty uncommunicative. The one thing he did tell us, though, is that the place is rigged with explosives—supposedly C4."

Brian's eyes shifted to the black bomb squad van that sat a short distance away as the man continued.

"You know this guy better than we do," Barnes went on. "Is that even possible? I mean, would he even have access to explosives? Especially C4. It's hard to come by unless you're associated with the military."

"Or if you work for a demolitions company, which Patten does," Brian put in.

Maria's gaze, too, shifted to Brian and she made the introductions. "This is Brian Koski. He's a private detective, former Cheyenne P.D. He's been working with the Pattens for almost a year on a case regarding a child who they claimed to be their daughter. In truth, she was another kidnap victim. You'd be wise to listen to him."

"So he *would* have access to C4?" the Colorado Springs detective confirmed.

"Undoubtedly," Brian returned. "He works with it every day."

"Shit," Barnes muttered. He turned to his partner, who stood within listening distance. "Cal, move everybody back...at least a hundred yards."

The man ran off to do his comrade's bidding.

"Can I try talking to him?" Brian asked. "Like Maria said, I know the guy, and he *did* trust me at one time."

"Yeah, before you found out he'd been molesting Angela—or rather, Courtney—and refused to bring her home," Maria added. "He's probably not too fond of you right now, either."

Brian shrugged. "It's worth a shot. If I can get him to let me inside—"

"No, Brian. It's too dangerous."

"We need to know if he's really got the place rigged with explosives, Maria, *and* we need to know if that little girl is okay." He looked at Detective Barnes. "What's her name?"

"Jennifer Marloe."

His gaze went back to Maria. "In order to do that, *someone* has to get inside, and the person he's most likely to let do that is me."

Maria looked at the other detective again. "It's your call. You're in charge here."

"I guess it's worth a shot. Like he said, we need to know what's going on in there. Be careful, though. Let him think you're coming in just to get his demands. We haven't had any luck there, either. Even our hostage negotiator couldn't get through to him. Like I said, the guy isn't talking."

"And *don't* tell him we found Angela's remains in his backyard," Maria added.

Detective Barnes' eyes widened. "You found *whose* remains?"

"His daughter's," the Cheyenne detective returned. "His *real* daughter's. She was only two years old when he killed her."

Barnes just shook his head slowly, then led Brian to a nearby squad and handed him the microphone attached to the interior radio. He pushed a switch that would enable the unit to project Brian's voice from the outside speakers.

"Don't promise him anything," Barnes warned.

Brian nodded. He held the microphone near his mouth and pushed the "Talk" button. "Jeff, it's Brian Koski. Just wanted to check and see that you all are doing okay in there."

"What in the hell are you doing here?" came his angry reply a moment later. "Wait. They notified you, didn't they, when they found your *dangerous* former clients."

"If you've really got that place rigged with C4, then they're right to think you're dangerous. I know different, Jeff, but it's up to you to prove them wrong, not me. You need to show them that you don't want to hurt anybody."

"I don't, but they're not giving me much choice."

"Look, why don't you let me come inside so we can talk about this—"

"No! Anybody comes near this place, and I *will* blow it. I swear!"

"You don't want to do that, Jeff. You know it and I know it. You don't want to hurt Melody or Jennifer."

"What difference does it make now? You're going to throw me in prison for the rest of my life, and probably Melody, too, for what you *say* I did to Angela."

"No one has accused you of anything yet, Jeff…"

"What do you mean? *You* accused me! And you said the police would want to talk to me after they talked to Angela. The insinuations were clear, Brian!"

"And if you did do those things to Angela, then all it means is that you need help, Jeff. I can see that you get that help."

"Yeah, right. *In prison!*"

"Maybe," Brian replied honestly. "You have to pay for your actions, like any man does, but it doesn't necessarily mean you'll spend the rest of your life there. If you get the help you need, hell, you could be out in four, five years," he lied.

"Really?"

"Yup. I've seen it happen." Again, he stretched the truth. "Look. Let me come inside. Let me see firsthand that you, Melody, and Jennifer are all right. I can tell you that it'll make everybody out here feel a lot better if they know that little girl is okay. And it'll also show that you're willing to be cooperative, and that alone makes you a little less dangerous."

An agonizingly long moment of silence followed as Jeff considered Brian's proposal. Finally the fugitive answered, and everyone breathed again.

"Okay. But just you. No dog and no gun."

"Not a problem. I'll leave the gun out here. Sinbad, too. There's no reason I should need either of them, right Jeff?"

"Right."

Brian took the gun from his shoulder holster and, in plain view, handed it to Maria. He couldn't see Jeff at either of the front windows in the cabin, but somehow he knew the man could see him. "Okay, Jeff, I got rid of the gun. I'm coming in. Is that all right?"

"Yeah."

"You're not going to shoot me, right?" he asked as he started slowly toward the house, his hands raised and palms outward.

He got the reaction he looked for when he heard the other man laugh. "I was tempted to the other day, but not now."

"I'm glad to hear that."

Brian was within three feet of the house now, and the door opened. He still couldn't see Jeff and assumed he was behind the portal. He stepped over the threshold.

"Over there," Jeff's voice ordered, "by the window."

Brian did as instructed, and then turned. His alert eyes took in his surroundings in an instant. The place was, indeed, wired with explosives. Enough to send him and all the cops outside to kingdom come. Even more disturbing, however, was the gun Jeff held in one hand, and the detonator he held in the other. Melody sat on the bed across the sixteen by sixteen foot room, a puffy-eyed, pale Jennifer Marloe wrapped in her arms.

"Hi." Brian smiled. "You must be Jennifer."

"Yes," the girl replied meekly.

"Now, silly," Melody chided gently, "why did you tell him that? You know your name is Angela."

The child started to sob again.

Melody pulled her closer. "Now, none of that. You know your daddy doesn't like it when you cry."

Jennifer started to struggle in her arms. "I told you! He's not my dad, and you're not my mom!"

Brian ignored the child's outburst and his gaze shifted to Jeff. "So, the cops outside want to know what they can do to defuse this situation—and so do I."

"They can let us leave," he returned simply.

"Somehow I don't think they're going to be willing to do that—unless you let me walk out of here with Jennifer."

"Yeah right, and they'll just pull back and have their sharpshooters open fire." He, too, looked at Jennifer. "That girl is the only thing keeping me and Melody alive."

"Okay. So, leave *with* the girl—and me. Your car is just down the hill. Get down the road a ways, let us go, and be on your merry way."

"We're not leaving here, Brian. *They* are going to leave, or I'll blow this place with Melody and the girl in it. And, trust me, the blast will take a lot of you with us."

Jennifer started to sob again and, this time, she let Melody do what she could to comfort her.

"So you'd kill your wife and an innocent child to save your own skin?"

"It's better than the alternative."

"Which is?"

"Prison," he returned simply. "You said yourself that they're going to hold Melody liable, too, for not *protecting* Angela. She wouldn't last a day in prison."

"And what about Jennifer? She's done nothing to deserve this."

He shrugged. "She'd be a casualty of war...and this is war, Brian."

"In your book, maybe. Those guys out there, though? They're just trying to get a little girl back safely. If you would just let her go, things would go a lot easier for you."

"And like I told you, if I let her go, I'm dead, no matter how you slice it."

"Not if you give yourself up."

"That's not going to happen."

Brian moved under Jeff's watchful eye to rest his hip on a corner of the table that sat in the middle of the room. "So, why don't you tell me about the night of the accident...the night you took Courtney Lanaski."

Jeff's gaze became guarded. "I don't know what you're talking about."

"Oh, I think you do. I think you were on your way home from work and either you witnessed the accident or you came upon the scene right after it happened." He shrugged. "There's no point in denying it, Jeff. There was *another* witness that night—one who saw a car just like yours pull away from the scene right after the Lanaski car exploded—with Lynn Lanaski and her *niece* still inside."

"That proves nothing."

"Maybe not, but the car seat I found in your garage does—the *Dora the Explorer* car seat. The *limited edition* car seat, just like the one the Lanaskis bought for Courtney. There was also a picture in a pocket in that car seat—a picture of Courtney Lanaski and her cousin sitting on Santa's lap on the day of the accident." Brian shook his head. "It was really stupid of you not to get rid of that car seat, Jeff."

The other man took a deep breath and glanced at his wife, who was still preoccupied with trying to calm Jennifer. "It wasn't like I *intended* to take Courtney that night. I was only trying to help."

"Help?" Brian asked doubtfully.

"Like you said, I was on my way home from work," Jeff began the explanation, however grudgingly. "I was maybe a half-mile behind Lynn Lanaski's car when a deer ran out in front of her. The roads were slippery and when she hit the brakes, the car started to skid. It hit the shoulder and plowed over an embankment. It rolled like two or three times, then hit a tree. I stopped my car and ran over to see if I could help."

"You didn't call 911?"

Jeff shook his head. "No. To be honest, I didn't even think of it. I just wanted to get to the car and see if everybody was okay. The car was really messed up, but it had landed right-side-up. It was already starting to smoke. I could hear kids crying, so I ran down the embankment. The driver, Lynn, was unconscious. She might have been dead already. I could see the babies inside. Both of them were in car seats. I couldn't get the rear driver's side door open, so I ran around to the passenger side. There were actual flames by that time, so I just yanked open the door and reached in to unbuckle the seat belt. I lifted Courtney out, car seat and all, and ran back up the hill. I had every intention of going back for the other child. She was still screaming, so I knew she was alive. That's when the car blew. The force of the blast knocked me down, but I still managed to keep Courtney from getting hurt. The other little girl, though...she wasn't crying anymore." Surprisingly, at least to Brian's state of mind, Jeff had tears in his eyes. He angrily brushed them away. "You have to understand, Brian. I was standing in the middle of that damned road, with a baby in my arms. Her mother and who I *thought* was her sister were dead. Melody and I had just lost our own daughter, a daughter who was about the same age, only three days before."

Brian held his tongue, adhering to Maria's wishes that he not reveal what they knew to be the truth about the real Angela Patten, but it was the hardest thing he had ever done. He wanted to scream at the man that he didn't just *lose* his daughter. He had sexually molested her, too, a two-year-old girl, and that molestation had killed her—and then he buried her in the backyard like a dead household pet.

"Melody was a wreck," Jeff went on. "She wouldn't stop crying. Even still, when I left that accident scene with Courtney, I had every intention of just taking her home where it was warm and calling the police from there. When I walked in the house, Melody was sitting in the living room, still in her nightgown from that morning. Her hair wasn't brushed, she was *still* sobbing... I had taken Courtney out of the car seat by that time and, when she saw the baby in my arms, *she stopped crying.* She ran to grab her from me and she kept screaming, 'Angela! Angela!' Courtney didn't look anything like Angela, but in Melody's messed-up mind, *she* was our daughter. I tried to tell her what had happened, about the accident and everything, but she wouldn't hear any of it. Over the next few minutes, Melody calmed down and was more herself again, but she still believed with her whole heart and soul that *that* little girl was our Angela. So...I just let it go. I figured I'd give it until morning, let Melody have her daughter back if only for the night. Well, *morning* turned into one day, then two, then a month. I just couldn't take the baby from her. I had my wife back, and I couldn't let her lose *another* child."

"So that's why, when I didn't bring Angela back after Collin took her, you felt it was necessary to get Melody a *third* child?" Brian glanced at Jennifer.

Jeff's jaw hardened. "And you should understand that better than anybody. You *saw* Melody after Lanaski kidnapped Angela. You saw what it did to her! I mean, look at her now. She's *normal* again!"

Brian stood and moved to stand nearer to Jeff and whisper harshly in his ear. "And what you should have done was gotten her help, *not* kidnapped another child!"

The gun came up between them, and Brian stepped back. Jeff also raised the hand holding the detonator. "Get out," he hissed in return.

Brian shook his head. "Jeff, you can't do this! You can't take another innocent child and expect the cops out there to just leave!"

"So what do you think they'll do?"

"Honestly, I have no idea."

"Come on! You were a cop once. A police captain. What would *you* do?"

"I can't speak for the detective in charge out there, Jeff."

"*What would you do?*"

Brian's jaw hardened. "I'd take your ass out the first chance I got."

"That's what I figured." Jeff moved to yank open the door. Once again, he was careful to stand behind the portal. "Get your ass out of here, and you tell them that either they leave or this is *not* going to have a happy ending."

Brian took a step toward the door, but paused when Jennifer struggled out of Melody's desperate embrace and ran to throw her arms about his waist.

"Don't leave me! Please, don't leave me! I'm not their little girl!"

Brian stooped and held the child at arm's length. "I know you're not, honey, and we're going to get you out of here. I promise."

"Please!" she sobbed.

"Get her, Melody," Jeff growled.

The woman approached, however hesitantly, and grabbed Jennifer's arm. The three of them were in range of the open door now—and a sharpshooter's bullet—but Brian only hoped Detective Barnes had the sense not to order the gunman to take out Jeff's wife. Not only would they risk hitting the flailing, near hysterical Jennifer, but Jeff—the most dangerous of them all—still held the detonator. Even a shot *through* the door, directed at him, could not guarantee that he would die before he pushed the trigger.

As difficult as it was, and despite the fact that it went against the grain of every fiber in his being, Brian let the sobbing, panic-stricken girl go and allowed Melody to drag her back onto the bed.

"I'll be back for you, Jennifer," he repeated the promise before he walked out the door and Jeff slammed it behind him.

"So?" Detective Barnes asked anxiously a few seconds later when Brian was again safely amid the ranks of the Colorado Springs police. Maria also stepped up to hear his answer.

"No dice. He's not coming out—until you guys leave."

"And is the place really rigged with explosives?"

"Oh, yeah. Fifteen to twenty pounds of it—enough to put a good dent in the side of that mountain," Brian returned as he tipped his head toward the Rockies, where they stood strong and silent just behind the cabin. "He had a remote detonator in his hand."

"So, if one of the sharpshooters had the opportunity to take him out, the C4 *still* might go off."

"I know I wouldn't want to take the chance," Brian confirmed.

"Great," Detective Barnes muttered. "So what in the hell are we supposed to do?"

Brian shrugged. "Wait him out. Their food and water will last only so long. Once he starts to get hungry, he might be a little more agreeable."

"How's Jennifer?" Barnes' partner, Cal Snyder, asked.

"Scared," was Brian's simple response. "Unhurt, though, from what I could tell."

A uniformed cop sprinted up to Detective Barnes. "We just got a call from dispatch. Apparently there's a thunderstorm headed our way. Pretty severe by the look of it. It should be overhead in a few hours."

"Wonderful. That's all we need," the detective grumbled. "Have dispatch get somebody to send a couple tents up here so at least we'll have some kind of cover."

The word "thunderstorm" was all it took for Brian to come up with an idea. He turned to the uniformed officer. "Is the storm supposed to hit Cheyenne, too?"

"I don't know."

"Can you check?"

"What difference does it make if it's going to hit Cheyenne or not when *we* are here?" Maria asked.

"Just humor me, okay?"

Maria looked at Barnes, who, in turn, just shook his head. "Go check," he told the patrol cop.

The man ran off and returned a few minutes later. "They said the storm is headed in from the west and, if anything, just the fringes of it will hit Cheyenne."

Maria turned to Brian. "So, *now* are you going to tell us why you're so interested in this storm?"

"Because I'd like to bring someone else up here to help."

"Who?"

"A...psychic." Brian almost cringed with the words.

The Cheyenne sex crimes detective just rolled her eyes.

"We already know where the Pattens and Jennifer are, Brian. We don't need a *psychic.*"

"No, but what we *do* need is some insight on how this whole thing is going to go down. Katrina Cordova can give us that. She gets her visions...during thunderstorms. If we bring her down here before the storm hits, she might be able to tell us if Patten actually has the guts—or the stupidity—to hit the trigger on that detonator."

Maria still looked doubtful. Detective Barnes, on the other hand, appeared to consider every word.

"Look, I was skeptical at first, too," Brian told Maria, "but *she* is the one who told me where Collin Lanaski was holding Angela. Her vision was right on the mark...and it contained specifics, not like other psychics who speak in generalities. She told me Angela was being held in a log cabin—" he glanced at the one behind them "—on an Ashley Road. She also saw an old windmill in the yard."

"And let me guess. You found Angela in a house on Ashley Road with a windmill in the yard," Maria interpreted.

"Yes, I did. She also had a second vision of a male figure looming over a *younger* Angela. She was in bed surrounded by stuffed animals, and the guy told her it was time to *play the game again.*" He lifted a dark eyebrow. "Sound familiar?"

Maria's growing interest manifested itself as a ripple in her brow. "Yeah, it sure does."

"She's good, Maria, and we could really use her right now. If the storm was going to hit Cheyenne, too, then I could just tell her about the situation on the phone and she might have a vision there. But it's not, so I have no choice but to bring her here. There's no guarantee that she will have a vision, but it's worth a try."

"And you actually think she'd be willing to come all the way down here?"

"I don't know. All I can do is ask her."

The detective sighed. "Okay. If she *is* willing, tell her I'll send a squad to pick her up. She'll get here a lot quicker."

Brian nodded and dug the cell phone from his jacket pocket.

It took some doing, but Brian managed to convince Katrina to make the trip to Colorado Springs. The storm was still just flashes on the horizon when the Cheyenne squad car delivered her just under two-and-a-half hours later. Brian met her at the foot of the hill and explained the situation in more detail as they made the half-mile trek to the command center, which was now housed in a large canvas tent.

"So, you actually think this will work?" she asked. "That I'll have a vision just because you *want* me to?"

He shrugged. "We've got all the ingredients. Or at least the last one is on its way." He directed her gaze to the continual flashes of lightning, accompanied by low rumbles of thunder, which cast the Rockies in an almost eerie glow.

"I told you on the phone, Brian, that it doesn't work like that. I can't *summon* a vision. It might not happen at all."

"I know that, and so do the others, but we have to try."

"You mean you have to know if that place is going to blow up or not," Katrina corrected as her onyx gaze drifted toward the small cabin immersed in floodlights that sat a hundred yards away, nestled between a stand of trees and the base of the mountain. She shook her dark head. "I still can't believe I actually agreed to come here knowing that place is set to explode."

"And hopefully that's what your vision—if you have one—will show us. It's one thing to *say* you'll blow yourself up, and another to actually do it—especially when it means killing your wife, too, not to mention an innocent child."

They had arrived at the tent by now, which sat in a small meadow also backed by the Rocky Mountains, and Brian quickly made the necessary introductions.

"So now what?" Maria asked as she looked at Katrina and tried to keep her continued skepticism out of her eyes.

Brian shrugged. "We wait."

Forty-five minutes later saw the storm arrive in full force. The tent whipped fiercely in the wind, and those inside the questionable safety of the structure wondered how long the makeshift command post would hold before joining all the cars at the bottom of the hill.

"Damn, I knew I should have had them send a couple of Crime Scene vans up here instead of this thing!" Barnes exclaimed above the roar of the combined wind and thunder. "And where are Patten and his wife? Inside a nice cozy little cabin while we get our asses kicked by Mother Nature."

"Yeah, a nice cozy little cabin loaded with a whole lot of C4," Brian returned. "I think I'd rather take my chances out here." He turned a rueful smile toward the Colorado Springs detective. "Besides, I don't think the vans would have made it up the hill."

"Which is why I opted for the tents, but you know... every good cop needs something to bitch about."

"Yeah, and Brian did a helluva lot of bitching when he was captain," Maria put in her two cents' worth as she cast a sly grin at her former boss. "I guess that's why he was such a good cop."

"So what made you quit?" Barnes asked. "Assuming that you *did* quit."

"I did," Brian answered slowly, "and for reasons I'd rather keep to myself." He turned to Maria. "You know, I never did ask you...were you able to get Collin Lanaski released?"

"No," she admitted. "The D.A. pulled a hissy fit, and Judge Reinhardt won't rule against him. Cochrane won't even consider that Lanaski might be Courtney's biological father until the DNA results come back. If and when they prove her true parentage, then and only then—his words, not mine—will he agree to release him."

"Yeah, well Cochrane always was a stubborn asshole." Brian shrugged. "I guess it really doesn't matter. The results should be back soon. Collin's already waited this long, so I guess a few more days won't kill him."

A sudden flash of lightning lit the interior of the tent as if it were high noon, when actually it was approaching seven p.m. Brian was the only one who glanced quickly at Katrina, only to find her calmly sitting before the opening in the tent watching the storm...and the small log cabin a hundred yards beyond.

He walked over to her, leaving a nervous Sinbad to pace the tent a few feet away. "Trying to target the cabin with your powerful psychic mind?" he joked.

She looked up at him. "Something like that."

Brian glanced over his shoulder to make sure the others weren't listening, then looked at Katrina again. "I wanted to apologize for the other night. I was out of line."

"Yes, you were." Her eyes moved back to the opening in the tent, and she quickly changed the subject. "So, do you think she's all right? The little girl, I mean."

"Jennifer?"

"Is that her name?"

He nodded as he stooped beside her folding chair. "Jennifer Marloe, and she was fine when I saw her. Scared, but fine. I think walking out of there and leaving her behind was the hardest thing I've ever done."

"I can't even imagine."

Another flash of lightning was followed by a loud crack of thunder that shook the sky. Katrina appeared unmoved. Sinbad, on the other hand, skulked to cower beneath a table, his tail between his legs.

"What's wrong with your dog?" Katrina asked. "He looks terrified."

Brian smiled as he glanced at the Belgian Malinois that was in the process of trying to dig himself even further into the hard ground. "He is. He doesn't like loud noises." He patted his leg. "Sinbad, *heir*."

For the first time since acquiring the dog, his partner disobeyed him.

"Sinbad," he said more forcefully this time, "*heir!*"

The canine reluctantly left his sanctuary and, tail still between his legs, crossed to stand at his master's heel. Brian rubbed his scruff vigorously and spoke near his ear. "It's okay, boy. Everything's okay." He looked at the smiling Katrina again. "I'm surprised the storms don't freak *you* out more, knowing what they can do to you."

She lifted her trim, jacketed shoulders in a shrug. "They used to. I've gotten so used to the visions that they don't really bother me much anymore."

"Except when they're about massive explosions and human body parts flying off, right?"

She managed a weak smile. "Yes." She looked at the cabin again. "So what are you going to do if I *don't* have a vision? Or if I do, and it's not helpful? How are you going to save Jennifer?"

"I have no idea. The local SWAT team had sharpshooters in the trees before the storm hit, but they couldn't be of much help when Patten never once so much as looked out a window. And, even if he had, shooting him might not end it...or at least not in the way we want it to end. He might still have time to detonate the bomb."

"So he carries the detonator with him?"

"He did when I was in there. It was in his left hand."

She shook her dark head. "I still can't believe you actually went in there. That took a lot of courage, Brian."

He smiled. "I'm not sure if it was courage or stupidity. I'm leaning more toward the latter, though. It really didn't accomplish anything, other than to see that Jeff was telling the truth about the C4."

"And you found out that Jenn—"

Another flash of lightning lit the sky and this time Katrina slumped in her chair. Brian caught her before she hit the ground. He eased her onto the rocky earth and rested her head in his lap just as Maria and Barnes bounded to his side. Sinbad retreated to his place under the table again, and his loud, agitated panting filled the tent.

"What happened? Is she all right?" Maria gasped.

Brian looked at Katrina's face. Her eyes were open and, as with the last time he witnessed the phenomenon, it appeared that she looked right through him. He couldn't suppress the shudder that wracked his body. "She's fine. This is what happens when she has a vision."

"What? She passes out?"

Brian nodded. He tested her pulse, just to be sure. Once again, her heart raced.

"And you're sure she's okay?" Maria pressed.

"Yeah…or at least I think she is. I've only witnessed this one time."

"All I know is it's freaky as hell," Detective Barnes commented. "The way she just stares like that…"

Brian looked up at him. "Tell me about it."

"So what do we do now?" It was Maria again who asked the question.

"We wait until she comes out of it."

That moment didn't come for nearly five minutes…the longest, Brian swore, of his life. Finally Katrina stirred in his arms, took a deep breath, and, with his help, sat up. She looked at all the worried faces surrounding her, but brushed off their concern and rattled off what she had seen.

"There *will* be an explosion. All that will be left of the cabin is a crater where it used to stand, and a bunch of blown-down trees around it. Many people are going to die, including police officers." She looked at Brian and, surprisingly, her eyes teared. "*You* are going to die, Brian…and so am I."

His face paled slightly in response to her words, but he didn't respond. Detective Barnes did.

"From the blast? Are we still too close?"

Katrina shook her head. "No, from a landslide. It'll come down behind us and cover the tent. There's no way to avoid it, short of leaving the scene."

"Son-of-a-bitch," the Colorado Springs detective ground out. "So he's really going to do it."

Katrina looked at Brian again. "There was something else, though, something that will happen just minutes *before* the explosion. I think that's what made him pull the trigger."

"What?"

"A bear, a grizzly I think—I know it was awfully big and had that silvery sheen to its fur like grizzlies do. It's going to come out of the woods over there." She stood and exited the tent, into the driving rain, and pointed to a spot off to their right near a set of trash cans. Brian, Barnes, and Maria were right behind her. "It will upset the trash cans. Jeff Patten will come to the window to check out the commotion. There was a gun in his right hand, but nothing in his left that I could see when he parted the curtains. At that moment, the bear turned on one of the officers." She pointed again, this time to a young uniformed police officer who stood with his shoulders hunched against the storm. "Him. The others will start shooting. It was only a few seconds later that the bomb went off."

"So Patten thought they were shooting at him," Brian surmised.

"Probably," Katrina agreed.

"This is ridiculous! Grizzly bears? Are you kidding me?" Maria spat. She turned and stomped back into the tent, ripped off her jacket, and shook it to free it of the excess rain.

Brian followed her in, with an equally saturated Barnes and Katrina right behind him. "It's the area for them, Maria. It's not that farfetched."

"Right. With all these people around? A bear would run a hundred miles an hour in the *opposite* direction."

"Or it would be attracted by all the commotion." Surprisingly, it was Barnes who countered her.

She whirled to face the other detective. "You don't actually believe her?"

"I've worked with psychics before, Maria, and I've learned not to ignore them."

As surprising as Barnes' words were, Brian got back to the matter at hand. "You're all missing the point here—that point being that, if what she's saying actually *does* happen, there will be a time when Patten will come to the window—without the detonator."

"And the sharpshooters will be able to take him out," Barnes concluded.

"Exactly." Brian turned to Katrina again. "Which window will he come to? The one to the right of the door, or the one to the left?"

"The left," she answered with certainty.

"So any idea *when* this is going to happen?" Barnes asked.

Maria just shook her head at the absurdity of it all and walked away.

"Not for a while yet," Katrina answered. "The storm was over, and it was really dark. Darker than it is now."

Another deafening crack of thunder accentuated her words, and a whimper came from under the table. Brian just looked at the dog, shook his head, and turned back to the others.

"Another reason to believe the bear theory," he said as he glanced at Maria's back. "In a raging storm like this, the animals move deep into the woods, under the shelter of the trees."

Another particularly strong gust of wind shook the tent, and they all held their breath and waited to see if the lines holding the structure would survive the impact. Thankfully, they did.

Maria turned back to them. "So what? We wait for the

storm to end, get the sharpshooters back into the trees, and wait for a *bear*?"

"Yup," Brian returned, "and we get all the officers away from the trash cans."

The brunette shook her head again. "I'm going to let *you* write the report on this one. I'll just sign it."

The storm had blown itself out an hour later, and the sharp-shooters moved quietly back into the trees in front of the cabin. All four rifles were aimed at the left hand window, and the elite members of the local SWAT team were instructed to let *nothing* distract them from their target—even a grizzly coming out of the woods to gorge itself in the trash cans fifty feet to the right of the house.

Word had spread. A psychic. A *vision*. It was laughable, yes. In fact, they had all *had* a good laugh when the story made the rounds. No one questioned the orders, however. Not when the life of a little girl, and their *own* lives, depended on professionalism.

Brian had insisted that Katrina allow the squad to take her back to Cheyenne. If they failed, if Jeff Patten succeeded in detonating the bomb, he was determined that part of her vision would *not* come true. She, at least, would live to tell the tale.

The more than twenty officers on the scene barely breathed as darkness engulfed them. The floodlights had been extinguished so Patten's predicted glance out the window wouldn't reveal those in the trees assigned to kill him. No one moved. The silence in and of itself was unnerving. Brian had even ordered the now alert Sinbad into a down, stay position where they waited an uncomfortable fifty feet from the house behind a huge oak. One of the sharpshooters was perched above him.

A sudden thrashing off to his right was enough to make

Brian jerk his head in that direction. Even he experienced a moment of disbelief when a massive bear lumbered from the woods. He laid a restraining hand on the suddenly tense Sinbad's back, silently ordering the dog to hold his position. The bear headed directly for the trash cans. Obviously, it had feasted there before. There were no officers in the vicinity to distract it this time, however, and the thundering crash as the animal rose to its full ten-foot height and knocked the first can over with a single swipe of its massive paw echoed through the mountains.

Brian's gaze flew back to the window. He held his breath for seemingly endless seconds until the curtains slowly parted in the center and a man's face appeared in the opening. Four consecutive shots rang through the trees. The startled bear headed for the hills, and Jeffrey Patten reeled backward as four bullets entered his brain. A woman's scream filled the night.

"Move!" Barnes' bellowed order set twenty officers into simultaneous motion.

Brian and Sinbad made it to the door first. He kicked it open and yet another resounding crash echoed through the mountains as the portal slammed against the wall. He halted immediately at the scene that lay within. Sinbad followed his partner's lead, a low growl rumbling in his chest. The bodies of a half-dozen police officers pushed the P.I. forward, their guns drawn and leveled at the terrified woman who sat on the bed, an eight-year-old girl clutched tightly to her breast.

"You killed him!" Melody screeched. "You killed Jeff!"

Brian glanced at Jeff's prone, lifeless body, and the gun lying next to him, before raising his right hand in a calming gesture. He used his left to wave the officers back, then returned his own pistol to the holster, lessening the threat he posed to the distraught woman. "Take it easy, Melody. Nobody else has to get hurt here."

"You killed him!" she repeated, the screech turning into a sob. She tightened her grip even further on the now struggling Jennifer and glared at Brian through tear saturated eyes. "You bastard! We trusted you!"

"I'm sorry, Melody, but this had to end, and the only way that was going to happen was if Jeff was taken down." He took a step toward her. Sinbad, too, crept closer. "Now, let Jennifer go."

"No!" she screamed and, once again, the sobbing, terrified child was pulled against her chest. "I won't let you take my daughter!"

"She's not your daughter, Melody. Her name is Jennifer Marloe. *Angela* died when she was only two years old. We found her, where Jeff buried her in your backyard."

"*No!* Angela is not dead. She's right here!"

"She is *not* Angela. I know you want her to be, but she isn't. She's just a frightened little girl that Jeff took from her real mother—"

"No! *She is mine!*" Melody stood, dragging Jennifer with her. She took a step toward the small table in the center of the room. "I will never let you take her!"

Her wild eyes locked on the detonator at the same time Brian's did. She shoved Jennifer aside and lunged toward the table. Brian, too, sprang into action, but Sinbad was quicker. The dog launched himself across the five feet between them and clamped down on her wrist just as Melody's hand closed around the device. The pressure of the canine's unrelenting jaw rendered the hand useless, and the detonator dropped harmlessly to the floor.

The officers moved in to subdue the woman as Brian scooped up the detonation device, then barked at his partner. "Sinbad, *aus!*"

The dog relinquished his prize immediately and returned to Brian's side. In the next instant, Jennifer was in his arms.

"It's okay, honey," he murmured as he handed off the detonator to Detective Barnes. "It's over."

"I want my mom," Jennifer sobbed. "Please, I just want my mom!"

"And we're going to take you to her, honey, real soon."
He started to lead the girl from the cabin, Melody's crazed
shrieking ringing in his ears.
"Don't you hear her? She wants her mother! Give her
to me!" Her pleas increased in volume and ferocity as Brian
and Jennifer disappeared into the night. "Please, Brian, don't
take my daughter! *Pleeeease!*"

CHAPTER TWENTY-ONE

Brian pulled up before Katrina's Victorian mansion and released an elongated yawn. It was nearing two a.m., yet he was not surprised to find her waiting in the open doorway clad in a long, fluffy robe. She had given him strict orders before leaving Colorado Springs that he was to "stop by" on his way home, and refused to take no for an answer. It was her way, he knew, of refusing to acknowledge that there was a strong possibility he would never return to Cheyenne.

"Hi," he said as he traversed the walk and approached the stoop.

"Hi, yourself." Katrina stepped back into the foyer. "Come on in."

Brian stepped inside and closed the door behind him.

"So, everything went okay?"

"Just like you said it would, minus the cabin and *us* being blown to smithereens. Once again, you were right on the mark, Katrina. I think the others were impressed." A tired grin curved his lips. "I know I was."

"And Jennifer is okay?"

"She's back with her very grateful parents as we speak."

"And Jeff and Melody Patten?"

"He's dead, which I'm sure you assumed. She was on her

way to a hospital, where I'm sure she'll undergo some extensive psychological testing. She may never stand trial. The woman was convinced, right up until the end, that Jennifer was her daughter."

"I almost feel sorry for her. I can't imagine losing a child the way she did. I mean, at the hands of her own husband…"

"And that child's father."

Katrina just shook her dark head, at a loss for further words.

"By the way," Brian continued, "I was thinking on the way home from Colorado Springs…was the explosion you saw tonight the same as the one in your other visions? Were you maybe tapping into what was going to happen with Jeff Patten?"

"No," she returned with conviction. "It was nothing like it. It was a lot bigger explosion, and a lot more people are going to die. Maybe *thousands*, Brian."

"Okay. Can't blame me for hoping."

"You know, there's something *I* was thinking about earlier, too, that I never asked you," Katrina went on.

Brian waited expectantly.

"I know you found the car seat and the picture, but did you ever find the dog tag? I mean, it stands to reason that if Jeff Patten wasn't worried enough to get rid of the car seat, that he wouldn't have gotten rid of the dog tag either."

Brian's brow furrowed suddenly. "I never thought about that…and I sure can't ask him now." He shrugged. "We may never know what happened to it."

"That's kind of sad. It would have been nice to give it back to Courtney."

"Yeah, it would have. Well…I think I'm gonna head home. It's been a long day." Brian reached out to touch her cheek in a gentle caress. "You look like you could use some sleep, too."

She smiled, though her state of exhaustion too was apparent in her eyes. "Not even going to try and convince me to let you stay the night?"

"Nope. You were right about that, too. You deserve better than what I'm capable of giving, Katrina. I'll always be the playboy. The one-night-stand man. *You*, on the other hand, need a forever type guy, and I'm definitely not him."

"We can stay friends, though, right? You can be my stop-by-for-a-cup-of-coffee once-in-a-while guy?"

Brian grinned. "*That* you can count on." He bent to press a kiss to her cheek. "I can also be your '*Shit, I had another vision of body parts flying through the air*' guy. Call me anytime, Katrina."

She moved closer to wrap her arms around his neck in a farewell hug. "That, Brian Koski, *you* can count on."

Brian stepped back, again one of the hardest things he had ever done, and turned to open the door. A flash of lightning in the distance, though, was enough to make him turn back. "Looks like the weather report was wrong. The storm *is* going to hit Cheyenne. Want me to hang around…just in case?"

"No. You're exhausted, and so am I. I'll be fine. Go home and get some sleep," she told him firmly.

"Yes, Mother." Brian grinned again just before he placed a very chaste kiss on her cheek.

In response, Katrina shoved him out the door, then closed and locked the portal behind him.

Brian groaned two hours later when the phone beside his bed woke him from a sound sleep. He looked at the caller I.D. and couldn't help but smile.

"Sorry, Katrina," he said into the mouthpiece, "no matter how much you beg, I'm not dragging my ass out of bed to come back over. I don't care what you promise. I've recently developed this aversion to nights filled with hot, steamy sex."

"Yeah, right, and I'm Mother Theresa, too."

"Well, now that you mention it, you do kind of resemble her, minus the wrinkles and the head thingy."

She laughed. "Will you just shut up!"

He released an exaggerated sigh. "Okay, fine. So, what's up?"

"I had another vision."

He sighed. "I told you I should have stayed when I saw the lightning. Are you okay?"

"I'm fine. The vision didn't last long...just like the storm. It was kind of weird, though, and rather benign. At first it didn't even seem important enough to bother you with, but then I decided that wasn't for me to determine."

"So what was the vision?"

"It was of Jeff Patten."

Brian sat up on the edge of the bed. "Really? What was he doing?"

"That's what was so strange. All I saw was him placing a cover on a small plastic container and then putting it in this wooden rack-type-thing. Then he just kind of stood there and stared at it for a minute..."

"Did you see where he was at the time?"

"No. It was black all around him."

"Huh. That *is* weird."

"Yes it is...and I'm sorry that I woke you. Like I said, it wasn't that important. It could have waited until morning."

"It's fine, Katrina."

"Well, I'll let you go back to sleep, and I promise I won't wake you again."

"I'd appreciate it...unless, of course, you have a vision about you and me and the hot, steamy sex I mentioned earlier."

He could almost see the smile in her words. "I thought you'd developed an aversion to it."

"Yeah, well in your case, I'd be more than willing to make an exception."

She laughed. "Good night, Brian."

"Night, honey, and sleep good."

Brian hung up the phone, turned onto his side, and closed his eyes. They flew open again a few moments later and he bolted to a sitting position. "Son-of-a-bitch!"

His feet found the floor, and a few minutes later he was dressed and out the door.

Brian arrived at the office later than normal the following morning. Sherry was already there, and so was Kathy. The former still looked far from healthy, but she was a trouper and already showing the newest B.K. Investigations employee the ropes.

"Hey, congratulations, boss!" Sherry exclaimed, her speech affected by a stuffy nose as she stood to give Brian a hug when he and Sinbad entered through the back door. "I saw the whole Patten thing on the morning news. You got them, huh?"

"With a little help," he acknowledged as Sherry stepped back. "That case is wrapped up. Or almost anyway. We just have to wait for the DNA results on Collin Lanaski and Courtney. The D.A. won't release him from jail, or acknowledge his paternity, until he sees those results."

"Well, then it's a good thing the mailman was on time this morning." Sherry moved to her desk to retrieve an envelope from Colorado DNA Service, Inc., in Denver. It was addressed to Collin Lanaski at the B.K. Investigations address. She handed the envelope to Brian. "Must be the week for DNA results. I figured you would want to open this one yourself, though."

Brian wasted no time in ripping open the letter. He scanned the results and looked at the two ladies with a smile. "It says there is a 99.99% chance that Collin Lanaski is Courtney's biological father."

"Did you ever doubt it?"

Brian laughed, a hearty, relief-born show of levity. "Only like a thousand times, until recently anyway." He held up the letter. "Well, I guess I'd better make a trip to the D.A.'s office so we can get Collin released."

"And back with his daughter," Sherry added.

"You got that right. It's long overdue." He pressed a kiss to Sherry's cheek and, to Kathy's surprise, hers also, and headed for the door again. "I'll be back!"

"Is that a threat or a promise?" Sherry called after him.

"Both!" Brian returned before he and Sinbad exited the office.

Brian spent the next hour arguing with David Cochrane, the Laramie County D.A. Yes, Collin Lanaski was guilty of kidnapping. He was also guilty of violating a restraining order and stalking. But he had *tried* to get the police to listen to him early on in the investigation, just as he had tried to get Brian to listen to him. He had tried to get *all* of them to believe his incredible story. The man had never faltered in his belief that Angela Patten was actually Courtney Lanaski, *his daughter* and, as it turned out, he was right. The DNA test results proved it. Collin Lanaski had tried to get help, but there was no help to be found for a man everyone considered to be crazy. So, Brian pleaded the man's case, could Cochrane blame him? Would he have done any different if Angela Patten had been *his* daughter? Jeff Patten had stolen Courtney from the scene of an accident and raised her as his own. He had been sexually molesting the child for *at least* two years. Could Collin Lanaski really be blamed for going a little off the deep end when his daughter's life was at stake—literally?

Finally, the D.A. relented. He would drop all charges, and Collin Lanaski would be released within the hour. Brian breathed a sigh of relief as he left the county courthouse and crossed the skywalk to the jail. He owed it to little Courtney Lanaski to see this case to its conclusion, and the only *just* conclusion was for her to be reunited with her father. That would happen now, as soon as Collin exited the elevator a free man and found Brian waiting in the hall to take him to his child.

The doors to the elevator slid open and, for what seemed the hundredth time in the past hour-and-a-half, Brian looked up from where he sat on a Formica bench, feet apart, forearms resting on his knees, hands clasped. This time, Collin Lanaski, dressed in jeans and a T-shirt and wrists and ankles free of restraints, exited the lift. Brian stood.

Collin paused for a moment, then walked up to the other man. "Are you responsible for this?"

The P.I. nodded. "I talked to the D.A., yes. He's the one truly responsible, though."

"But it was you who talked him into letting me go?"

"I got the DNA results this morning," Brian said in the form of an answer. "They prove that Courtney is your biological daughter."

Sudden tears shined in Collin's eyes. "So it's over then?"

"Yeah, Collin, it's over."

"What about the Pattens? They won't try to get her back?"

"No. Jeff is dead, and Melody is in the hospital. She'll be lucky if she ever sees the outside of a psychiatric ward again."

Collin's eyes had widened through Brian's statement. "Jeff is *dead*?"

"It's a long story, Collin. What do you say we get out of here, and I'll explain on the way to pick up your daughter?"

251

The first genuine smile Brian had seen from the man lit Collin's face. "Sounds good to me."

"Daddy!" Courtney cried when Brian and Collin entered the Riker house through the back door. Sinbad followed them in. The family sat at the island in the kitchen eating lunch, and the little girl scrambled down from her stool and raced across the short space to be swept into her father's arms.

"God, I missed you!" Collin said, not bothering to wipe at the unmanly tears that streamed down his face as he hugged his daughter to him.

"I missed you, too, Daddy." She wiggled free of her father's embrace and moved to wrap her small arms around Brian's waist. "Thank you for getting my daddy out of the jail, Brian."

"You're welcome, honey," he said as he smoothed the blonde hair atop her head.

Collin moved to stand before Zach and Caryn, who still stood near the counter, smiles broadening both their faces. He gave the latter a hug. "I can't tell you how grateful I am, Caryn, for your taking care of Courtney."

She smiled at her former co-worker as she stepped back. "No problem, Collin. She's a wonderful little girl, and we had a really good time." Caryn moved to stoop before Courtney. "But I bet you'll be happy to finally go home with your daddy, won't you, honey?"

"Uh-huh." She turned to Collin. "Can we go now, Daddy?"

He laughed. "In a minute, honey."

"And we have to pack your things first," Caryn told the child.

"Okay." Courtney took Caryn's hand. "Let's go!"

Caryn smiled at Collin before she allowed the little girl to lead her through the great room and up to the loft.

"So, I bet you're happy all this is over," Zach told Collin.

"You can't even imagine," the other man replied with heartfelt sincerity. He looked at Brian. "None of it would have been possible without this guy, though."

"Right." Brian chuckled. "Like I was so cooperative in the beginning."

"Granted, I was a little upset with you at first," Collin admitted, "but I can't blame you for doubting my story. I mean, for a man's *dead* daughter to miraculously reappear after four years? Hell, even I thought I was crazy there for a while."

"Yeah, well, like Zach said, it's over now. You've got your daughter back, and hopefully you'll have your job back at the school soon, too."

"We saw on the morning news about the whole standoff with the Pattens last night," Zach told his friend. "Sounded like it was a little scary there for a while."

"That's putting it mildly. I thought we were all going to be blown to smithereens...or die in a rockslide."

Zach's tanned brow knitted in confusion. "A rockslide?"

Brian brushed off the other man's bewilderment. "I'll explain later."

"If I were you, I'd have been more concerned about someone being mauled by a grizzly." Zach shook his sandy head. "That was incredible. That it came out of the woods just at the right moment, and allowed the SWAT team to take Patten out. It was almost like they knew it was going to happen."

"Yeah, it was pretty freaky." Brian chose not to elaborate on that point either, at least not with Collin present.

Caryn and Courtney returned to the kitchen, small suitcase and an obviously new blonde-haired, porcelain doll in hand. Blondie also tagged at her heels. "Look at the dolly Mrs. Riker bought me, Daddy. Isn't she pretty?"

"She sure is." Collin stooped before his daughter and touched a finger to her nose. "In fact, she looks just like you."

Courtney smiled her pleasure. "Can we go to your house now, Daddy?"

Collin looked up at Brian for the answer, since he no longer had a vehicle of his own.

"We sure can," the P.I. returned. "In fact, it's *your* house now, too, Courtney." It was Brian's turn to stoop before the child. "But first there's something I need to give you...something you lost a long time ago."

Courtney's brow wrinkled in an adorable show of confusion. Collin, Zach, and Caryn appeared just as bewildered. "What?" the little girl asked.

Brian reached into his pants pocket and, a moment later, a chain emerged. Dangling from the end of the chain was a military-style dog tag.

Collin's eyes widened in disbelief, mirroring Zach and Caryn's reaction. Courtney started to jump up and down excitedly.

"Is it my daddy's dog tag? The one he gave me when I was little?"

Brian smiled. "It sure is." He pointed to the face of the engraved piece of metal. "It says your daddy's name right there. Lieutenant Collin James Lanaski." Brian reached out to slip the chain over the eager Courtney's head. "And now it's back where it belongs."

"So nobody can ever hurt me again, because the dog tag will protect me?"

Sudden tears shined in Brian's eyes. Collin and the other two adults in the room suffered the same affliction. "That's right," the P.I. said. "Nobody can ever hurt you again."

Courtney went into Brian's arms and he hugged the little girl to him before he stood to face Collin upon his next question.

"Where in the heck did you find it?"

"I...got a tip last night after I got back to Cheyenne that they might be in a container in the Patten garage. I went over there to check, and sure enough—"

"And knowing you," Zach interrupted, "I'll bet you didn't get permission from Maria Parenteau to enter the crime scene again, did you?"

Brian grinned at his friend. "Minor technicality. And, besides, if I had, she'd have wanted to put them into evidence until the case against Melody is resolved, and it could've been six months or better before they were returned to their rightful owner." He reached out to ruffle the hair on Courtney's head.

"I can't believe the guy was stupid enough to keep them all these years," Collin exclaimed. "I mean, they're proof positive that I was telling the truth."

"Yeah, well obviously Jeff wasn't too worried about anyone ever finding out that *Angela*—" he smiled at Courtney "—wasn't really his daughter. If he was, he would have gotten rid of the car seat, too."

"I guess, but he still took an awfully big risk."

"That he did," Brian agreed, "and that risk cost him everything...including his life."

"Daddy?" Courtney looked at her father again.

"Yes, honey?"

"When we get to our house, is it okay if I don't have any stuffed animals? I don't like them anymore."

Collin had to battle a new set of tears. The healing would be a long time in coming for his daughter, but now that they were together again, he could see to it that it *would* come. "No problem, honey. No stuffed animals." He looked at the porcelain doll. "Just lots of pretty dollies for a pretty little girl."

Collin, his daughter, and a puppy named Blondie followed Brian and Sinbad out the door, leaving Zach and Caryn to watch from the back deck as the Dodge Ram headed down the driveway. A smile creased both their faces. For the first time in four long years, little Courtney Lanaski was going home.

AFTERWORD

B rian crossed the living room of his downtown apartment the following evening and, TV dinner in hand, plopped down in an old tan recliner formerly belonging to his father. The chair was one of the few things he had claimed for himself while cleaning out his parents' home after their deaths. It wasn't the most comfortable piece of furniture in the world, but it had been David Koski's favorite for more than ten years and served as a constant reminder of the man who worked so hard to ensure his son's success in life.

Brian pulled the lever on the side of the La-Z-Boy and the footrest slid easily into the reclining position. He grabbed the remote from the end table, clicked on the TV for the nine o'clock news, and took the first bite of mashed potatoes from the *Hungry Man* Swiss Steak meal.

"And now our top story of the day," the KQCK news anchor was saying. *"The Albany County Sheriff announced this afternoon that there have been several arrests in the Medicine Bow National Forest murders earlier this month. In police custody are fifteen-year-old Brandon Breighton, thirteen-year-old Kevin Breighton, and ten-year-old Paul Breighton. The three oldest Breighton children told police right after the murders of their parents and younger brother and sister that they were fishing on Lake Owen and returned to*

their campsite to find their remaining family members bludgeoned to death. The boys then hiked to the Laramie Ranger District station to report the murders to authorities. Albany County Sheriff, Richard Marks, stated in a press conference this afternoon that they have a multitude of verifiable evidence that the boys were actually involved in the murders. A preliminary hearing will be held in Albany County Circuit Court on September 3 to determine if the three Breighton brothers will be charged as adults. If convicted, the three minors will be constitutionally precluded from receiving the death penalty.

The Breighton family, James Breighton, forty-two, his wife Donna, forty, and their two youngest children, Cole, age seven, and Brianna, age four, were found bludgeoned to death at their wilderness campsite near Lake Owen on August 3 of this year. The multiple murders have been declared the worst in Wyoming history."

Brian shook his dark head slowly. "Kids killing their family. What in the hell is wrong with this world?" A rueful smile touched his lips. "For the first time since Stanley booted me off the force, I think I'm glad I'm no longer a cop."

He finished the TV dinner, then waited for the weather report before clicking off the television and turning in for the night.

ABOUT JEAN HACKENSMITH...

I have been writing since the age of twenty. (That's thirty-seven years and, yes, I'm disclosing my age.) I am the proud mother of three, stepmother of two, and grandmother to twelve wonderful children. I lost the love of my life, my husband Ron, in November of 2011 when he died in an accident at work. He took my heart with him and, for a time, my desire to write. Time, as they say, heals all wounds, and I have again discovered my passion for the written word. In fact, I find it strangely comforting to delve into the intricate webs that are my character's lives and immerse myself in their existence instead of dwelling on my own.

Next to writing, my second passion is live theater. I founded a local community theater group back in 1992 and directed upwards of forty shows, including three that I authored. I also appeared *on* stage a few times, portraying Anna in *The King and I* and Miss Hannigan in *Annie*. I am sad to say that the theater group closed its final curtain in 2008, but those sixteen years will always hold some of my fondest memories.

My husband and I moved from Superior, Wisconsin, five years ago, seeking the serenity of country living. We also wanted to get away from the natural air conditioning provided by Lake Superior. We moved only fifty miles south, but the temperature can vary by 20-30 degrees. I guess I'm a country girl at heart. I simply love this area, even though I must now enjoy its beauty alone. I love the solitude, the picturesque beauty of the sun rising over the water, the strangely calming effect of watching a deer graze outside your kitchen window. Never again will I live in the city. I am an author, after all, and what better place to be inspired than in God's own backyard.

CPSIA information can be obtained
at www.ICGtesting.com
Printed in the USA
FFOW02n1956070514
5259FF